"I'M GOING TO HAVE TO KISS YOU. AND WHEN I DO, I CAN'T PROMISE I'll STOP . . ."

Marilee stood very still, heart pounding. "How do you know I'll ask you to?"

Wyatt stared at her with naked hunger. "Careful. Because unless you tell me to stop, you have to know where this is heading . . . "

In reply Marilee stood on tiptoe to brush her mouth to his, stopping his words. Stopping his heart.

He drew in a deep breath and stared into her eyes. "I hope you meant that."

"With all my heart."

"Thank God." Wyatt dragged her against him and covered her lips with his. Inside her mouth he whispered, "Because, baby, I mean this."

This kiss was so hot, so hungry, Marilee felt the rush of desire from the top of her head all the way to her toes. Wyatt changed the angle of the kiss and took it deeper until she could feel her flesh heating, her bones melting like hot wax. With but a single kiss her brain had been wiped clear of every thought but one. She wanted this man. Wanted him now . . .

Also by R. C. Ryan

Montana Legacy

MONTANA DESTINY

R.C. RYAN

WITHDRAWN

FOREVER

NEW YORK   BOSTON

This book is a work of fiction. Names, characters, places, and incidents are the product of the author's imagination or are used fictitiously. Any resemblance to actual events, locales, or persons, living or dead, is coincidental.

Copyright © 2010 by Ruth Ryan Langan
Excerpt from *Montana Glory* copyright © 2010 Ruth Ryan Langan
Excerpt from *Montana Legacy* copyright © 2010 Ruth Ryan Langan

R. C. Ryan has been previously published under the name Ruth Ryan Langan.

Cover design by Christine Foltzer
Cover photograph by Herman Estevez
Handlettering by Ron Zinn
Book design by Giorgetta Bell McRee

Forever
Hachette Book Group
237 Park Avenue
New York, NY 10017
Visit our website at www.HachetteBookGroup.com.

Forever is an imprint of Grand Central Publishing.
The Forever name and logo is a trademark of Hachette Book Group, Inc.

Printed in the United States of America

First Printing, May 2010

10 9 8 7 6 5 4 3 2 1

ATTENTION CORPORATIONS AND ORGANIZATIONS:
Most HACHETTE BOOK GROUP books are available at quantity discounts with bulk purchase for educational, business, or sales promotional use. For information, please call or write:

Special Markets Department, Hachette Book Group
237 Park Avenue, New York, NY 10017
Telephone: 1-800-222-6747 Fax: 1-800-477-5925

To my beautiful daughter, Mary Margaret

And to her beautiful daughters, Caitlin, Ally, Taylor, Isabella, and Maggie

And, of course, to Tom, my fearless protector

And a special thank you to Gary Fitzsimmons for his generosity in sharing his valuable expertise in the field of emergency responders.

MONTANA DESTINY

PROLOGUE

———◆◆◆———

Gold Fever, Montana—1992

Hang on, Clint." Twelve-year-old Wyatt McCord hung on the wooden fence at the town's rodeo grounds, shouting encouragement to the cowboy fighting to stay in the saddle of the meanest bucking bronco on the rodeo circuit.

Beside him, his cousins, Jesse and Zane, watched wide-eyed as the rider was tossed high in the air before landing facedown in the dirt. While two cowboys in clown costumes distracted the crazed animal, a handler hustled the cowboy through a gate to safety.

"Wow!" Eleven-year-old Zane looked properly impressed. "Did you see how close he came to being trampled?"

"He didn't stick long enough to qualify." Wyatt couldn't hide his scorn.

"You think you could?" Jesse, at fourteen the oldest of the three, shot his cousin a knowing look.

"Maybe not now. But I bet a couple of years from now, I'll do better'n old Clint."

Jesse spit in the dirt, the way he'd seen his grandfather's wranglers do along the trail. "I'll take that bet. A couple of years from now." He shared a grin with Zane. "And I'm betting we'll be picking you up out of the dirt and hauling you home in pieces."

"Not me. Haven't you heard? I'm Superman." Wyatt watched as the next cowboy climbed atop the rail, preparing to drop into the saddle when the gate opened. "I figure if I'm going to carry on Coot's name, I'd better be good at everything I try. Especially in this town."

"Why bother?" Jesse looked around at the sea of faces in town for the annual rodeo, completely unaware of the cluster of preteen girls who watched from a distance, sighing over him and his cousins. "They all figure our grandpa's crazy anyway. Why should we bother trying to impress them?"

"It's not about them." Wyatt turned away from the railing as yet another cowboy bit the dust.

His two cousins followed.

The three cousins looked more like brothers, with the same dark, curly hair and the McCord laughing blue eyes. They and their families shared the sprawling ranch house that was home to three generations of McCords. Homeschooled, they were best friends. Their bond, forged since birth, was wide and deep.

"It's about proving to Grandpa that we don't feel the same way as the folks here in town do. They might call him a crazy old coot, but we know better. Our ancestor's treasure really is out there somewhere. And we've got to be stronger, and smarter, so that when the day comes that we can join Coot in his search, we'll be ready."

Zane stopped and studied the booth selling corn dogs

and chili fries. "I'd be a whole lot stronger and smarter with a couple of those."

Laughing, the three pooled their money and invested in as many dogs and fries as they could afford.

They sat cross-legged in the shade and polished off their lunch, believing, with all the innocence of youth, that the only life they'd ever known could not possibly end, even though the fabric of their family had already begun to unravel. All three of them had heard voices, often late at night, raised in protest. Grumblings about too much togetherness. Complaints about the restrictions of ranch life. Coot's once loyal sons were being asked to choose between a father's lifelong search for lost treasure and the needs of wives who yearned for a future far from the Montana wilderness.

Unknown to these three carefree boys, this would be the last rodeo they would share for many years to come.

CHAPTER ONE

———◆◆◆———

Present Day

Wyatt." Amy McCord turned to watch as her husband's cousin paused at one of the food booths set up at the rodeo grounds. "You've already had two corn dogs. Don't tell me you're buying another one."

"All right. I won't tell you." Despite his faded denims and scuffed boots, with his hair blowing in the wind, Wyatt McCord looked more like an eternal surfer than a cowboy. "But I can't get enough of these." He took a big bite, closed his eyes on a sigh, and polished off the corn dog in three bites.

Wiping his hands down his jeans he caught up with his cousins, Jesse and Zane, and Jesse's bride, Amy.

Their grandfather's funeral had brought the cousins together after years of separation. Now the three had begun to resolve years of old differences and were quickly becoming the same inseparable friends they'd been in their childhood.

Wyatt glanced around. "Where did all these people come from? It looks like half of Montana is here."

Jesse grinned. "Gold Fever might be a small town, but when it's rodeo time, every cowboy worth his spurs makes it here. In the past couple of years it's become one of the best in the West."

The four paused at the main corral, where a cowboy was roping a calf. While they hung on the rail and marveled at his skill, Zane whipped out his ever-present video camera to film the action. During his years in California he'd worked with famed director Steven Michaelson filming an award-winning documentary on wild mustangs. Now he'd become obsessed with making a documentary of life in Montana, featuring their ongoing search for a treasure stolen from their ancestors over a hundred years ago.

The search had consumed their grandfather's entire adult life, causing the people who knew him to give him the nickname Crazy Old Coot. He'd embraced the name, and in his will, he'd managed to entice his three grandsons to take up his search, no matter where it might lead them.

Jesse looked over at a holding pen, where riders were drawing numbers for the bull-riding contest. "There's one you ought to try, cuz." He laughed at Wyatt's arched brow. "It doesn't take just skill, but a really hard head to survive."

"Not to mention balls of steel," Zane remarked while keeping his focus on the action in the ring.

Wyatt merely grinned. "Piece of cake."

Jesse couldn't resist. He reached into his pocket and withdrew a roll of bills. "Twenty says you can't stick in the saddle for more than ten seconds."

"Make it a hundred and I'll take that bet."

Jesse threw back his head and roared. "Cuz, you couldn't stay on a bull's back for a thousand."

"Is it a bet?" Wyatt sent him a steely look.

"Damned straight. My hundred calls your bluff."

Wyatt turned to Zane. "You're my witness. And you might want to film this. I doubt I'll offer to do a repeat."

Without waiting for a reply he sauntered away and approached the cluster of cowboys eyeing the bulls.

Half an hour later, wearing a number on his back and having parted with the fifty-dollar entry fee, he stood with the others and waited his turn to ride a bull.

While he watched the action in the ring he noticed the ambulance parked just outside the ring. In case any fool wasn't already aware of the danger, that brought home the point. But it wasn't the emergency vehicle that caught his attention; it was the woman standing beside it. There was no way he could mistake those long, long legs encased in lean denims, or that mass of fiery hair spilling over her shoulders and framing the prettiest face he'd ever seen. Marilee Trainor had been the first woman to catch Wyatt's eye the moment he got back in town scant months ago. He'd seen her dozens of times since, but she'd always managed to slip away before he'd had time to engage her in conversation.

Not this time, he thought with a wicked grin.

"McCord." A voice behind him had him turning.

"You're up. You drew number nine."

A chorus of nervous laughter greeted that announcement, followed by a round of relieved voices.

"Rather you than me, cowboy."

"Man, I'm sure glad I ducked that bullet."

"I hope your life insurance is paid up."

Wyatt studied the bull snorting and kicking its hind legs against the confining pen, sending a shudder through the entire ring of spectators. If he didn't know better, Wyatt would have sworn he'd seen fire coming out of the bull's eyes.

"What's his name?" He climbed the wood slats and prepared to drop into the saddle atop the enraged animal's back.

"Devil. And believe me, sonny, he lives up to it." The grizzled old cowboy handed Wyatt the lead rope and watched while he twisted it around and around his hand before dropping into the saddle.

In the same instant the gate was opened, and bull and rider stormed into the center ring to a chorus of shouts and cries and whistles from the crowd.

Devil jerked, twisted, kicked, and even crashed headlong into the boards in an attempt to dislodge its hated rider. For his part, Wyatt had no control over his body as it left the saddle, suspended in midair, before snapping forward and back like a rag doll, all the while remaining connected by the tenuous rope coiled around his hand.

Though it lasted only sixty seconds, it was the longest ride of his life.

When the bullhorn signaled that he'd met the qualifying time, he struggled to gather his wits, waiting until Devil was right alongside the gate before he freed his hand, cutting himself loose. He flew through the air and over the corral fence, landing in the dirt at Marilee Trainor's feet.

"My God! Don't move." She was beside him in the blink of an eye, kneeling in the dirt, probing for broken bones.

Wyatt lay perfectly still, enjoying the feel of those clever, practiced hands moving over him. When she moved from his legs to his torso and arms, he opened his eyes to narrow slits and watched her from beneath lowered lids.

She was the perfect combination of beauty and brains. He could see the wheels turning as she did a thorough exam. Even her brow, furrowed in concentration, couldn't mar that flawless complexion. Her eyes, the color of the palest milk chocolate, were narrowed in thought. Strands of red hair dipped over one cheek, giving her a sultry look.

Satisfied that nothing was broken, she sat back on her heels, feeling a moment of giddy relief. That was when she realized that he was staring.

She waved a hand before his eyes. "How many fingers can you see?"

"Four fingers and a thumb. Or should I say four beautiful, long, slender fingers and one perfect thumb, connected to one perfect arm of one perfectly gorgeous female? And, I'm happy to add, there's no ring on the third finger of that hand."

She caught the smug little grin on his lips. Her tone hardened. "I get it. A showboat. I should have known. I don't have time to waste on some silver-tongued actor."

"Why, thank you. I had no idea you'd examined my tongue. Mind if I examine yours?"

She started to stand but his hand shot out, catching her by the wrist. "Sorry. That was really cheesy, but I couldn't resist teasing you."

His tone altered, deepened, just enough to have her glancing over to see if he was still teasing.

He met her look. "Are you always this serious?"

Despite his apology, she wasn't about to let him off the

hook, or change her mind about him. "In case you haven't noticed, rodeos are a serious business. Careless cowboys tend to break bones, or even their skulls, as hard as that may be to believe."

She stared down at the hand holding her wrist. Despite his smile, she could feel the strength in his grip. If he wanted to, he could no doubt break her bones with a single snap. But she wasn't concerned with his strength, only with the heat his touch was generating. She felt the tingle of warmth all the way up her arm. It alarmed her more than she cared to admit.

"My job is to minimize damage to anyone who is actually hurt."

"I'm grateful." He sat up so his laughing blue eyes were even with hers. If possible, his were even bluer than the perfect Montana sky above them. "What do you think? Any damage from that fall?"

Her instinct was to move back, but his fingers were still around her wrist, holding her close. "I'm beginning to wonder if you were actually tossed from that bull or deliberately fell."

"I'd have to be a little bit crazy to deliberately jump from the back of a raging bull just to get your attention, wouldn't I?"

"Yeah." She felt the pull of that magnetic smile that had so many of the local females lusting after Wyatt McCord. Now she knew why he'd gained such a reputation in such a short time. "I'm beginning to think maybe you are. In fact, more than a little. A whole lot crazy."

"I figured it was the best possible way to get you to actually talk to me. You couldn't ignore me as long as there was even the slightest chance that I might be hurt."

There was enough romance in her nature to feel flattered that he'd go to so much trouble just to arrange to meet her. At least, she thought, it was original. And just dangerous enough to appeal to a certain wild-and-free spirit that dominated her own life.

Then her practical side kicked in, and she felt an irrational sense of annoyance that he'd wasted so much of her time and energy on his weird idea of a joke.

"Oh, brother." She scrambled to her feet and dusted off her backside.

"Want me to do that for you?"

She paused and shot him a look guaranteed to freeze most men.

He merely kept that charming smile in place. "Mind if we start over?" He held out his hand. "Wyatt McCord."

"I know who you are."

"Okay. I'll handle both introductions. Nice to meet you, Marilee Trainor. Now that we have that out of the way, when do you get off work?"

"Not until the last bull rider has finished."

"Want to grab a bite to eat? When the last rider is done, of course."

"Sorry. I'll be heading home."

"Why, thanks for the invitation. I'd be happy to join you. We could take along some pizza from one of the vendors."

She looked him up and down. "I go home alone."

"Sorry to hear it." There was that grin again, doing strange things to her heart. "You're missing out on a really fun evening."

"You have a high opinion of yourself, McCord."

He chuckled. Without warning he touched a finger to

her lips. "Trust me. I'd do my best to turn that pretty little frown into an even prettier smile."

Marilee couldn't believe the feelings that collided along her spine. Splinters of fire and ice had her fighting to keep from shivering despite the broiling sun.

Because she didn't trust her voice, she merely turned on her heel and walked away from him.

It was harder to do than she'd expected. And though she kept her spine rigid and her head high, she swore she could feel the heat of that gaze burning right through her flesh.

It sent one more furnace blast rushing through her system. A system already overheated by her encounter with the bold, brash, irritatingly charming Wyatt McCord.

"A hundred bucks, cuz. And judging by that spectacular toss over the rail, I'd say you earned it."

Wyatt tucked the money into his pocket. "It was pretty spectacular, wasn't it? And it worked. It got the attention of our pretty little medic."

Jesse, Amy, and Zane stopped dead in their tracks.

Amy laughed. "You did all that to get Lee's attention?"

"Nothing else I've tried has worked. I was desperate."

Jesse shook his head in disbelief. "Did you ever think about just buying her a beer at the Fortune Saloon? I'd think that would be a whole lot simpler than risking broken bones leaping off a bull."

"But not nearly as memorable. The next time she sees me at the saloon, she'll know my name."

Zane threw back his head and roared. "So will every shrink from here to Helena. You have to be certifiably nuts to do all that just for the sake of a pretty face."

"Hey." Wyatt slapped his cousin on the back. "Whatever works."

Zane pulled out a roll of bills. "Ten says she's already written you off as someone to avoid at all costs."

Wyatt's smile brightened. "Chump change. If you want to bet me, make it a hundred."

"You got it." Zane pulled a hundred from the roll and handed it to Jesse. "Now match it, cuz. I was going to bet that you can't persuade Marilee Trainor to even speak to you again. But just to make things interesting, I'm betting that you can't get her to have dinner with you tonight."

"Dinner? Tonight? Now you're pushing the limits, cuz. She's already refused me."

"Put up or shut up."

Wyatt arched a brow. "You want me to kiss and tell?"

"I don't say anything about kissing. I don't care what you do, after you get her to have dinner with you. That's the bet. So if you're ready to admit defeat, just give me the hundred now."

"Uh-oh." Wyatt stopped dead in his tracks. "Is that a dare?"

Amy stood between them, shaking her head. "You sound like two little kids."

Wyatt shot her a wicked grin. "Didn't you know that all men are just boys at heart?"

He reached into his pocket and handed Zane a bill before he strolled away.

Over his shoulder he called, "I'll catch you back at the ranch. You can pay me then."

He left his cousins laughing and shaking their heads.

CHAPTER TWO

❧

Marilee stepped from the shower and turbaned her hair in a towel before slathering her fair skin with lotion. After toweling her hair she stepped into a pair of boy-style boxer shorts and tied a cotton shirt at her midriff.

Leaving her damp hair streaming down her back in a riot of tangles, she padded barefoot to the tiny kitchen of her apartment and set a kettle on for tea. After rummaging through the refrigerator, she decided her supper would have to be a peanut butter and jelly sandwich. She was too tired to bother with a grilled cheese. That would require taking out a pan, turning on the burner, and watching to see that she didn't burn it. Too much wasted energy.

While she waited for the water to boil, she sank down onto a barstool at the tiny kitchen counter. It had been a good day. Except for a run to Dr. Wheeler's clinic with an out-of-towner who needed stitches, there'd been no serious injuries. No broken bones. No head injuries. During rodeo time, this was considered a very good day indeed.

Rodeo. The very word had her smiling. She loved the sights and sounds and smells of the fairgrounds. Reveled in the people and animals and pageantry. Like the men and women who followed the circuit, she appreciated the athletic ability required to win an event. The professionals were superb athletes. But she also enjoyed the pure freedom expressed by the ordinary cowboys who showed up year after year just to compete with fellow wranglers. Not for fame, or money, or trophies, but for the pure love of the sport.

She loved mingling with the men and women who spent their lives doing the backbreaking work required to keep a ranch going. These were the people to whom rodeo meant the most. The same men and women who competed in hog-tying, calf-roping, and bull-riding for sport did the same thing all year on their ranches, not for sport but out of necessity. They honed their skills in the real world, far away from the glamour of these few days in the limelight.

In many ways this lifestyle was far removed from the life she'd lived growing up. Maybe that was why Gold Fever satisfied her so. After a lifetime of enduring the strict military code that had colored her childhood, she felt as though she'd somehow stepped into an alternate universe, where the only rules were those she set for herself.

She loved being in charge. Loved choosing the path less traveled by most of her friends. As a girl forced to pull up stakes at a moment's notice, she'd dreamed of putting down roots and staying long enough to really know the people around her. Though many of the ranchers in these parts rarely made the long drive to town, they always remembered her name and offered their hands in friendship. These were good, hardworking people, and she felt fortunate to live among them and call them friends.

When the kettle whistled, she sighed and heaved herself to her feet. Before she could reach it, there was a knock on the door.

While she tried to decide which one to deal with, there was a second knock. Curiosity won out, and she chose to ignore the kettle and see who was at her door at this late hour.

After peering through the tiny hole, she opened the door. "What are you . . . ? How did you find out where I live?"

"This is Gold Fever, remember? Everybody knows everything about everybody. I could have asked a dozen people, and they'd all know that Marilee Trainor lives in the apartment above the emergency medical garage on Nugget Street in downtown Gold Fever." Wyatt brushed past her and placed a cardboard box on the kitchen counter.

She barely remembered to close the door before following him. "Just a minute. I don't recall inviting you in."

"You didn't. I invited myself."

She stared at the box. "Is that pizza?"

"It is. But if you'd like me to leave . . ." He picked up the box and made a move to go.

"Wait." Without thinking, she put a hand on his arm. And became instantly aware of the ripple of muscle beneath the shirt sleeve.

He paused. "Hungry?"

Relieved to let go of him, she put a hand to her middle. "Starving. But I was too tired to do much about it."

He reached over and lifted the whistling teakettle off

the burner. "That's piercing. How can you stand it?" He turned to her. "Now, what were you saying? Did I hear you say 'Come on in, Wyatt'? 'I'm so thankful that you came along just in time to save me from starvation'?"

Though she wanted to laugh at his silly sense of humor, she managed to stop herself just in time. "I told you I wanted to be alone."

"And you will be. I'm leaving. Right after you guess what's on the pizza."

"I don't play games."

"Your loss. Try to guess anyway."

"Why don't I just peek?"

As she reached for the lid he put a hand over hers. "First, tell me what you like."

There it was again. That sizzle of electricity from the mere touch of him. "All right. I'll play along. But just to get you moving toward the door. The only things I like on my pizza are sausage, mushrooms, green pepper, and onion."

"Your wish . . ." He lifted the lid and she stared in surprise.

"Who told you?" Before he could say a word, she held up a hand. "Never mind. As you said, this is Gold Fever. Ask half the town what I like on my pizza, and they could probably tell you."

"Or, I could be a really gifted mind reader."

She couldn't hold back the laughter. "You could be. But I'll stick with door number one. What's in the bag?"

"Wine." He lifted it from the slim bag and pulled a corkscrew from his pocket.

At her arched brow, he grinned. "Just in case you didn't have one."

"My my. What a handyman. You do think of everything, don't you?"

"I try. Glasses?"

"You're assuming that I'm inviting you to stay."

"I'm assuming that you're as hungry as I am, and that the smell of this pizza is driving you crazy."

"You're right." She pointed to the cupboard above the stove. "The glasses are there."

He filled two stem glasses and handed one to her before leading her to the little sofa across the room.

"Here. Put your feet up. You've put in a long day."

"I have. And I will." She propped her feet on a little footstool and lifted the glass to her lips.

In his best Anthony Hopkins imitation, Wyatt purred, "A nice little glass of Chianti to go with the fava beans and the body I'm about to cut up for you."

She was still laughing as he rummaged in her cupboards and found two plates. Minutes later he settled himself beside her, and they ate and drank in companionable silence.

"Oh." Marilee sat back with a sigh. "I can't even tell you what that tasted like. I think I inhaled it."

"I know what you mean." Wyatt filled their plates a second time and topped off their glasses. "Now we can actually take our time and enjoy."

She did. And then followed up with a third slice of pizza before sitting back with a sigh of satisfaction while sipping her wine.

She glanced over. "I should be mad. I told you I wanted to be alone."

"Okay. I can take a hint." He started to get up. "I'll leave you now."

"Too late." She put a hand on his arm. "I've already accepted your hospitality. Now I invite you to accept mine."

He turned to her with a smile. "I was hoping you'd say that."

She studied him, from the wild mane of dark hair to the scuffed boots propped up beside her bare feet on the hassock. "Are you always so pushy, McCord?"

"What you call pushy, others might call confident."

"A rose by any other name . . ."

"Is what you remind me of."

She blinked at his sudden change of direction.

Before she could say a word he merely smiled. "One of those pale English roses, all cool and pink, with drops of dew still on the petals." He leaned close and breathed her in. "You smell like crushed roses."

"Body lotion." Her heart was hammering, and that knowledge had color rising to her cheeks. Damn him.

"I smelled you as soon as I walked in. You had my head swimming."

There was that smile again. She'd have called it cocky, except that it was beginning to grow on her. Or else she was a lot more tired than she realized. No energy left to fight. Yeah. That was the reason.

"I'll give you this, McCord. You certainly know how to think on your feet. I'm betting you've managed to use that line to get all kinds of girls to do your bidding."

"It's a curse, but I've learned to endure it." He topped off her glass and then his own. "Would you like me to start some coffee?"

"Not this late. The caffeine will have me tossing and turning all night long."

"Okay." He crossed one ankle over the other and leaned

his head back against the back of the sofa. "I like your place. It looks like you."

"All prim and tidy?"

"I was going to say fascinating." He pointed to the exotic piece of silk displayed in a simple black-lacquered frame hanging on the opposite wall, and the ornate shelves displaying a collection of Oriental masks and woven baskets. "Looks like you've done some traveling."

She nodded. "An Army brat. I never stayed in one school long enough to learn my classmates' names. My father said I was getting a better education than all those kids who lived in one town all their lives."

"That's one way of looking at it. How'd you end up in Gold Fever?"

She shrugged, uncomfortable talking about herself. "My mother and I came here after . . . my dad died, because her only living relative was here."

He'd noticed her slight hesitation. Did he detect an issue between Marilee and her father? Or was he reading more into this than was here? "A relative? Somebody I know?"

"Reese Trainor."

"I didn't know her well, but I remember that she ran a boardinghouse here in town."

"That's right. She was a third cousin. After she died, my mother moved on to Florida. She wanted me to join her, but I'm glad I chose not to."

"Why?" He was watching her eyes while she spoke. He loved the way they sparkled in the lamplight.

"Mom's passed away now, too. I would have been alone again. After a lifetime of traveling, it's nice to finally sink some roots." She looked over and saw him watching her. "I guess that sounds crazy."

He shook his head. "Not at all. I've been gone a long time, but I never stopped missing this place. The minute I returned, I knew I was home to stay."

"Oh, yeah. On your family's crazy treasure hunt." At his arched brow she added, "Big news in Gold Fever."

"Why do you call it crazy?"

"Isn't that what they said about old Coot?"

He laughed. "Runs in the family. I take it you're not a believer."

"Not at all."

"Even though you were dispatched to Treasure Chest Mountain after Vernon McVicker killed Rafe Spindler and tried to kill Jesse and Amy, as well? You still don't believe there's really a lost fortune?"

She shivered, recalling the grisly scene when one of the wranglers from the Lost Nugget Ranch was shot and killed by Coot McCord's trusted lawyer, who was in turn brought down by a team of sharpshooters from the state police. It was an ugly, twisted scheme designed to derail the McCord family from continuing their search for the lost treasure.

"Maybe your grandfather's lawyer believed in the treasure. Or maybe he just went off the deep end. Frankly, I don't care one way or the other how the rest of you spend your lives. But I think the whole lost-treasure lore is nothing more than a really good yarn."

"I'll accept an apology when you're forced to eat those words." He looked up. "Speaking of eating, we're not finished yet. There's dessert in that bag."

"Dessert?" Her head came up sharply. "What did you bring?"

"Tiramisu. Guaranteed to be the gooiest, yummiest confection you'll ever sink your teeth into."

"Bring it on."

As he got to his feet she carried her wine to the bar and set it aside before putting the kettle on the stove. Minutes later, with two huge slices of dessert, they perched on barstools and devoured every crumb before washing it down with steaming cups of tea.

He held up his cup. "Decaf?"

"Naturally. I'd like to get a little sleep tonight."

"I know something that will relax you even more than a cup of tea."

At his offhand remark she glanced over.

His lips quirked. "I give really great back rubs."

"I think I'll stick with tea."

"Your loss." He filled the sink with hot, soapy water and proceeded to wash their dishes.

Marilee picked up a linen towel and stood beside him, drying.

"Are you always this handy in a stranger's kitchen?"

He looked over at her. "I don't consider you a stranger. But in my travels, I've learned that I'm a more welcome guest if I clean up after myself."

"Where have your travels taken you?"

He shrugged. "I've been to a lot of places. Both here in the country and around the world."

"Was your father in the Army, too?"

He rinsed a plate and handed it to her. "Both of my parents suffered from wanderlust. They just had to see every exotic place they'd ever read about. I was still a kid when they pulled up stakes and left the Lost Nugget. I turned into the typical rebellious teen. I let them know, in every possible way, just how furious I was that they'd uprooted me and taken away my greatest pleasures in life.

My cousins, who were my best friends. My grandfather, who was my hero. And this countryside, that was as familiar to me as these rooms are to you."

"How did you rebel?"

He gave a laugh. "Think about every rotten thing a teen can do, and I did them all. Dropped out of school. Experimented with wine, women, and song. Explored cults, religions you've never heard of, and even lost myself in a few mountains and jungles."

"I'm sure that got their attention."

He shared her laughter. "Yeah. They got the message that I was mad as hell. Thankfully, I finally woke up to the fact that it was my life I was about to ruin, and not theirs. I finished college, tried my hand at a few respectable jobs, and made my parents proud before they died."

"I'm sorry, Wyatt. How did they die?"

His hands stilled. "Plane crash. They were off on another world adventure, this time to South America. When I got the word, I had just signed on as a counselor for troubled teens. I tendered my resignation and made a trek to Tibet to meditate for a month with some monks. Then I returned to civilization and decided to spend the rest of my life doing exactly as I pleased."

"And what is it that pleases you?"

"I thought I'd spend my time wandering the world. Funny how life hands us all these little surprises." He rinsed the last of the forks before draining the water from the sink and drying his hands. "When I got the message that Coot had died, I knew I had to come back. And the minute I got here, I knew I was home for good."

"Just like that?"

He smiled. "Just like that."

"It wouldn't have anything to do with the chance to find Coot's lost treasure?"

"The treasure you don't believe in." He shot her a dangerous smile. "I'm sure that has something to do with it. Coot made it possible for me to stay, and to feel useful. But I'm not sure now if I could have ever left. The pull of this place has always been strong. The minute I returned, I knew I was in over my head."

"Yeah. Me, too, but probably for a very different reason. You're here because it's home. I'm here because I always wanted one. And since my parents wouldn't make one for me, I decided to make one for myself."

He turned to study her. "Lots of Army brats feel at home all over the world."

"I'm sure I could have, too, if my parents had ever tried to make a home for us. My father . . ." She shrugged. "He was into issuing orders and having them followed to the letter. My mother and I were his troops, and when he didn't like what he saw, we paid for it."

"Your mother allowed that?"

"My mother bought into it. I doubt she ever made a simple decision in her life without my father's approval."

"And how did their daughter fit into all this?"

She smiled. "You know that rebel you talked about, who broke the rules and his parents' hearts?" When Wyatt nodded she added, "I fought my whole life for the right to make my own decisions and live with the consequences. It was a long, hard battle, with me acting like an out-of-control car and my father the brick wall I kept hitting. Until the day that wall crumbled, all I could do was keep revving my engine and dreaming of one day having my own power."

"And now you have it. Was it worth the fight?"

"I'll tell you when I quit fighting." Marilee hung the damp towel on a hook by the stove. When she turned, she stifled a yawn.

At once Wyatt turned away. "Time to head back to the ranch."

She followed him to the door. "Thanks for feeding me."

"Anytime." He stared at her mouth.

Seeing the direction of his gaze, she absorbed a jolt that brought a rush of color to her cheeks.

She leaned in slightly, anticipating his kiss. "'Night, rebel."

"Good night, Marilee."

"My friends call me Lee."

"Yeah. That's what Amy calls you. Lee." He tried it, then shook his head. "Sorry. I think I'd like to be more than your friend. But for now . . ." He touched his hand to her cheek, then turned and stepped through the doorway. "Good night, . . . Marilee."

The way he said her name, soft, almost a whisper, reminded her of a prayer.

She closed the door and latched it, all the while listening to the sound of his footsteps as he descended the outer stairs.

Her face felt flushed from his touch. To cool it, she pressed her forehead to the door and listened to the roar of the engine as he gunned his Harley. Lights flashed across her windows for a brief moment as he turned his motorcycle toward the distant ranch.

She'd been pleasantly surprised by Wyatt McCord. Oh, she'd seen him often in town, hair streaming behind him on his bike, or at the Fortune Saloon, surrounded by his family or a crew of wranglers from the ranch. She'd written him off as too handsome, too privileged, and probably completely self-absorbed.

Instead, he'd been funny and charming and interesting to talk to. And he was a good listener. She'd opened up to him the way she rarely opened up to anyone.

She smiled. It hadn't hurt that he'd brought her favorite pizza.

As she switched off the lights and made her way to her bedroom, Marilee decided that she was going to have to change her opinion of him. The brash, bold, annoying rebel was a man of many surprises. And the fact that he hadn't tried to turn his visit into an all-nighter was another point in his favor.

He hadn't even tried to kiss her.

As she made ready to sleep she had to brush aside the feeling of frustration over that. The truth was, a part of her had wanted him to. Another part was afraid he might.

Had she somehow conveyed her feelings to him? Maybe, she thought, he really was a mind reader.

She was too weary to puzzle over it.

After the day she'd put in, she was asleep as soon as her head touched the pillow.

CHAPTER THREE

The morning sky outside the kitchen window of the Lost Nugget Ranch was a clear, cloudless blue when Wyatt swaggered into the big ranch kitchen whistling a little tune.

That had the others looking up with interest.

"Sounds like you had a good night." Zane turned to his cousin as he helped himself to a glass of freshly squeezed orange juice from the counter before taking his seat across the table. "Does this mean you won the bet?"

Their great-aunt Cora, Coot's seventy-year-old sister, was seated across the table from rugged, white-haired Cal Randall, longtime foreman of the Lost Nugget. Cal was devoted to the ranch and to the woman seated across from him.

Though Cora was a world-renowned artist whose wild-life paintings sold for outrageous sums of money, she continued to live a simple life in her childhood home, where she was more comfortable wearing her brother's cast-offs than her own clothes. In the town of Gold Fever she was known as an odd eccentric, as out-of-step as her crazy brother had been.

Cora's head came up, and she studied her nephews with interest. "What bet?"

Jesse heard the note of disapproval in her tone. Their aunt, who willingly shared her home with her nephews, detested gambling. "Wyatt bet me a hundred dollars that he'd be having dinner last night with Marilee Trainor."

Wyatt gave a smug smile. "I'll take that hundred now, if you don't mind."

"Not so fast." Zane glanced around at the others. "What proof do we have that you actually won? For all we know, you could have stopped off at the Fortune Saloon for one of Daffy's greasy burgers before driving back to the ranch."

"I could have. But then I wouldn't be able to describe Marilee's apartment in detail."

Amy took that moment to enter the room, looking pretty in fresh denims and a gauzy shirt. She paused to brush a kiss over Jesse's cheek before taking the seat beside him. "I've been in Lee's apartment dozens of times. Go ahead, Wyatt. Describe it."

"Small, efficient kitchen with two barstools." He arched a brow. "Where we shared tiramisu and decaf tea. Cozy sofa along one wall, with a little fancy embroidered footstool. A lot of interesting artifacts collected on her life of travels as an Army brat. Exotic silk framed in black on one wall, and lots of masks and baskets on her shelves."

Amy nodded before saying to the others, "He nailed it."

"Yeah. But what proof do we have that he actually ate there?" Jesse shot his cousin a triumphant look.

"I suppose I could demand an autopsy, to prove what the poor victim ate at her last meal." That had everyone around the table grinning at his outrageous sense of humor. "But since that seems a bit radical, you'll have to take my word for it. We shared a pizza with her favorite toppings— sausage, mushrooms, onions, and green pepper—as well as a bottle of Chianti and, to top it off, tiramisu."

"Be still my heart." Amy mockingly touched a hand to her heart. "What single woman wouldn't welcome a man bearing such gifts?"

Wyatt shot her a killer grin. "My thoughts exactly."

"Oh, you're good, cuz." Jesse slapped him on the back while Zane handed over his money.

"Of course, as pretty as she is, Marilee has a flaw."

They all waited as Wyatt sipped his coffee.

"Okay, cuz. Out with it." Zane leaned forward.

"She thinks Coot deserved his nickname. She doesn't believe there ever was a fortune, and that anybody who's willing to join in the search for it is just as crazy."

Jesse laughed. "Is that all? Hell, half the town of Gold Fever figures we're all loony. I wouldn't be surprised if they're taking bets to see which one of us crashes and burns first."

"So," Zane asked casually, "does this mean you've lost interest in pretty little Marilee Trainor?"

"Not at all." Wyatt glanced around the table. "I figure I'll just have to pour on a little more charm until she's willing to see the light."

"I think I ought to warn you." Amy nibbled a light-as-air biscuit. "Lee is well-liked by everyone in Gold Fever, and she returns the sentiment. She genuinely likes people, and they're drawn to her. But she's really careful about letting anyone get too close. She guards her friendships, and she's single by choice."

"So, you're saying I'll have an uphill climb."

Amy smiled. "More like an impossible climb."

"Thanks for the warning. I love a challenge."

Jesse turned to Zane. "This should prove interesting. Maybe we ought to take a couple more bets."

Throughout all of this, Cora sat back sipping her coffee and enjoying the easy banter between her grandnephews. When Zane and Wyatt had returned to the Lost Nugget Ranch for her brother's funeral, she'd feared their relationships had been too badly damaged to ever be repaired. Now the old friendship they'd once enjoyed had blossomed anew, and they had once again become the easy, fun-loving family she'd hoped they could be.

Cal Randall winked at Cora across the table. "Who do they remind you of, Cora?"

"Coot." She glanced around, meeting their smiles. "You're all so much like your grandfather. I find myself thinking several times a day how much he would have enjoyed all this."

"He is enjoying it, Aunt Cora." Jesse circled the table to brush a kiss over her cheek. "He's the one who set the terms and conditions in his will, and he knew exactly what he was doing. Thrown together again, we had to learn to swim or sink. Nobody but Coot would have been so sly. You don't think he'd leave all this behind without sticking around to watch, do you?"

Cora blinked away the tears that sprang to her eyes before touching a hand to her nephew's cheek. "You're right, of course, Jess. I feel him here so often."

"Me, too." He straightened and caught his bride's hand. "Come on. I promised you a grand tour of the property."

"Tour?" Cora looked puzzled. "I would think, growing up right next door to our ranch, you'd know this land as intimately as you do your father's place."

"We're scouting locations to build our own ranch." Amy blew a kiss to Cora and allowed herself to be led from the room.

Zane looked around the table. "Why would anyone want to leave this to build their own?"

Wyatt shrugged. "You think we're in the way? Maybe the newlyweds aren't getting enough privacy."

Zane winked at his aunt. "Or maybe they're thinking about adding to the nest."

They all saw the sudden light that came into Cora's eyes.

Cal got to his feet. "I'm heading up to the north range. Either of you interested in riding along?"

"I'm up for it." Zane was on his feet, touching a hand to the ever-present movie camera in his shirt pocket.

"I think I'll go, too." Wyatt polished off the last of his omelet and turned to the cook. "Great breakfast, Dandy."

"Wait'll you try my dinner. Slow-cooked roast beef tonight, with garden vegetables."

"I'll be here." Wyatt called.

Zane's voice drifted from the mudroom where he was busy taking a wide-brimmed hat from a hook by the door. "Count me in."

When they were gone Dandy topped off Cora's cup. "Nice to see the house alive with all those young stallions, Miss Cora."

She nodded. "I was just thinking the same thing." She picked up her cup and started toward the door. As always, she was wearing her brother's old overalls and a paint-stained shirt. "I'll be in my studio, Dandy."

The cook was already busy cleaning off the table, the countertops, the floor. He wouldn't stop, she knew, until the kitchen sparkled. It was his trademark, and everyone at the Lost Nugget Ranch had learned to respect his rules. No dirty boots leaving marks on his floor. No dirty hands at the table. No hats allowed past the hooks on the mud-room wall.

They were all willing to do whatever it took to keep the obsessively neat Dandy happy so that he was free to make the best food in the state of Montana.

As she headed toward her studio, Cora's heart felt light. Could it be that Jesse and Amy were thinking about starting a family? Though she couldn't imagine this house without Jesse here under the same roof, it was enticing to think about another generation growing up on this land she and her brother loved with such passion.

Once inside her barnlike studio she set to work, her mind focused on capturing the intricate light she'd seen just before the sun dipped beneath the peaks of Treasure Chest Mountain. Though her paintings fetched obscene amounts of money in the international art world, Cora never thought about that. Her only concern was capturing the beauty of her beloved countryside on canvas. It was her pride, her passion, her life.

As always, she was soon lost in her latest work of art.

Marilee showered and dressed, all the while sipping coffee and listening to the drone of news on the local

TV station. After clipping her cell phone to her belt, she headed downstairs to spend a pleasant hour cleaning her rescue vehicle. Although it was owned by the county, she took pride in always having it ready for any emergency. That meant a full tank of gas, along with a fresh supply of linens, blankets, cots, and first-aid supplies.

Parked alongside it was her ancient truck, which she drove when she was on her own time.

When the rescue vehicle was clean, she drove to the clinic, also owned by the city of Gold Fever, and staffed by Dr. Frank Wheeler and Elly Carson, his trusted nurse-practitioner.

Marilee stepped inside the clinic and breathed in the familiar scent of disinfectant.

Elly looked up from the phone and waved without missing a beat of her conversation.

"Are the spots on Timmy's stomach flat or raised, Paula?" She paused. "Uh-huh. Oozy?" She winced. "Okay. Chicken pox. You'll have to keep him quarantined." She laughed. "I know, Paula. And I'm sure he was contagious for the past forty-eight hours, which means half the class will be down with it in the next week or so. Can't be helped. You'll have to miss work until Dr. Wheeler says you can send him back to school. He'll want to see him first. Call when the rash is gone."

She hung up, grinning. "Poor Paula Henning. She said she'll go stir-crazy if she can't leave her ranch. I can hardly wait to talk to Kristy O'Conner and tell her that one of her students has come down with chicken pox."

"Now I remember why I didn't go into teaching." Marilee opened a cabinet and began filling a plastic tub with supplies. "Any emergencies?"

Elly gave a shake of her head. "A quiet night for a change. I bet, after all those hours at the rodeo, you were glad for the break."

"Yeah." Marilee decided not to mention her visitor. Though Elly was a good friend, she wasn't ready to share this with her yet. Everybody in Gold Fever loved knowing everybody else's business, almost as much as they loved sharing it with the world. At least for now, she would keep Wyatt McCord to herself. Besides, she reminded herself, it wasn't as though anything was going to come of it.

When the phone rang, Elly picked it up and gave her usual cheerful response. "'Morning. Gold Fever Clinic." In the blink of an eye her tone changed to that of a professional. "Is she bleeding? No, Frances. Don't try to move her. Stay with her. Marilee is here now. She'll be right over. Is the front door unlocked? Five minutes. Stay put."

She replaced the receiver. "Delia Cowling didn't answer her door when her neighbor Fran Tucker got there for coffee. Apparently Delia took a fall in her basement. She's lucid and isn't bleeding. That's all I know."

Marilee turned away, hugging the plastic tub of supplies to her chest. "I'm on it."

Elly put a hand on her arm. "A word of warning, Lee. I don't know if you've had much contact with Delia, but you certainly know her reputation. She's practically made a career out of being nasty. With that vile temper of hers, you'll need to handle her with kid gloves."

"Thanks. I'll keep that in mind." Marilee headed for the door. "I'll report in as soon as I've determined the extent of her injuries."

Minutes later she was pulling up outside the home of the woman who proudly called herself the town's historian. Delia Cowling knew everything that had gone on in Gold Fever for the past sixty years. And was more than happy to share her knowledge with anyone willing to listen. That was why most who knew her well referred to her not as the town historian, but as the town gossip, who had managed to offend nearly everyone in Gold Fever with her wicked tongue at one time or another.

Thankfully, Marilee thought as she climbed the steps of the neat white frame house and let herself in the front door, she'd never personally been on the receiving end of Delia's famous temper.

The smell of coffee wafted from the kitchen.

Though she hadn't been in Delia's house before, Marilee quickly located the open door leading to the basement stairs.

"Delia?" She descended the stairs. "Frances?"

"We're down here."

The lights were on, and Delia lay on the cold, damp cement floor, surrounded by the littered contents of an upended box.

An afghan had been tossed over her.

"She was shivering when I found her." Fran Tucker knelt beside her neighbor, looking absolutely terrified. "I ran upstairs to call the clinic and grabbed this. I hope it's okay."

Marilee nodded as she removed the afghan and began a quick examination of the woman on the floor.

"Any pain, Delia?"

"Of course. How do you think you'd feel if you fell? I hurt all over." Her voice trembled.

Marilee probed gently. "Where is the worst pain?"

"My ankle. I slipped and tried to catch myself, but I went down so fast there wasn't time. And then I heard a knocking on my door, and I was terrified that whoever was there would just give up and leave me down here." Her voice rose. "I could have died down here and nobody would have even known."

"Hush now, Delia." Her neighbor stood, wringing her hands. "You're not going to die."

"But I could have."

Hearing the bubble of hysteria in her tone, Marilee was quick to soothe. "Thank heavens for good neighbors."

Delia nodded. "I was so grateful to see Fran coming down those stairs."

Her neighbor shrugged. "I felt like an intruder letting myself in like that, without an invitation. I know how Delia guards her privacy." Her tone became more accusing. "It wouldn't be the first time that she ignored my knock and refused to come to the door."

"Sometimes I just don't feel like company." Delia's tone was sharp.

"More often than not." Frances brought her hands to her hips, ready to do battle.

Marilee decided to intervene before these two went at each other's throats. "What made you come inside, Fran?"

"I thought I heard Delia calling for help. Once I stepped inside, I was able to follow the sound of her voice."

"Apparently you had some angels on your side, Delia."

"Angels? More like demons, sending me flying like this."

Marilee was accustomed to patients babbling. It was a good sign that the adrenaline was kicking in. But in Delia's case, the quick temper was a sign she wasn't badly hurt.

Marilee did a quick check of the older woman's vitals. Though her blood pressure was a bit high, that was to be

expected under the circumstances. Fortunately, except
for some swelling in her ankle, she seemed in very good
condition.

"Nothing's broken. I'm going to get you up slowly.
Don't do a thing. Just let me do the lifting, all right?"

"If you say so." Delia's tone was petulant as she was
helped to a sitting position.

Marilee noted her pallor and gave her time to clear her
head before taking the next step. "Frances and I are going
to get you up those stairs."

"I can do it myself. I've been climbing those stairs for
more than sixty years."

"Not today. I insist you let us help." Marilee's tone
was firm.

With Marilee on one side and her sturdy neighbor on
the other, they got the older woman up the stairs and to
her bedroom.

Once there Marilee got Delia comfortably into bed
before retrieving supplies from her vehicle and wrapping
the ankle.

"Dr. Wheeler will want to take a look at this."

Frances caught Delia's hand. "I'll take you over there
later today. Do you want me to stay with you, or would
you rather rest?"

Delia looked away, clearly annoyed at being helpless
and at the mercy of others. "If you don't mind, I think I'll
sleep a bit. We'll have coffee another time."

Frances nodded. "I'll turn off the coffeemaker and
we'll start a fresh pot later."

"There's no need . . ."

Delia's voice trailed off when she realized her neighbor had ignored her protest.

She turned to Marilee. "I can't believe this happened. I've always been so careful when I go downstairs. That old cement floor is cracked and dangerous. But Frances had been bragging about her excellent spiced-apple cake that had taken a blue ribbon at the fair, and I went in search of my mother's old recipe, hoping I'd find it in my keepsake box of her things."

"Were you thinking of competing with Frances in this year's competition?"

Delia blushed, her only admission of guilt. "The next thing I knew I was slipping. I remember grabbing onto the edge of the shelf to stop my fall, but I caught a cardboard box by mistake and then I was down. No fool like an old fool."

Marilee placed a hand over Delia's. "Don't beat yourself up over it. These things happen. That's why they're called accidents. At least nothing's broken."

"Oh, my." Delia touched a hand to her throat and gave a gasp. "My mother's locket. It must have broken free when I fell." She clutched Marilee's wrist. "Would you mind going downstairs to find it? It's a small gold heart on a chain. It means the world to me."

"I'll look for it. You rest now." Marilee pulled the bed linens over her patient and made her way down the stairs.

"What a mess," she muttered as she looked around.

It was obvious that Delia had tried to break her fall by grabbing hold of the stash of old boxes that littered the shelves. The one she'd managed to snag had broken open, spilling yellowed letters and documents all over the floor.

It wasn't going to be an easy matter to find one small locket and chain in all this mess.

"Just part of the job," Marilee sighed as she dropped to her knees and began trying to make order out of the chaos.

She set the empty box in the middle of the mess and began picking up the papers, placing them one by one in a neat pile inside. She was nearly done when she came to a torn scrap of yellowed paper. Underneath it lay Delia's locket and chain. Tucking the jewelry into her pocket, Marilee was about to add this paper to the pile when her eye caught the word in a large scrawl.

Gold.

She paused to read more and made out the words:

Can't believe my good fortune. I found gold nuggets the size of a man's fist.

Marilee's heart started pounding. Everyone in Gold Fever talked about the diary kept by Nathanial McCord, the McCord ancestor who had originally found the treasure in 1862 at Grasshopper Creek. Though much of his journal had been found, there were thought to be many more pages missing.

She studied the paper, which was worn, wrinkled, and water-stained. Could this be part of that journal? If so, what was it doing in Delia Cowling's basement, in this old box of papers?

She picked up another paper. Though it didn't appear to be nearly as old as the first, it contained crude drawings of hills, with X's marked over certain ones, and notations about possible places to hide a fortune.

Electrified, Marilee sat back on her heels.

Though this was none of her business, she felt a need to ask Delia about what she'd found.

Keeping these two pages, she placed the box and its contents back on the shelf before making her way up the stairs.

In the bedroom, Delia was sound asleep.

Marilee stood for several seconds before coming to

a decision. She set the old woman's locket and broken chain on the night table and then made her way outside to phone a report to the clinic.

As for the papers in Delia's possession, no matter what reason she might give for having them, Marilee believed the McCord family had a right to know about their existence.

Though she had steadfastly refused to believe that old Coot McCord's hunt for his ancestor's lost treasure would ever lead to anything, she couldn't deny the quick little flutter around her heart. Maybe it was the thought that she could add to the lore of the lost treasure.

Or maybe, she thought with a sigh, it was simply because she'd come up with the perfect excuse to see Wyatt McCord again.

Chapter Four

———◆◆◆———

Marilee parked the rescue vehicle in the garage before climbing into her old, battered truck. Digging out her cell phone, she dialed the medical clinic.

At the familiar voice she said, "Elly? I'm headed out to the Lost Nugget Ranch."

At Elly's note of concern, she was quick to reply. "Oh, no. Don't worry. Nobody's sick or hurt at the ranch. I just have something that needs to be delivered."

She knew she was being deliberately evasive, but there was no way she could explain. "I hope you and Doc don't have to make a run while I'm gone. But if you do, I wanted you to be prepared. You know where I keep the spare keys."

She could hear the smile in Elly's voice on the cell phone. "You give Miss Cora my best, you hear?"

"I sure will. I'll check back with you on my way home." Marilee tucked away her cell phone and turned up the radio, singing along with Taylor Swift at the top of her lungs. With the windows open and her hair blowing on the breeze, she felt a bubble of happiness that wasn't entirely caused by the gentle weather or the brilliant sunshine. Part of it was, she knew, the fact that she was about to see Wyatt. And part of it was simply that she was enjoying the aura of mystery and anticipation surrounding the papers she'd found in Delia's basement.

"Hey, Cal." Wyatt's voice from the bed of the truck had Cal and Zane, seated in the cab, glancing out the back window. "Could you be a little more careful going over this rise?"

He had both arms around the bawling heifer that they'd found tangled in barbed wire. After a quick examination of the injuries, Cal had decided to bring the heifer in to the main barn, where they could keep an eye on her while her injured leg mended.

Zane aimed his camera out the open window, capturing the image of his cousin, shirtfront stained with the heifer's blood, trying his best to calm the frightened animal while the truck rocked from side to side, taking the dips and curves at breakneck speed.

"Hold on. We're almost there." Cal sped through an open gate and took the last hundred yards like Mario Andretti.

Zane leaped out to open the barn door. The truck came to a halt inside, and within minutes a couple of the wranglers had the heifer in a stall, where Cal and a grizzled cowboy knelt, applying an antibiotic to the cuts.

Wyatt and Zane watched until the animal was treated before they headed out into the sunlight.

Marilee's old truck wheezed to a stop and she stepped out.

One look at Wyatt's shirt, covered in blood, had her racing toward him. "You idiot. What did you do this time? Try to ride one of the bulls out on the range?"

He was too startled by the sight of her, all tidy and springtime-fresh, to do more than gape. Then, as he realized what she was talking about, he stared down at his bloody clothing before shooting her that killer smile. "All in a day's work, ma'am."

"Get that shirt off and let me look at the cuts."

"Can't wait to get me naked, is that it?"

She was already reaching for the buttons of his shirt, while Zane stood to one side, watching and grinning.

"See what happens, cuz?" Wyatt went very still while she fumbled with the damp fabric. Though he was cracking jokes, he couldn't completely ignore the little thrill that raced up his spine when she freed first one button, then the next. "I feed a woman, and right away she wants to undress me. It's been the story of my life."

Marilee parted his shirt, then seemed startled by the absence of blood on his chest.

"What . . . ?" She stared again at the bloody shirt, then looked up to find him grinning from ear to ear.

"A poor helpless heifer got caught in some barbed wire. We brought her back for observation. But I didn't want to spoil your chance to do your Florence Nightingale routine."

Though she drew back and huffed out a breath, she couldn't help laughing at herself. "Okay. You got me." She looked over at Zane, who joined in the laughter. "Hi. I'm Marilee Trainor."

"Nice to meet you, Marilee. Zane McCord. You already know my cousin, the jokester. He makes quite an impression, doesn't he?"

"Oh, yeah." She tried not to stare at the ripple of muscle she'd bared during that comedy routine.

"What brings you all this way?" Wyatt tucked his hands in his back pockets to keep from touching her and rocked on the heels of his boots. "Thinking of feeding me?"

"I suppose I do owe you dinner. But I'll leave that for another night." She pointed to her truck. "I brought something I think will interest you and your family."

"Why don't you bring it inside?" He started toward the back porch. "I'll just wash up and dig out a clean shirt."

She watched him saunter away and had to admit that his backside looked as good in those faded denims as his bare chest had just seconds ago.

When she realized that Zane was watching her, she turned away to fetch the papers from her truck. Minutes later she and Zane walked into the kitchen.

Zane handled the introductions. Afterward, Dandy welcomed her with a choice of iced tea or lemonade.

She stared at the plate of fruit. "Did you actually squeeze fresh lemons?"

He looked offended. "Is there any other way?"

She shared a laugh with Zane. "I see you haven't heard of instant lemonade."

Dandy sniffed. "That's for amateurs." He handed her a frosty glass with a slice of fresh lemon decorating the sugar-dipped rim.

By the time Wyatt had returned from his room, tucking a clean shirt into his waistband, she was sitting at the kitchen table, sipping lemonade and talking with Zane and Dandy.

"I passed Aunt Cora in her studio and told her you'd come by for a visit." Wyatt snagged a glass of lemonade from the counter and pulled up a chair beside Marilee's. "She's cleaning up before coming to say hi."

Cora bustled into the kitchen, still wiping her hands on a rag that reeked of paint thinner. "Marilee. How grand to see you." She tucked the rag in the back pocket of her bib overalls as she rounded the table and engulfed the young woman in a bear hug. "It's been too long."

"Yes, ma'am. It has." Marilee kissed the older woman's cheek. "How're you doing, Miss Cora?"

"Fine. It's been quite a comfort to have these boys back home." Cora glanced around the table, her smile radiant as she took in Wyatt and Zane.

"Elly wanted me to say hi. She sends you her best."

Cora accepted a glass of lemonade from Dandy before settling herself at the table beside Zane. "How's Elly's husband, Mac?"

"According to Elly, Mac's as ornery as ever."

The two women shared an easy laugh just as Jesse and Amy came strolling into the kitchen.

When Amy spotted Marilee she danced across the floor to hug her.

After returning the hug Marilee held her a little away and gave her old friend a long look. "Marriage agrees with you."

"Thanks." Amy shot a quick glance at her husband. "Jess and I have been scouting locations for our spread."

"You're leaving the Lost Nugget?"

"Oh, no." Amy was quick to correct her. "Jesse could never leave here. But we thought we'd start looking for a site to build our own house. Not right away, but maybe in a year or two."

Out of the corner of his eye, Wyatt saw his aunt give

a long sigh. To her credit, her smile remained in place. A year or more would definitely give her time to get used to the idea of Jesse moving. He'd lived his entire life in this house, and he was more like a son to her than a great-nephew.

Jesse held Amy's chair and handed her a glass of lemonade before sitting down beside her. "I didn't see your rescue vehicle, so I guess this is a social call." He glanced beyond her to Wyatt and arched a brow. "What brings you out to the Lost Nugget, Lee?"

The look hadn't been lost on Marilee. It was obvious that Jesse, not to mention the rest of his family, was aware of Wyatt's nighttime visit to her apartment.

So much for keeping secrets.

She felt her palms sweating. It was difficult for her to comprehend so many people living in such close quarters. All of them here, under this roof, and knowing one another's business.

Knowing her business.

It occurred to her that as an only child she wasn't at all prepared for this big, open, inquisitive family. What's more, having moved so often, she'd rarely had a chance to develop the sort of close friendships that allowed her to share her most intimate thoughts and feelings with other people. In fact, she had become very good at keeping people from getting too close.

She felt, as she had so often in the past, like an outsider. Not really connected to anyone, and especially these people who seemed so comfortable with one another.

With an effort she pulled herself back from her troubling thoughts. "I had an emergency call this morning. Delia Cowling took a fall in her basement."

Cora lowered her drink. "I hope she's all right."

"She's fine. A sprained ankle, but nothing broken except her mother's locket. After making her comfortable I went back downstairs to hunt for the locket and chain. She'd overturned a box of old papers, and while cleaning them up I found some things I thought just might be of interest to all of you."

Because Wyatt was beside her, she handed the papers to him and watched as he read the first, then the second.

He shot her an incredulous look before handing them over to his aunt. As soon as she looked at the first page she let out a cry, and the others left their places at the table to crowd around her and read over her shoulder.

"This"—Cora lifted the stained, wrinkled paper—"has to be part of Nathanial's diary." She turned to her nephew. "Jesse, would you mind fetching that box from Coot's room? You know the one I mean."

He raced from the room and returned minutes later bearing a leather-bound box. Lifting the lid, he removed the crumbling notebook.

Cora studied it almost reverently as she explained to Marilee. "This is what remains of Nathanial McCord's diary. Some of it was found in the rotted cabin he shared that winter in 1862 when he and his father, Jasper, came to Montana to seek their fortune."

Wyatt picked up the thread. "Over the years a lot of the pages were lost, blown about the countryside by storms. But from what we've read, fourteen-year-old Nathanial was close to starvation and half-frozen when he stumbled onto a fortune in gold nuggets at Grasshopper Creek."

Marilee gasped. "I guess that would go a long way to ease his hunger and cold."

"You bet." Wyatt grinned. "The only trouble is, it was stolen that night at a room above the saloon, and Jasper was murdered."

Cora nodded. "At the time, everybody believed the crime was committed by Grizzly Markham, a fearsome miner who'd been drinking with Jasper and listening to him boast of his newly discovered fortune. Jasper had foolishly allowed everyone in the saloon that night to see the nuggets. When young Nathanial woke in the morning to find the fortune gone and his father's throat slashed, he set off to avenge his father's murder and retrieve the gold."

Marilee was clearly caught up in the tale. "I guess he wasn't successful, or you wouldn't still be searching."

Cora's voice lowered to a hush. "Markham was found weeks later, dead in the same manner as Jasper, and the gold missing. Some said Nathanial had his revenge. Others pointed out that he was only a boy, not capable of such a thing. Whatever the truth, Nathanial spent the rest of his life searching for the gold, which he believed to be stashed somewhere nearby, and which we still consider our legacy." She held the newly discovered page next to the open notebook and waited for the others to see what was so obvious.

Jesse swore under his breath. "Look at the scrawled handwriting. And the size and texture of the paper. It's a perfect match."

The others crowded around.

"And this." Cora held up the second paper. "It's undeniably Coot's. Everyone in this town is familiar with his doodles and drawings and markings."

Jesse's eyes narrowed on Marilee. "How did Delia Cowling explain what these were doing in her basement?"

"She was asleep. I . . ." Marilee spread her hands. "I knew I had no right to bring these out here, but I just thought you had the right to know about them."

Seeing her embarrassment, Wyatt laid a hand over hers. "You did the right thing. And now it's up to us to find out how these came to be in Delia's possession."

Around the table, the others nodded.

Marilee met his stare. "I'll need to go with you when you talk to her. I owe her an explanation for daring to take something of hers without permission. This was totally unprofessional. A medic is expected to treat the patients and their possessions with respect." She turned to the others. "And even though I felt this would be a matter of importance to all of you, I still had no right to reveal her secret without her knowledge and explicit permission."

Cora spoke for all of them. "Marilee, you have the respect of everyone in this community. I can't imagine that Delia would find fault with what you did."

Wyatt shrugged. "How can you be so sure of that, Aunt Cora? If Marilee made the connection to our family with only a glance at these papers, why wouldn't Delia have done the right thing years ago and returned them to their rightful owners? Unless," he added, "she had every intention of keeping them a secret."

"For what reason?"

At Jesse's question, Wyatt's tone lowered. "That what I intend to find out. We all thought, after that incident with Vernon McVicker, that he'd been acting alone. What if there were others who coveted the gold?"

Jesse nodded. "I agree. But I'm finding it pretty hard to believe that Delia Cowling would have been involved in some sort of conspiracy."

Zane set aside his lemonade. "We need to find out the truth."

Jesse glanced around. "I say we confront Delia now."

His two cousins nodded.

Cora lifted the lemonade to her lips and drank. "I believe I'll wait here while you confront Delia."

When Jesse frowned, she set down her glass and met his look, as though daring him to argue with her decision. "Delia and I haven't spoken in years. I intend to go back to my studio and finish my work before the light fades." When she saw that her nephew was about to protest, she said firmly, "You can let me know what you find out when you return."

"Yes, ma'am." He caught Amy's hand. "I'll drive."

Zane picked up his video camera and followed.

Behind them, Wyatt called, "I'll ride along with Marilee."

When they were settled in her truck he stretched out his long legs and watched her drive as she followed behind Jesse's ranch truck.

"Last I heard, you didn't believe in old Coot's lost fortune." Wyatt shot her one of those mellow smiles when she turned to look at him. "Am I mistaken, or have you had a change of heart?"

Marilee couldn't help laughing. "I would have been the last one in this town to believe in the McCord pipe dream. But that old paper really got to me. Just reading the word *gold* had me sweating." She shook her head. "I still can't believe I'd violate my own code of ethics like that and bring you something of Delia's without her permission."

"Except that this doesn't belong to Delia Cowling. It's ours. Plain and simple. And she'd better have a really good explanation for having those papers locked away in her basement for all these years, or she'll be answering to Ernie Wycliff."

At the mention of the police chief, Marilee's hands tightened on the wheel of her truck.

She'd opened a real can of worms. And now, ready or not, she would just have to deal with it.

CHAPTER FIVE

Jesse, always the hothead, was out of his truck and sprinting up the walkway to Delia's house before the others had even exited their vehicles. By the time they joined him, he was frowning.

"Delia isn't answering the door."

Marilee checked her watch. "She's probably at the clinic. I told her to have Dr. Wheeler check her ankle. Her neighbor Frances Tucker offered to drive her."

They trailed back to their trucks and headed over to the clinic across town.

Elly was just tidying up one of the examination rooms when they strode inside.

She looked up. "Which one of you needs to see the doctor?"

Marilee stepped around the others. "Nobody here needs to see Dr. Wheeler. We're looking for Delia Cowling."

"Oh." Elly stepped to the sink and washed her hands with disinfectant soap. "She's gone. Nothing to worry about. Doc said it was just a bad sprain. But she'll have to stay off her foot for a while. Frances agreed to drive her to Shelbyville to stay with her cousin." Elly chuckled. "Her poor cousin. Delia was already feeling grumpy when she arrived. By the time she left, she was indulging in a huge pity-party. I hope her cousin has some Valium."

Marilee arched a brow. "Did Dr. Wheeler prescribe it for Delia?"

Elly shook her head. "Not for Delia. For her cousin. By the time Delia leaves, she's going to need it. That woman's mean mouth would give the angels a headache."

Though Marilee enjoyed Elly's joke, the others weren't laughing.

Jesse gave a hiss of impatience. "Did Delia say when she was coming home?"

"Not exactly. I guess she'll lean on her cousin until she can easily put her full weight on that ankle." The nurse glanced from Jesse to Zane to Wyatt, who wore matching looks of disgust. "Something wrong?"

"Nothing." Marilee was quick to smile. "We had something to ask her, but it can wait until she gets back in town."

"All right then." Elly began switching off lights as she trailed them to the front door. "It's been a full day. Doc was heading home, and I'm on my way to meet Harding Jessup over at the hardware store. He swears his newest faucet is guaranteed not to leak. I'm going to hold him to it. This will be the third replacement in a year."

When she left, the three cousins paused outside the clinic, feeling a letdown after the adrenaline rush they'd experienced earlier.

Jesse looked around. "I guess there's nothing to do but wait until Delia gets back."

Zane nodded.

Jesse turned to Marilee. "Thanks again. I really appreciate what you did."

"I wish it could have been more."

He shrugged. "It's not your fault that Delia decided to leave town." He caught his wife's hand. "I'm starving. Want to eat in town or head back to the ranch?"

Amy looked up at him. "I'd rather go back. I think Aunt Cora will want to hear how our meeting went."

"You're right." He looked over at Zane. "Coming with us?"

"Sure thing." Disappointed that the adventure hadn't turned out as he'd hoped, Zane tucked his video camera in his pocket.

As they started toward the truck, Wyatt held back and touched a hand to Marilee's shoulder. "I can ride back with them, and save you a trip. Or if you'd like, I'll spring for supper at the Fortune Saloon."

She grinned. "I believe I owe you a meal. If you stay, I'll buy."

"We'll flip for it later." He held the door for her, then circled around and climbed into the passenger side. "But remember, if I stay, you'll have that long drive back to the ranch, and then home alone."

She laughed. "I'm a big girl. I think I can handle it."

He shrugged. "Your call."

As the others settled into the ranch truck, he motioned for Zane to lower the window.

Cupping his hand to his mouth he shouted, "I'll catch you back at the ranch later."

Marilee couldn't miss the wide smiles on his cousins' faces. They thought Wyatt McCord was going to get lucky.

Maybe he was. And then again, maybe he wasn't. She had no idea how the night would end. She was allowing Wyatt McCord to get too close, too quickly. She'd been there a time or two before and had been burned every time. Now that she felt stronger and wiser, she had no intention of simply falling into a relationship. But there were times, like right now, that she could feel herself sliding along, unsure of where she might land. And that bothered her much more than she cared to admit, because she was a person who needed to be in charge of every aspect of her life.

Still, he was such fun to be with. And what was the harm in having a little fun? She hadn't felt this comfortable with a man in a very long time.

Comfortable? Who was she kidding? Whenever she was with Wyatt, she was forced to deal with all kinds of strange, new emotions, not one of which was comfort.

The sudden tingle along her spine meant she was beginning to realize that she may have stepped into something over her head.

She intended to take this slow and easy. Tonight was nothing more than a meal and a few laughs. After that, she would just have to take charge and see that she didn't allow the night and her charming companion to take this to a level she wasn't prepared to deal with.

"Why, just look at you, big as life." Daffodil Spence, who owned the Fortune Saloon with her sister, Violet, opened her arms as Wyatt sauntered through the doorway.

As expected, he returned the embrace and kissed her cheek. "Hey, Daffy. How's business?"

"It just got better with you here, honey." She turned to include Marilee. "Well, don't you two make a pretty picture." Her smoky, rusty-nails voice lowered. "You two want to be seen? Or would you rather sit in the shadows?"

Wyatt leaned close, as though delivering a state secret. "Find us a dark corner, Daffy."

"You got it, honey." She winked at him and led the way through the smoke-filled room.

Though Wyatt and Marilee had hoped to be invisible, there was no escape from the curious stares of the towns-people. They were forced to pause at each table to speak a few words. There was the mayor, Rowe Stafford, who was, as always, surrounded by a cluster of old cronies hanging on his every word. At the next table was Stan Novak, a local building contractor who had let it be known around town that he was furious with the McCord family for not releasing any of their vast holdings for development. Their next stop was to speak with Orley Peterson, owner of the grain and feed store, who'd been talking to Judge Wilbur Manning about suing a local rancher who refused to pay for a year's worth of supplies. Sheriff Ernest Wycliff was sitting with his deputy, Harrison Atkins, and Harrison's daughter, Charity, who handled the emergency phone at the jail during the night shift.

Daffy led them past the busy pool tables, where several cowboys from the Lost Nugget Ranch were engaged in matches with cowboys from nearby ranches. They smiled and waved at Wyatt, and he returned their greetings.

Daffy skirted the small, empty dance floor and moved on to a far corner of the cavernous room. "This dark enough for you, honey?"

"Perfect." Wyatt waited for Marilee to slide into the booth before settling himself beside her.

"You want to start with a couple of chilled longnecks?" Daffy dropped two menus in front of them.

Wyatt glanced at Marilee, who nodded.

When Daffy returned, she set the beers down and slid into the opposite side of the booth, kicking off her spike-heeled shoes and wiggling her toes.

"Been on my feet for eight hours now. Thought I'd just sit here while you two decide what to order."

"What're the specials?" Marilee asked.

"Vi started a pot of chili at noon. Right about now it's hot enough to start a fire in your gut that won't burn out until next Friday." She threw her head back and laughed at her own joke. "She's also got barbecued ribs, chicken, and her pound-and-a-half burger with onions, mushrooms, peppers, and cheese." Without missing a beat she added, "I recommend the ribs. They're so tender they're falling off the bone."

"I'll have that." Wyatt turned to Marilee. "How about you?"

"Absolutely. With a side of Vi's famous onion rings."

"You've got good taste, honey." Daffy winked. "In food and in men."

As Daffy walked away, Marilee chuckled. "You realize," she said as she lifted the frosty bottle to her lips and drank, "that Daffy was practically drooling when she looked at you."

"She drools over every cowboy that walks through the door. Now if you'd drool"—he touched a finger to her jaw—"my ego would definitely be stroked."

"I doubt your ego needs stroking. I'm thinking you have a very high opinion of yourself, rebel."

He gave an easy laugh. "Does this mean you're not going to buy into my shy-guy routine?"

"Not likely."

They sipped their beers and watched the ebb and flow of customers, some drinking, some eating, some playing pool or darts. When Daffy delivered their meals, they both dived in.

"Um." Marilee closed her eyes on the first bite of soft-as-butter ribs. "Daffy wasn't kidding. These are the best."

Wyatt nodded. "I'll never let Dandy know, but these are every bit as good as his." He reached for an onion ring. "Of course, it could be because I haven't eaten a thing since breakfast."

"Did you say breakfast?" She sighed and touched a hand to her middle. "I even forgot about that."

"No wonder you're starving. I can see that I'm going to have to feed you more often."

"Somebody ought to." She laughed. "Food's not high on my list of priorities."

"What is?" He sat back, sipping his beer and watching her eyes. He loved the light that sparkled in them.

"My independence. I fought long and hard for it."

"So you've said."

"And my job. I'm really happy when I'm doing whatever I can for the people of this town."

"Why a medic?"

"I was always patching up something or somebody. I remember a friend when I was about seven. He fell off the monkey bars at school. I knew instinctively that he shouldn't try to stand. I sent one of our classmates to find a teacher. I went with him to the nurse's office, and I held his hand until the ambulance arrived to take him to the hospital to cast his broken leg."

"That's pretty young to be so smart."

"I guess it was. I was always stumbling across wounded animals in the woods or backyards. My mom got sick at the sight of blood. She'd get weak and have to go sit down and rub her hands together until the sickness passed. I was determined to be just the opposite. I seem to have this sixth sense about injuries. I don't panic. I don't sweat. I just . . ." She looked over at him. "I just do what's needed."

"Why not go back to school and become a doctor?"

She shrugged. "I've thought about it. I don't know why, but I'm not sure I want to go that far with it. I really enjoy my life the way it is. I like the freedom this job gives me. It allows me to see a lot of the countryside. And it pays me enough to afford the plane I keep out at the airport."

"The plane is yours?" He sat up. "I figured it belonged to the town or the county."

She shook her head. "It's all mine. It doesn't have a lot of bells and whistles, but it gives me a lot of pleasure." She glanced over. "Would you like to go up in it some time?"

"I'd like that." He gave a snort of laughter. "I might have to white-knuckle it, but I'd still like it."

"That's natural enough, considering how your parents died."

He nodded. "Until their accident, I was able to fly anywhere without a thought. Since their crash, I have a few issues with flying."

She laid a hand over his. "I'd say you have good reason to have some issues."

He absorbed the warmth of her touch. "I've flown since then. Plenty of times, as a matter of fact. But every time, on takeoff, I feel the butterflies. Then, once I'm airborne, I get past it. How about you? Any fear of flying?"

"None. As long as I'm at the controls, I don't have any second thoughts."

"A woman who likes to be in control." He closed a hand over hers. "I like that."

Marilee absorbed the quick little flutter of awareness. Wyatt McCord did have a way about him. And probably knew exactly what he had and how to use it.

To fill the silence she said, "I don't get as much flying time as I'd like. But whenever I get a chance to make money while flying, I leap at the offer."

"Who pays you?"

She shrugged. "The town. The county. Sometimes the state or even the federal government. But mostly it's businessmen who need me to pick up something in a distant town and deliver it the same day. With gas so expensive, I never refuse the offer to fly at someone else's expense." She looked over. "Want to join me the next time I'm flying on business?"

"Yeah. I'll be your copilot."

"You're on."

They both looked over at the roar of laughter coming from two cowboys engaged in a game of darts. When the last dart was tossed, one of the players reached into his pocket and withdrew a handful of bills, which he slapped into the palm of the other player before storming away.

"Wow." Marilee chuckled. "Now there's a happy loser."

"And an even happier winner." Wyatt nodded toward

the second player, who walked away whistling while he stuffed his winnings in his pocket.

"Do you play?" Marilee drained her beer.

"A little. You?"

She nodded. "I've played a time or two."

"To sweeten the pot, let's play for the bill. Loser pays. You willing?"

She thought about it for less than an instant before saying, "Okay. You're on."

Wyatt slid from the booth and caught her hand.

Minutes later they stood at the line, each one prepared to toss a single dart. The one with the higher score would become the first player of the match.

"Ladies first." Wyatt stepped back and watched as Marilee tossed her dart, landing in the inner circle for a triple.

He arched a brow. "I'm thinking you've played this more than a time or two."

"It could be beginner's luck."

"It could. Or you could be setting me up." He stepped up to the line and tossed, landing in the outer circle for a double.

He walked to the board and withdrew both darts before handing one to Marilee.

With a bow he said, "Looks like you get to go first."

He stood back, admiring her technique. She kept her eye firmly on the board while tossing the first dart. It landed with precision in the inner circle.

"Triple points."

Wyatt tossed and landed just beside hers.

She caught the smug look on his face. "Don't get cocky, rebel. You still have two darts to toss." She stepped up to the line and without hesitation tossed her second dart, which landed again in the triple area.

Wyatt was shaking his head. "Now I know I've been hustled. Nobody can do that twice. Except"—he wiggled his brows like a movie villain—"yours truly."

He stood at the line, assessed the distance, and tossed his dart. It landed directly beside Marilee's.

She was laughing. "If I hadn't seen it with my own eyes, I'd have never believed this." She took a moment to concentrate, then tossed her last dart. It landed squarely in the center. "Bull's-eye. See if you can match that."

"You don't make it easy, do you?" He studied the board, then tossed his last dart.

It landed beside hers in the center. Just as she was about to congratulate him, the dart slipped from the board and dropped to the floor.

They looked at each other and started laughing so hard they had to cling together for a moment.

"Oh, you should have seen your face," she said, still laughing.

"Are you sure you didn't have a magnet somewhere? I would have sworn that dart was a solid hit."

"Sorry about your bad luck, loser." Still laughing, she walked over to their table and picked up the bill Daffy had left there. "I believe this is yours."

He tucked it into his pocket and caught her hand. As they passed the dance floor he suddenly pulled back. Caught by surprise, she turned to look at him.

"They're playing my favorite song." He swept her into his arms and began to move with her around the floor.

The honky-tonk music was something low and bluesy.

Marilee looked up into his face. "I don't recognize this song. What is it?"

He gave her that soulful smile. "I don't know. But from now on it's going to be my favorite."

She felt her heart stutter.

He closed both arms around her, drawing her close.

She knew that everyone in the saloon was watching. At the moment, she didn't care. She couldn't think about anything except the press of his body to hers. The feel of those strong, muscled arms around her. The warmth of his thighs molded to hers. The touch of his mouth against her temple, his warm breath feathering her hair.

"This is nice." His voice vibrated through her, sending a series of delicious tingles along her spine.

"Yeah." She looked up into his eyes and could feel herself drowning in them.

She was melting all over him, with the entire town watching. She could actually feel her heart beginning to drum in her temples.

She knew she ought to draw back, but she couldn't. She didn't want the song to end. Or this night.

Oh, hell. Just look at her. She was falling for a foot-loose rebel with a smooth line who'd probably left a trail of broken hearts from Toledo to Timbuktu. The kind of guy she'd made a career of staying as far away from as possible. And here she was. Falling hard. Willingly. Right in front of the entire town. And loving every minute of it.

CHAPTER SIX

———◆———

Y ou leaving?" Daffy paused, balancing a tray of drinks.

"Yeah. I left your money on the table, Daffy." Wyatt waved to her sister, Vi, sweating over the grill, who blew him a kiss. He returned his attention to Daffy. "You were right about those ribs. Be sure and tell Vi. They were the best ever."

"I told you so. You behave now, honey." She shot a knowing glance at Marilee. "Don't go doing anything I wouldn't do, girl."

She was still cackling over her joke as they walked out the door.

Wyatt kept his hand at the small of Marilee's back as they made their way to her truck.

She liked the way his big hand felt there. Not possessive. She would have resented that. But it definitely felt protective. She had the keen sense that he would be a fierce protector of anything or anyone he cared about. It was, she decided, just one more thing she liked about

Wyatt McCord. And this evening had revealed a treasure trove of good things about him.

He held her door and waited until she'd settled herself behind the wheel before circling around to the passenger side.

He fastened his seat belt. "You up for the long drive back to the ranch? Or would you rather save yourself the trip and just invite me to spend the night at your place?"

She saw the teasing laughter in his eyes. "Did I forget to tell you? I love long drives. They invigorate me."

"I was afraid of that." He was chuckling as they pulled out onto the street and headed through town.

"So." He turned toward her. "Seeing the way you tossed those darts, I think we can put to rest the lie that you've only played once or twice."

"Oh, did I forget to mention that I was the champion chucker in my dorm in college?"

"Yeah. You kept that a big, bad secret. At least the champion part. Judging by the way you aim, you're no chucker. You know exactly where your dart will land."

"Thank you, sir." She bowed her head. "What about you? This wasn't your first time. Not the way you matched me play for play."

"I may have played a time or two in a London pub during my rebellious days."

Marilee's laughter faded as a new thought dawned. "And that unfortunate loss? Was that really an accident, or did you lose deliberately so I wouldn't have to pay the bill?"

He shrugged. "My lips are sealed."

"I should have known."

Once on the open highway he turned on the radio, and

they both sang along with Garth as he lamented his papa being a rolling stone.

When the song ended, Marilee looked over. "I'll consider that a sermon. According to Garth, a woman would be a fool to lose her heart to a man who'd rather drive a truck than be home with her."

Wyatt winked, and in his best imitation of Daffy's smoky voice he said, "Honey, a man may love the open road, but any female with half a brain can figure out how to compete with a truck. Just bat those pretty little red-tipped lashes at any male over the age of twelve, and his brain turns to mush. Next thing you know, instead of revving up his engine, he's on his hands and knees, carrying a toddler on his back around a living room full of toys and baby gear."

Though the image was a surprisingly pretty one, Marilee had to wipe tears from her eyes, she was laughing so hard. When she caught her breath she managed to say, "You've got Daffy down so perfectly, you could probably answer the phone at the Fortune Saloon and no one would believe it wasn't her."

"She's easy." He chuckled. "I think she's the only female with a voice that's deeper than mine."

He looked out the window at the full moon above Treasure Chest Mountain in the distance. "It's a shame to waste such a pretty night. Maybe you ought to pull over and park. We can make out like teenagers."

"Not a bad idea." At his arched brow she added, "It would give me a chance to see if I could turn your brain to mush."

"Believe it."

Marilee felt the tingle of awareness as she turned

the truck into the long gravel lane that led to the ranch house. The truth was, she'd been half tempted to park and make out. She had no doubt that Wyatt would make it memorable.

She brought the vehicle to a halt and glanced at the darkened windows. "Looks like everybody's asleep. Don't they keep a light on for you?"

"They probably figured I wouldn't be needing it."

"Sorry to disappoint your cousins."

"Not to mention me. I'm gravely disappointed at the way this evening has ended. You're going to ruin my reputation as a lady-killer." He flashed her one of his famous smiles.

He opened the door and climbed down. When he rounded the front of the truck, he paused beside her open window. "Good night, Marilee. I appreciate the ride home. I just wish you didn't have to make that long drive back to town all alone."

"I'll be fine. I've got my radio to keep me company."

"You could always come inside and bunk in my room."

"What a generous offer. But once again, I'm afraid I'll have to decline, though I have to admit that I've had more fun in a few hours with you than I've had in years."

The minute the words were out of her mouth, she wanted to call them back. What was it about Wyatt that had her trusting him enough to reveal such a thing?

Though she barely knew him, she'd uncovered an inherent goodness in him that was rare and wonderful.

This had been one of the best nights of her life.

Still, he'd gone very quiet. As though digesting her words and searching for hidden meanings.

As he turned away she called boldly, "What? No kiss

good night? Just because I refused to spend the night with you?"

He turned back with a smile, but it wasn't his usual silly grin. Instead, she noted, there was a hint of danger in that smile.

He studied her intently before reaching out as though to touch her face. Then he seemed to think better of it and withdrew his hand as if he'd been burned.

His eyes locked on hers. "I've already decided that I'll never be able to just kiss you and walk away. So a word of warning, pretty little Marilee. When I kiss you, and I fully intend to kiss you breathless, be prepared to go the distance. There's a powerful storm building up inside me, and when it's unleashed, it's going to be one hell of an earth-shattering explosion. For both of us."

He walked away then and didn't look back until he'd reached the back door.

Startled by the unexpected intensity of his words, Marilee put the truck in gear and started along the gravel lane.

As her vehicle ate up the miles back to town, she couldn't put aside the look she'd seen in his eyes. The carefully banked passion he'd taken such pains to hide had left her more shaken than she cared to admit.

In truth, she was still trembling.

And he hadn't even touched her.

When Marilee climbed the stairs to her apartment, her cell phone rang. She was accustomed to getting emergency calls day and night.

She automatically flipped open her phone as she stepped inside and turned on the lights. "Emergency One. What's the problem?"

"It's my heart."

The familiar deep voice had her pausing mid-stride. "Wyatt?"

"Yeah. I meant to ask you to call me when you got home so I'd know you were safe. Now I've been having heart palpitations worrying about you all alone on that long stretch of highway."

"Pretty good timing, rebel. That highway is just a memory now. I'm already inside my apartment and heading toward the bedroom."

"I'm betting you set a new speed record."

She laughed. "And broke a few speeding laws along the way. But I'm home now, safe and sound. I hope this eases your worries about me."

"Yeah. I can sleep now. But I still wish you'd agreed to bunk out here with me. Good night, Marilee."

As she disconnected and set her cell phone on the night table, she paused to look out the window at the starry sky. Her hard-nosed father had treated her like a fresh recruit her entire life, undermining even the slightest hint of pride in her accomplishments. Her mother had been a clinging vine who couldn't make a single decision on her own. After her father's death her mother had spent years in a fog before discovering her own strengths. Marilee had fought long and hard to achieve any sort of independence. By design she'd been on her own for years. It had been a long time since anybody had worried about her.

She was oddly touched by Wyatt's concern.

"Oh, Amy." Marilee opened the door of her apartment and greeted her friend with a hug. "I'm so glad you could come by for a visit."

"Me, too." Amy stepped inside and sniffed the air. "Something smells yummy."

"Quiche. It's quick and easy." Marilee led the way to the kitchen.

Amy took a seat at the counter and watched as her friend removed a pan from the oven before putting the kettle on. Minutes later the two young women were enjoying salads and quiche, and steaming cups of tea.

Amy sipped her tea and looked over at her friend. "Okay, Lee, what's up?"

Marilee looked appropriately offended. "What's that supposed to mean? Can't a friend invite a friend to lunch?"

"We've been sharing lunch for years, Lee. As well as gossip. But something tells me there's something else going on here."

Marilee took her time setting aside her fork, avoiding Amy's eyes.

Finally she looked over. "Tell me about Wyatt."

Amy's smile bloomed. "I knew it. He's getting to you."

Marilee ducked her head. "I keep trying to write him off as just another charming bachelor looking to score. But every time I think I've got him pegged, he manages to surprise me. I know he's Jesse's cousin, and you probably feel an obligation to keep a few family secrets, but I really need to know more about him."

Amy sat back. "What would you like to know?"

"Whether he's the real deal or just a very good actor."

Amy hesitated. "Tell me how you see him."

"He's nice. Almost too nice. And sweet and funny and charming. He makes me laugh. And sometimes, when I least expect it, he makes my heart pound."

"Oh-oh." Amy chuckled. "This sounds serious."

"No. Really. You know me. I'm not interested in serious. No commitments. But . . ."

"But what?" Amy prodded.

"I can't stop thinking about him."

Amy caught her friend's hands. "Lee, it's like I said. He's getting to you."

"But is he just playing me? Is this all just a game with him? Does he see me as the latest conquest?"

"Hey." Amy studied her more closely. "This really matters to you, doesn't it?"

"I just don't want to be played for a fool." Marilee slid off the stool. Needing to be busy, she picked up their plates and walked to the sink. When she'd finished rinsing them, she looked up. "I've always been such a good judge of character, and all of a sudden, I'm not sure just what to make of Wyatt McCord."

Amy gave her friend a gentle smile. "Lee, in the short time that I've been in the family, I've found Wyatt to be everything you said. He's naturally charming, and that outrageous sense of humor is his most endearing quality. But I've never known Wyatt to be phony. He's the real thing. He's honest and up front with everyone he meets."

When Marilee remained silent she added, "For now, why not just enjoy his company. And if things start heating up, you're going to have to trust your instincts. Hey. You're a big girl now, playing in the big-girl league. I'm betting on you to make wise choices."

Wise choices.

By the time her best friend left, Marilee had decided to take her advice. For now she would relax and enjoy the ride. And if it got too bumpy, she'd simply bail.

*   *   *

"Hey, rebel."

At the sound of Marilee's voice on his cell phone, Wyatt was instantly awake.

"You free to go flying today?"

He thought about the crew heading up to the north range. He'd agreed to go along. He'd have to twist Zane's arm to be his substitute on such short notice. But there was no way he'd let this opportunity slip away. Especially since he'd just spent the past three days looking for an excuse to see Marilee again while working his tail off with Cal Randall and his wranglers.

"Free as a bird. What time are we leaving?"

"As soon as you get here."

"I'm on my way."

Marilee turned on the coffeemaker before stepping into the shower. By the time she was enjoying her second cup of coffee, she heard the roar of Wyatt's Harley, followed by the sound of his boots on the stairs.

She tore open the door. "'Morning, rebel."

"'Morning." A smile of pure pleasure lit his eyes. "Is this what the well-dressed pilots are wearing this year?"

She twirled, showing off a denim miniskirt and trim white shirt with the sleeves rolled to her elbows. "You like my uniform?"

"It beats the leather bomber jacket and flyboy hat with goggles that I was expecting." He inhaled. "Is that coffee I smell?"

"And here I thought you were about to compliment me on my perfume."

"I will. Right after my jolt of caffeine."

"Over there." She pointed to the mug on the countertop.

He filled the mug and drank it down in one long swallow.

Then he set down the empty mug and crossed to her, dipping his head to the column of her throat. "Great perfume, by the way."

She absorbed an unexpected sizzle of heat.

How did he always manage to catch her off-guard?

To cover her confusion, she grabbed her keys. "Come on. I've got a plane to fly."

Wyatt stood back watching as Marilee went through her routine at the airport, filling out a flight plan and conferring with Craig Matson, the mechanic, before doing a thorough physical check of her bright yellow, fixed-wing aircraft that bore the license MON342.

Satisfied, she opened the door of the plane and motioned for Wyatt to follow.

"Did I hear you mention Helena?"

She nodded as she fiddled with dials, adjusted her earphones, and slid on a pair of sunglasses. "Harding Jessup is paying me to deliver some plumbing supplies. So I promised Dr. Wheeler I'd pick up some medical supplies he'd ordered while I'm there. It will all be handled at the airport, so we can just do a quick turnaround."

"No overnighter?"

She arched a brow. "You sound disappointed."

"Not at all." He grinned. "But I was willing to sacrifice my time, not to mention my body, if you needed to stay over."

"Really decent of you, rebel. Maybe next time."

"That's what they all say." He glanced at the small, cramped space behind the pilot and copilot seats. "You think there's room for anything more than a postage stamp back there?"

She laughed. "That's why it's called a small craft."

"A mini, if you ask me."

He fell silent as the voice of the controller came over her earphones. She followed directions, steering her craft along the runway until she reached the turn. With the length of another runway ahead of them, the little plane picked up speed.

Wyatt adjusted his sunglasses and sucked in a breath, the only sign of nerves.

When the plane was airborne, he slowly exhaled.

Marilee glanced over. "You okay?"

"Fine. Now." And he was.

He understood his reaction to takeoff. From all accounts, something had gone very wrong with the plane his parents had chartered in the jungles of South America. It had barely made it off the makeshift runway of the small village when it had crashed into the trees and burst into flames.

How many times had he imagined their reaction? Had there been time for fear to set in? Panic? Had they had a moment to clasp hands? Whisper words of love? Had they thought about the son they might never see again? Felt a flash of regret? Or had it been over in an instant?

He hoped so. He fervently hoped there had been no time to suffer.

He touched a hand to his breast pocket. In it he carried the watch his grandfather Coot had given to his father when he'd graduated from college. It was the only thing of his father's that had been salvaged from the burning rubble. Along with that he had his mother's wedding ring, a simple band of platinum engraved with the word *Forever*. It currently resided in a small, velvet-lined box in his room.

He'd never had a chance to say good-bye. But then,

he thought, they weren't really gone. They'd just stepped into a place he couldn't see. That thought had given him a lot of comfort through the years.

"You're quiet." Marilee studied his profile as he stared out the window.

"I'm enjoying the view." He turned to her. "The one outside the window, as well as the one in here."

"Thanks." She smiled. "Just so you're not going to get sick on me."

"No need to worry. I can handle my nerves."

And a lot of other things, she figured. Aloud she merely said, "There's a thermos of coffee behind you. And a couple of bottles of water."

"What would you prefer?"

"I'll take a bottle of water. I've had enough caffeine."

He twisted off the cap before handing her the plastic bottle.

She took a long pull and set it in the cup-holder.

Wyatt watched as the small town of Gold Fever drifted out of his line of vision, to be replaced by acres and acres of grazing land and then, slowly, mile after mile of wilderness.

Marilee arched a brow. "What's with the smile?"

"I was just thinking how much I love this place. When I was traveling the world, all I wanted was to be here." He sighed. "Just here."

"Do you know how many kids growing up in small towns nurture the dream of leaving it all behind to explore the world?"

He shrugged. "Nothing wrong with that. We all have a right to our dreams. But it was never mine. It was the dream of my parents, and I was dragged kicking and screaming away from everything I loved."

"I'm sorry."

He glanced over. "Don't be. Everything in my wild youth was leading me back here. Even Coot's death. I felt so guilty, knowing I hadn't seen my own grandfather in years. But the minute I set foot on McCord land, I had the strangest feeling that I'd never leave again."

She reached over to lay a hand on his. "That's nice."

"So is this." He looked down at their hands. "You couldn't have picked a prettier day to fly."

"Yeah. That's why I called you. I figured since you'd admitted to being a nervous flier, I'd introduce you to my plane on a perfect day. No weather to worry about. No storms between here and Helena."

"Smart." He squeezed her hand. "And, by the way, I like your plane. Almost as much as its pilot."

"Thank you, sir." She removed her hand to fiddle with the controls. And noted that she could still feel the heat of his touch on her skin.

Their descent into Helena Regional Airport was as smooth as the entire flight had been.

Once again Wyatt stood back to watch Marilee at work. At the terminal she signed a stack of papers and supervised the unloading of plumbing supplies and the loading of the medical supplies.

Satisfied, she turned to him. "Are you up for lunch?"

At his nod she added, "The grill offers a hot dog or a burger."

"A dog. With chili if they have it."

"They do, and it's so hot your mouth will be on fire for hours."

"My kind of chili dog."

She was laughing. "I thought I'd order them to go. That way we can take our time eating while we enjoy the view on the ride home."

He caught her hand, linking his fingers with hers. "I like the way you think."

A short time later, after filing her return flight plan, she did a thorough examination of the plane before inviting Wyatt to join her in the cockpit.

Once they were airborne, she motioned toward the sack of food. "Think you can handle lunch, or do you need time to settle?"

"I'm fine. Let's eat." He opened the bag and unwrapped the chili dogs.

After his first bite he hissed through his teeth. "You weren't kidding." He reached for a bottle of water and took a long, deep drink. "These ought to come with a warning label."

"I told you so."

"Yeah." He grinned and took another bite.

Marilee arched a brow. "Getting used to it?"

"I guess so. By the time I dig into my second or third, I won't even notice the fire in my mouth."

He set a carton of chili fries between them.

Marilee adjusted her sunglasses and popped a fry into her mouth. "On a day like this, with the sky a perfect blue and the sun so bright it almost hurts, I always wonder what it would feel like to just keep on flying, with no end in sight."

"I've tried it. Believe me, it's exhilarating. For a while." Wyatt tipped up his water bottle and took another drink. His voice lowered with feeling. "But after a while, I realized that rebelling and flying aimlessly just isn't all that satisfying. I need to have a goal. These days, I like to know where I'm headed. And what I'm going to do when I get there."

Marilee shivered at the intensity of his tone, though she wasn't at all surprised by his admission. Wyatt McCord struck her as a man who set goals and met them. And despite all the years of aimless wandering in his misspent youth, he knew exactly who he was and where he was going at all times.

CHAPTER SEVEN

————◆◆◆————

The landing was as smooth as the entire flight had been. But Wyatt felt a rush of relief to be on the ground. As much as he trusted Marilee's competence, he couldn't completely shake the lingering dread of flying. Maybe he would have to fight these feelings for a lifetime. But at least he wasn't allowing them to control his life. That gave him a measure of satisfaction.

As they taxied to the small terminal and came to a stop, his cell phone vibrated.

He pulled it from his pocket. "Yeah?"

"Hey, cuz." Zane's voice sounded breathless. "Where've you been?"

"Helena. We just landed back in Gold Fever."

"Perfect timing. Stay in town. Jesse and Amy and I are headed there. We just got word that Delia Cowling is home."

"About time." Wyatt stepped into the sunlight and followed Marilee down the steps of the plane. "I'll wait for you at her place."

As he tucked his phone away, Marilee shot him a glance. "Delia?"

He nodded. "Back home."

"Her poor cousin probably couldn't take any more." Marilee paused. "I hope you and your cousins don't mind if I go along. I owe Delia an apology for taking those papers without her permission."

"And she owes us an even bigger apology for keeping them a secret from our family for all these years."

"I think I see a confrontation in our future." Marilee pulled a set of keys from her pocket. "If you wouldn't mind driving my truck across the tarmac, I'd like to unload the medical supplies and deliver them to the clinic on the way to Delia's."

"Good idea. Let's kill two birds."

Marilee shook her head. "Please. I'd rather not talk about killing any birds."

Wyatt paused and touched a hand to her cheek.

She felt the heat all the way to her toes.

He stared down into her eyes, and his lips curved into a killer smile that had those same toes curling with pleasure.

"My fearless, independent adventurer. You handle a plane like you were born with wings. I've watched you patch up battered, bloody cowboys without flinching. But you can't even think about harming a bird."

She couldn't say a word. Her throat was dry as dust.

With a thoughtful look he rubbed a thumb over her lower lip, then turned away and headed toward her truck.

Marilee remained where she was, absorbing the aftershock of his touch. She'd thought he would kiss her. Had wanted him to. Desperately. Instead, all he'd done was touch her. And that had been enough to reduce her to a weak, trembling mass of jelly.

She was going to have to do something about these jumbled hormones.

She sucked in a deep breath and got to work hauling the cases of medical supplies.

By the time Wyatt drove the truck close to the plane, she was in control and able to work alongside him without sighing like a girl with her first crush.

But just barely.

Wyatt and Marilee pulled up in her truck outside Delia Cowling's house within minutes of the ranch truck bearing Zane, Jesse, and Amy. They came together on the little walkway in front of her house to plan their strategy.

Jesse, always the hothead, was clearly in the mood for a fight. Being forced to wait these past few days had added to his temper.

"She'd better have a really good explanation for keeping these papers a secret." He held up the faded pages fisted in his hand.

Zane nodded. "I can't wait to hear what she has to say."

Marilee lifted a palm. "I hope you'll allow me to apologize to her first."

"For what?" Amy asked.

"For taking those papers from her home without her permission."

"They clearly weren't hers. You could see that they belonged to us," Jesse said reasonably.

"Which is why I brought them to you. But still, I had no right to take anything from her home without first asking. My job brings me into people's lives and into their homes. If Delia wanted, she could make trouble for me."

Jesse gave a snort of anger. "I'd like to see her try."

Wyatt decided to try to cool his cousin's heated temper. "We have a right to get some answers. But only after Marilee has had her chance to explain." He glanced around the circle. "Agreed?"

Jesse jammed his hands into his pockets and stared down at the ground.

Amy tucked her arm through his, knowing her touch would be enough to soften his attitude.

Zane nodded.

"All right then." Wyatt took the lead and walked up on the porch before knocking.

Minutes later the door was opened.

Delia Cowling peered at them in surprise. "What's this? A welcome committee?"

"Something like that." Marilee managed a smile. "How's your ankle?"

"Still sore. Most of the swelling's gone down. But since I can walk, and I'd had enough of my cousin and her grumbling, I figured it was time to come home. My cousin agreed with me."

That brought a round of silent glances and a few knowing smiles.

Delia stood in the doorway, looking distinctly unnerved by their presence. It was obvious that she wasn't accustomed to having visitors drop by unannounced.

After an uncomfortable pause, she reluctantly held open the door. "I suppose you'd like to come inside."

"Thank you." Marilee stepped in, followed by the

others. "Delia, I wanted you to know that when I returned to your basement to look for your mother's locket . . ."

"Oh." Delia put a hand to her mouth. "I never thanked you for that. I guess I was asleep when you came upstairs. But I found Mama's locket on my night table when I woke up and knew you'd been the one to put it there. I was so happy to have it back." She touched a hand to her throat. "My cousin had the chain repaired, and now it's back where it belongs, thanks to you, Marilee."

Marilee cleared her throat. "As I was saying, when I was searching for the locket, I had to wade through a pile of papers that had fallen from a cardboard box that you'd knocked over."

"Quite a mess, as I recall. I never expected you to clean it up."

Marilee shook her head. "I didn't mind. As I was returning the papers to their box, I came across these." She turned to Jesse, who handed the faded pages to the old woman.

Delia glanced at them, then looked from Marilee to Jesse. "You found these on the floor of my basement?"

"That's right."

The old woman peered at them more closely. "Does this say gold?"

Jesse started to answer but Wyatt cut him off, allowing Marilee to speak her piece.

"It does. As you can see, they're very old. And from things I'd heard over the years, I realized that they would be of special interest to the McCord family, since they've spent a lifetime searching for their ancestor's lost gold. I brought these upstairs to ask you about them, but since you were asleep, I decided to take them out to the ranch. I'm sorry that I did that without your permission."

The old woman shrugged. "These are nothing to me. I can't imagine what they would be doing in my basement." Hearing the whistle of her kettle, Delia frowned. "I was just making some tea." After a prolonged pause she said almost hesitantly, "Would you like some?"

Marilee spoke for the others. "That's not necessary. We don't want to make extra work for you."

"It's just tea." Delia started toward the back of the house, clearly favoring her sore ankle, while the others trailed behind.

Jesse spoke to Delia's back. "Are you saying you've never seen these papers before?"

Delia nodded. "That's what I'm saying. This is the first I've seen of them."

The three cousins exchanged a glance.

Jesse's anger had just been deflected. In its place was curiosity.

Wyatt spoke for all of them. "Would you allow us to go downstairs and look around?"

"Whatever for?" Delia crossed to the stove and removed a whistling teakettle.

"There could be more of these."

"More? Where?"

"Maybe in the box where Marilee found these. I'm sure she could show us which one it is."

Delia's tea was forgotten. "I believe I'd like to see that myself. I can't imagine where they've been all these years."

With Wyatt assisting the older woman down the stairs, the others followed.

"Careful," Delia cautioned. "This floor is old and damp and cracked. I wouldn't want any of you to fall the way I did." She winced, just thinking about that morning and the pain she'd been forced to endure. "I've paid a dear price for my carelessness."

In the glare of the single dangling lightbulb, Marilee looked over the row of boxes lined up on the metal shelving and lifted one down. "This is the box you upended when you fell, Delia."

As Marilee lifted aside the cover, Delia knelt down and began to sift through the papers inside. "Why, this is filled with nothing but faded papers. Most of them appear to be old college papers of Ledge's." She looked up. "Whatever would my brother be doing with your ancestor's papers?"

"That's what we came here to find out." Jesse's temper was back.

Delia didn't seem to notice. Distracted, she continued sifting through the box until she suddenly held up a scrap of yellowed paper. "Does this say murdered?"

Jesse, Zane, and Wyatt dropped down beside her and stared at the paper in her hand.

It bore the same scrawl as the other page taken from Nathanial's diary.

Jesse's voice grew thoughtful. "According to family lore, Coot's great-great-grandfather, Jasper McCord, was murdered. Most folks believe by a prospector named Grizzly Markham. Some of the pages recounting his son Nathanial's account of the incident were missing from his diary."

Delia nodded. "I'm aware of all that. But why is it here, in Ledge's papers?"

Wyatt's tone was sharp. "That's what we'd like to know. Would Ledge be at his bank right now?"

"Hmmm?" Delia glanced up. Seeing the looks being exchanged by the three cousins, she shook her head, as though slipping from a fog. Her tone sharpened. "Of course I couldn't say. I've only just returned to town today."

Wyatt helped the old woman to her feet. "Would you be willing to let us go through the rest of his papers? Just in case there could be something more?"

She gave a firm shake of her head. "It's not that I believe Ledge has anything to hide, you understand. But I would never give you permission to look through his personal papers without his consent."

They were so close. The three cousins could hardly contain their impatience to sift through the contents of the box.

"You're sure, Delia?" Marilee pressed.

"You'll have to get Ledge's permission." She placed the lid back on the box.

With a last reluctant look, Wyatt returned the box to the shelf before taking Delia's arm and walking alongside her as they climbed the stairs.

Once upstairs, he helped her to the kitchen. Without a word Marilee filled the old woman's cup with water from the kettle.

She turned. "What do you take in your tea, Delia?"

"Nothing. Thank you." She accepted the steaming cup and sipped.

As they turned to leave, her tone grew more stern. "I hope you believe me when I say that I never knew about those papers."

Wyatt paused in the doorway. "I believe you, Delia. Thank you for all your help."

He followed the others out of the house and to their trucks.

Jesse's voice was tight with anger. "I don't believe a word that old gossip said. She knows more about everything that goes on in this town than anybody else alive. I say we get to the bank and confront Ledge Cowling before his sister has a chance to warn him about what we've discovered."

Zane and Wyatt nodded in agreement.

Wyatt said aloud what they all were thinking. "I'm dying to know why the president of the town bank, knowing about our family's search, would keep something this important hidden for all these years."

It took them only minutes to drive from Delia's house to the bank, situated on the main street alongside the courthouse. It was a small, brick, one-story building with a row of windows overlooking the street.

As they stepped inside, they could see Ledge Cowling talking on the telephone and pacing behind the glass wall that separated his office from the rest of the business. When he spotted the McCord cousins, along with Amy and Marilee, he quickly returned the phone to its cradle and dropped into the chair behind his desk.

His secretary, Paula Henning, looked up with a smile. When she wasn't tending her small ranch and her son, Timmy, she worked at the bank to supplement her income. "Hey, Lee." When she spotted Jesse, Zane, and Wyatt, as well as Jesse's wife, Amy, her smile grew. "My goodness. I don't think I've ever had all of you here at one time. Is this something special?"

"Just business." Wyatt studied Ledge through the glass. "We'd like to talk to your boss."

"Of course. Let me tell him you're here." She stood and made her way to Ledge's office.

A minute later she returned. "Right this way."

She held the door until they were crowded inside his office. When Ledge lifted a hand in dismissal, she withdrew and closed the door before returning to her desk.

"Well. This is an honor." Ledge indicated the leather chairs in a half-circle facing his desk. When everyone was seated he settled himself in his big armchair and steepled his hands on the desktop. "Now what brings the McCord family to my humble bank? I know you aren't here for a loan. In all the years I've been in business, your family has never once asked for my help."

"It's comforting to know that you'd be here if we needed your help, Ledge." Without bothering to make further small talk, Jesse dropped the yellowed paper on his desk. "Do you recognize this?"

Ledge took his time studying it. When he looked up, he arched a brow. "I'm sorry. Should this mean something to me?"

Jesse frowned. "It was in your sister's basement. According to her, the box it was in contained old papers of yours."

Ledge gave a negligent shrug of his shoulder. "I have no idea what box that might be. Of course, Delia lives in our parents' old home, so there could be all sorts of things in that basement that neither of us could possibly identify. If you ever get down there, you'll notice that our parents saved everything from our childhood. Report cards, awards, trophies."

Wyatt picked up the page. "And you're saying you've never seen this before?"

"Afraid not." Ledge glanced around, allowing his gaze to linger on Amy, then on Marilee, favoring each with his best banker's smile. "Apparently this means a good deal more to you than it does to me. And for good reason. After all, everybody knows about your ancestor's lost treasure. I surely wish I could be more help to you."

He stood, indicating an end to the meeting. "If you're ever in the market for a loan, I hope you'll come see me. Now, if you don't mind, I have a meeting with Orley Peterson. He's thinking of adding to his feed and grain store and needs a bank loan. I always have time to do business with the folks who need me."

He offered his hand to each of them in turn, and they had no choice but to return the handshake.

As they made their way back to their trucks, Zane voiced what they'd all surmised.

"I'd bet any amount of money that the caller on his phone when we pulled up outside the bank was Delia. Ledge was way too cool to be caught by surprise."

"Yeah. Poor Aunt Cora. We told her where we were going and promised that we'd be coming back with some answers." Jesse's frustration was obvious. "And Ledge Cowling flicked us off like annoying flies."

"It doesn't matter." Wyatt's tone was low and even, a certain sign that he was fighting to control his temper. "He may have won the first round. But he'd better not mistake our departure for defeat. There are lots more rounds before the final bell. Ledge is going to find out that the McCords have the staying power to last as long as it takes to win it all."

As the others turned toward the ranch truck, Wyatt caught Marilee's hand. "I'm sorry the day has ended like this." He managed a quick smile. "And just when I'd planned a lovely evening of seduction. But I think I'd better go back with the others while they explain to Aunt Cora."

She felt her heart do a sudden flip and hoped she looked as cool as he did. "Well then, the seduction will just have to wait."

He squeezed her hand. "Not too long, I hope."

She watched him walk away and wondered at the way her pulse was pounding in her temples.

If she didn't soon get her hands on him, she might just have an explosion to match the one he'd promised.

The man definitely had a way about him.

Despite her best intentions to keep things light and impersonal, he'd managed to get under her skin the way no other man ever had.

Chapter Eight

"Morning, Aunt Cora." Wyatt glanced around the kitchen, empty except for his aunt, busy loading supplies into an insulated box, and Dandy, stirring something over the stove.

"Good morning." Cora looked over with a smile. "You're up early."

"I might say the same for you." Wyatt didn't want to admit that his sleep had been disturbed by erotic dreams of Marilee. He was going to have to do something about her, and soon.

"Ever since this business with Ledge Cowling, I've been feeling uneasy." Cora finished what she'd been doing and picked up her coffee to sip. "I know it's irrational. Those papers could have been in Delia's basement for fifty years or more, when Ledge and Delia's parents were still alive. But now that we've found another piece of the puzzle, it's as though Coot is reaching out to us, urging us to move ahead with more purpose. I do so want to see my brother's dream to its conclusion."

He nodded. "I know what you mean. We've been making progress on tracking Coot's trail. But I think we need to start charting our own course. Ever since Jesse's wedding, we've been slacking off. But now, finding this latest clue . . ." He let his words die as Cal stepped into the kitchen.

The ranch foreman glanced toward the box of food, then over at Cora. "Another overnighter?"

She could tell, by the look on his face, that he disapproved. "I need to take advantage of the summer sunlight before it's gone, Cal. I need some alone time. I thought I'd camp out at Treasure Chest for a week or two and work on some of my canvases."

He accepted a cup of coffee from Dandy before pulling up a chair beside hers. "I wish you'd take somebody along. I don't like knowing you're out there all alone."

"Now, Cal." She laid a hand over his. "I've been doing this all my life."

"That doesn't mean I have to like it. It isn't safe for you to be alone in the wilderness."

She gave him a gentle smile. "I'll be on McCord land the entire time."

"There aren't any herds up there. And that means there are no wranglers, either."

She touched a hand to the pocket of her brother's old shirt, which she hadn't been able to discard. She still wore it for luck. "I have my cell phone. And you know I always carry a rifle in my Jeep and a handgun."

"Just the same . . ."

"You sound like a mother hen clucking at her chicks."

She set aside her empty cup and got to her feet. "Come on. You can help me carry my supplies out to the truck. I'm just too restless to stay here another minute."

The older man heaved to his feet and picked up the box of food, setting it on the wheeled cart he'd designed just for Cora's jaunts into the wilderness.

Cora kissed Wyatt's cheek. "I won't be gone more than a week or two. If you get any news, you can always call me."

Wyatt watched as she followed Cal through the mudroom.

He understood her need to cope with all that nervous energy and frustration. At least she had her art, which filled her hours from dawn to dusk. She often confessed to turning out some of her finest work when she was feeling stressed.

If only he had an outlet for his own frustrations.

Restless, he left the kitchen and walked to the great room, knowing the others would be downstairs shortly. On a ranch this size, chores started early. Dandy was up before dawn, preparing breakfast, and everyone was expected to eat a hearty meal before beginning a day that often didn't end until well past dark.

On the oversize coffee table lay a map of the area. It was dotted with sticky notes and pins that he and his cousins used to mark the places they believed their grandfather had already searched. From the various scraps of paper and doodles that Coot had left through the years, they'd mapped out a tentative trail.

Wyatt stood mulling the huge expanse of land between the last note they'd charted and the end of the McCord property, just beyond Treasure Chest Mountain. How many scraps of paper were lying around in waste bins all over Montana? Coot's absentmindedness was legendary. He'd been known to allow his drawings and maps to spill from his pockets along the trail, where they were often carried on the breeze for miles. Folks around these parts who recognized them returned them to their rightful owner. Others just tossed the papers away like so much litter.

He looked up when Jesse and Amy strolled down the stairs. "'Morning."

"'Morning." Jesse caught Amy's hand and the two paused beside Wyatt. "Something wrong?"

Jesse looked as sleek and happy as a mountain cat. Wyatt was betting it wasn't just his morning shower that put such a gleam in his eye. He was so much in love with his wife, he was practically glowing.

Wyatt thought of Marilee, fresh from her shower in her tidy little apartment, and felt a quick tug of desire.

"Nope. Just studying the map we made. I'm thinking we need to get more serious about searching for Coot's treasure."

Jesse grinned. "I've been thinking the same thing. Just knowing Ledge Cowling was sitting on something that could have been a clue has me champing at the bit."

Amy squeezed his hand. "We talked about it last night."

"What're we talking about?" Zane descended the stairs and joined them.

"Searching for Coot's treasure." Wyatt pointed to the map. "We had a plan. Then, in the afterglow of a certain wedding"—he shot a meaningful glance at Jesse and Amy—"we got lazy. I say it's time we get serious about this. As serious as Coot was."

"I agree." Zane lifted his latest camera from his pocket and took aim at his cousins. One day he planned to edit miles of film into a documentary that would end, hopefully, with the discovery of the lost fortune. It had been Coot's dream; now it was his. "Since this is being recorded for posterity, what do you say we make a pact to really bust our butts chasing Coot's dream."

"You mean our dream," Wyatt corrected.

He and Jesse sandwiched Amy between them and lifted their fists in a salute, mugging for the camera.

Wyatt spoke for all of them. "Let the record show that from this day forward, we intend to spend whatever time we can spare from ranch chores to continue our search for the lost fortune."

"And when it's found," Jesse added, "we'll just see who's crazy as a coot."

"Amen to that, cuz." Zane clicked off the recorder.

Wyatt's cell phone rang more than a dozen times before he managed to free it from his shirt pocket. "Hold on," he shouted before dropping it into the dirt.

After a very long pause he retrieved it. "Yeah. Hello."

"Hey, rebel." The sound of Marilee's voice on the phone had Wyatt's heart rate speeding up. "I hope I haven't caught you in the middle of driving a herd of cattle."

"Nothing quite so glamorous. I was trying to hold a heifer still so Jesse could inject her with a dose of antibiotic. Hold on again."

Marilee grinned at the sound of the bawling animal in the background.

"Okay." Wyatt rubbed his hand down his dusty jeans while retrieving the phone. "Job finished. What's up?"

"Orley Peterson hired me to fly up to Razorback Ridge to deliver some supplies. Want to tag along?"

He glanced at his watch. "I can be there in an hour."

"Why don't you drive directly to the airstrip? That'll give me time to do my preflight."

"I'll see you there." He tucked his cell phone into his pocket and turned to Jesse and Zane, who were grinning like fools. "What's so funny?"

"Another flying date with Marilee?" Zane exchanged a look with his cousin. "For a guy who's not fond of airplanes, I'd say this is getting serious."

Instead of the denial they'd been expecting, he shocked them both by tucking his hands in his back pockets before strolling away.

Jesse watched him, before turning to Zane. "Uh-oh. I think loverboy is hooked."

"Wyatt?" Zane started to grin, then frowned instead. "Oh, man." He dug out a bandanna and mopped at the sweat beading his forehead. "Before you know it, I'll be the only sensible one left."

"That was quick and easy." Wyatt felt the sudden rush of adrenaline as the plane lifted off the tiny airstrip at Razorback Ridge.

The flight from Gold Fever to the little town two hundred miles away had been smooth and uneventful, and now, with day turning into a golden, glorious evening, he was feeling mellow.

As they gained altitude, Marilee adjusted her sunglasses and glanced over. "You okay?"

"Fine." He waited for his heart to settle. Except for that

quick blip of his pulse when they became airborne, this had been an easy takeoff.

"Good. We should be landing in Gold Fever shortly after dark. Sorry there wasn't time for a leisurely dinner while we were at Razorback."

He pointed to the bag of burgers and fries he'd ordered from the little airport grill while Marilee filed her return flight plan. "This will fortify us. Want to eat now, or wait awhile?"

"I'll wait. But you go ahead."

He shook his head. "There's plenty of time."

"Okay. Then just sit back, relax, and enjoy the view before it gets too dark."

Wyatt found himself doing just that. It was one of those perfect, cloudless evenings, the sky a clear blue, the sun just beginning to set behind Treasure Chest Mountain, turning the peaks to an amazing purple and pink glow.

He uncapped a bottle of water and took a long pull. "So, you get these fly dates often enough to pay the bills?"

She nodded. "Some months are busier than others. And most are just a quick flight from home base to some of the smaller towns that have airstrips."

"Does each town maintain its own airport, or is this a state-run operation?"

She shook her head. "Neither. Most are privately owned. Our little airport in Gold Fever is owned by Orley Peterson, Stan Novak, and Ledge Cowling. The one we just left is owned by Orley and Ledge. In fact, they've invested in a number of small airports in the state." She paused. "Speaking of Ledge, Paula Henning told me that he's out of town. He left right after we met with him."

Wyatt capped the bottle and set it aside. "Did she say where he went?"

"He didn't tell her. Just said he had some business to take care of." She pointed. "If you look straight ahead, you'll see the beginning of your land."

Wyatt peered through the windshield. As far as the eye could see was the most breathtaking landscape imaginable.

"It's funny. In my travels, I was always looking for that perfect place, where I would be free of all the anger and baggage I was carrying. I did a lot of soul-searching while I meditated in Tibet. I tried to"—he shrugged—"I guess the word would be *atone*, for all the grief I gave my parents by taking on really thankless tasks in far-flung places like Africa and South America. And those things worked for a while. But then I'd have the urge to move on again, looking for some new freedom, some noble endeavor." There was a fierceness in his tone that had her looking at him as he studied the land below. "Then I came home for Coot's funeral and was persuaded to stay, and I discovered everything I was searching for right here. I've never felt freer or more genuinely myself than right here, doing all the filthy, backbreaking chores needed to keep this ranch going."

In silence they flew over vast herds of cattle dotting the lush hillsides. Wyatt pointed out the occasional ranches where wranglers lived with their families and tended the herds in the more isolated sections of McCord land.

"We'll be passing over Treasure Chest." Marilee had a firm grip on the controls as they caught the sudden downdrafts and air currents always present above the mountains.

Wyatt felt his stomach take a quick dip.

To distract himself from the turbulence, he peered down, searching vainly for a sign of Aunt Cora's Jeep, even though he knew that she could be hidden behind dozens of jagged ridges and outcroppings of rock.

As they crossed over the mountain range he spotted something puzzling. Craning his neck for a better look, he touched a hand to her arm.

"Is there time to circle back and make that run again?"

"Sure. What did you see?"

"I don't know." He scanned the ground below before pointing. "Does that look like a trail?"

Marilee studied the landscape below in the fading light. "Oh, yeah. Definitely a trail. A wide one. Looks like it might have been made by a horse and wagon." She pointed ahead. "Looks like it goes all the way from Treasure Chest to the river."

"That's odd."

"The trail? What's odd about a trail?"

"We don't have any herds in this area. In fact, we don't have any ranches or bunkhouses in this stretch of wilderness."

She shrugged. "Maybe it's an old prospector's trail."

"After more than a hundred years, wouldn't it have been covered over by vegetation?"

"You told me your aunt was painting somewhere out here. Could it have been made by her vehicle?"

"It appears to begin or end at the river. She would have been coming from our ranch"—he pointed—"in that direction."

"Yeah. Strange." Marilee's eyes widened as she suddenly tapped her instrument panel.

At her look of alarm, Wyatt tensed. "What's wrong?"

"This gauge. It should read full. It did in my preflight. Now it's showing no fuel and blinking an alarm."

"Didn't you refuel at Razorback?"

"Yes. And I have the receipt to prove it. This can't be right." She tapped the instrument panel again. "The gauge must be faulty. I saw one of the ground crew handling the refueling while our cargo was being unloaded."

"Could there be a leak in the fuel line?"

"I doubt . . ."

The engine sputtered, and Wyatt automatically clutched the armrests. "I don't like the sound of this. What can I do to help?"

The aircraft shuddered and did a sudden shift from side to side, dipping the wings.

Marilee's voice was calm and cool, as if she were declaring it a lovely day. "Make sure your seat belt is secure. Brace yourself for a rough landing. We're going down."

"How soon?"

"Now."

With absolute clarity Wyatt watched as Marilee calmly adjusted her earphones and spoke to the nameless, face-less entity at a control tower too far away to do more than listen and record.

There was an odd sound that Wyatt recognized in the dim recesses of his mind as wind, whistling past the plane as it hurtled toward the ground at a speed that seemed a hundred times faster than his thundering heart.

He thought about his parents, going down in a small jungle clearing, far from home and family.

He thought about Marilee, sitting beside him, calmly doing her job, as though it were a day in the park.

And then there was no time for thought.

Wyatt felt a strange sense of peace settle over him as the ground rushed up at them, blurring his vision.

CHAPTER NINE

The plane cleared the tree line, sailed over a swollen stream, and skimmed the ground before touching down with teeth-rattling force.

MON342 continued on, bumping over ruts and gullies with bone-jarring speed until at last it came to a wheezing stop. Just inches from the windshield loomed an enormous boulder.

Wyatt didn't permit himself to think what would have happened if they hadn't avoided that disastrous encounter.

After the whistle of air rushing past the little plane, the sudden silence was shocking.

Wyatt sat perfectly still, as though anticipating another crisis.

His first thought was Marilee. He looked over. Her hands were still tightly gripping the controls. Her eyes stared unblinking at the view outside her windshield.

At last she let out an audible sigh.

He touched a hand to her arm. "You all right?"

"Yeah." She relaxed her hands and let them drop to her lap before looking over at him. "You?"

"Not a scratch." He took her hand in his. "You sure you're okay?"

"I'm fine now." She let him continue to hold her hand. She needed the connection. It felt so good to know that he was here beside her.

"All right. No blood," she said with a sigh. "No broken bones. This is all good."

"How about the plane?" Wyatt looked around. "Since there aren't any flames coming from the engine, I'm guessing we're not in any immediate danger."

"Not from a fire. But I'd better check for structural damage before it gets too dark to see."

She released her seat belt, and he followed suit.

Her legs were none too steady as she stepped from the plane. Nerves were setting in now, big-time, and she could feel a weakness slowing her movements.

They circled the plane, noting the damage done to the tail and one wing as they'd scraped over rocks and low-growing brush and shrubs.

Wyatt leaned a hand against the wing to steady himself. "You think the plane is sound enough to take off?"

She shook her head. "I wouldn't risk it. I'll need a crew to go over every inch of it before I'll take it up again."

His mind began working overtime. They weren't going to simply lift off and fly home as he'd first imagined when he'd stepped outside the plane. Not that he was in any hurry to be airborne again, but if they were stuck here, he needed to readjust his thinking.

"How did this happen? What happened to the fuel?" Wyatt paused beside Marilee.

"There's no way to tell until I get the plane back to the hangar and have a crew check out the fuel line. There had to be a leak. I just don't understand how it was missed during refueling."

"Unless it happened after takeoff."

She nodded, deep in thought. "There was no collision. No jolt. No extreme wind or weather, or sign of any problem."

"Old age?"

She shrugged. "The plane isn't that old. And I have a maintenance contract with a really reliable crew to keep it in tip-top shape."

While she spoke, Wyatt dug out his cell phone and called Jesse to explain their situation. "Hold on." He turned to Marilee. "Jesse can get a crew out here in the morning. He'll try to locate a flatbed truck, too. Do you mind spending the night with the plane?"

She shook her head. "I don't see that we have any choice. There are no visible lights in the area. There's nothing out here but wilderness. It's only for one night. And we've got everything we need on board. Food. Water. There are emergency supplies I always carry."

Wyatt spoke into the phone. "Marilee's fine with it, and so am I. I'll hand the phone to her, and she can check the coordinates on the panel to let you know exactly where we are."

Marilee took his phone and climbed into the plane. A short time later she stepped out.

"I notified the control tower in Razorback about our situation. They'll contact Gold Fever's airport and alert them that we won't be returning tonight." She laughed. "Old Randy, who takes the evening shift, will be happy to know he doesn't have to miss a night with Vi and Daffy at the Fortune Saloon."

"Never let it be said that a plane crash kept good old Randy from happy hour."

The two shared a chuckle.

Wyatt rubbed his hands up and down her arms. "It's so good to be able to laugh."

"Yeah." She looked up at him, eyes shiny. "For a few minutes I wondered whether there'd be anything left to laugh about when this was over."

His eyes narrowed on her. "You were worried?"

"You bet."

"It didn't show."

She shrugged. "I had to stay focused on all the things I've learned through the years about how to handle the unexpected. And believe me, this was totally unexpected. Good thing I didn't have time to think about what was happening, or I'd have been scared to death."

He gave a quick shake of his head. "You had me fooled. You looked and sounded cool as a cucumber."

"You know what they say. Never let 'em see you sweat."

"I did enough sweating for both of us."

She lifted a hand to his cheek. "I hate that you had to go through this, Wyatt. Knowing what I do about your parents, I feel so guilty that you had to worry for even a few minutes. Thank heaven for happy endings."

Seeing the way his gaze intensified, she turned away, suddenly feeling the need to be busy. "There's a chill in the air. I'm going to gather up some wood for a fire."

Wyatt remained where he was, unable to shake the realization that, despite all the drama of a pending crash, Marilee had been worried about him.

When was the last time someone had done that? He couldn't recall. He'd been on his own for so long now, he'd grown accustomed to feeling alone in the universe. He'd even managed to convince himself that he didn't mind. But her simple admission touched him more deeply than anything else she could have said.

"Hey, rebel." Marilee's voice had his head coming up sharply. "You going to lend a hand, or just stand there watching the colorful sunset?"

With a thoughtful expression, he bent to the task of gathering wood.

"Oh, this is nice." Marilee sat with her back against a rock, nibbling the last of the cold hamburger Wyatt had bought at the airport grill. "I'm glad now that you stocked up on some dinner."

"Nothing like good food and a cozy campfire." Beside her he tipped back his head and took a long drink from the water bottle.

"I suppose, in your world travels, you've had your share of campfires."

He nodded.

"I'd like to hear about them."

He leaned back, remembering. "Some, like the ones in Nepal, were necessary for survival from the bitter cold."

"Why Nepal?"

"Why not? It sounded like a good idea at the time."

She gave a mock shiver. "Tell me about a warmer place."

"How about the jungles of South America? Those campfires were strictly for cooking the fish we caught in the rivers."

"And I suppose you had to avoid crocodiles while fishing?"

"A few."

"You've had some amazing adventures."

"Yeah. But I like this one best."

"In the middle of nowhere?" She glanced over. "Why?"

"I'm sharing it with you."

At his unexpected admission, her eyes widened. "Thank you. That's . . . nice to know. The funny thing is, I'm enjoying it, too."

"You seem surprised by that."

She tossed the paper bag into the fire and watched the flames consume it. "I guess I am. When I was fighting to bring down my plane, I was going over the rules of survival in my mind. Keep the nose up. Wings level. Stay focused. There isn't anything in the book about turning a crash landing into a cozy evening around a soothing campfire."

Because she was worrying the edges of her miniskirt, he caught her hand in his to still the movement. "You know what they say about rules."

When she looked over he was smiling, that dangerous, killer smile that had the power to make her heart stammer.

"They're meant to be broken."

"I don't think . . ."

He twined his fingers with hers and she felt a quick flare of heat race up her arm. "I do. Think," he added with a grin. "Probably way more than I should. And what I've been thinking is bound to affect both of us."

"Really? What have you been thinking about?"

"You and me. Where we're going. What we'll do when we get there."

When she opened her mouth he surprised her by pressing a finger to her lips to still her words.

At that simple touch she absorbed the most amazing collision of icy splinters along her spine.

"Earlier tonight, when we came through that crazy landing, you told me you'd been worried about me." He looked at their joined hands. "That's what I love about you, Marilee. No matter how much is going on in your life, you make room for everyone around you."

"This is getting way too serious." Nervous, she got to her feet.

He stood beside her, turning her to face him.

Her eyes, he noted, were misty.

He framed her face with his big hands. "What's wrong?"

"Nothing." She gave him a shaky smile.

He tipped up her face. "You're lying. I can tell. What's wrong? What did I say?"

"I'm just being foolish."

When she tried to pull away his fingers gripped the tops of her arms. "There's no place to run. No place to hide. We're about to spend the night alone out here in the middle of nowhere. So don't turn away from me. Tell me what's on your mind. Did I say something to hurt you?"

She lowered her head, refusing to meet his eyes. Her voice was little more than a whisper. "I'm giving you fair warning. It's silly." She swallowed. "You said that's what you love about me."

"Ah." He drew out the word as he studied her eyes. "And you're thinking I just tossed out some casual phrase that you've heard from dozens of guys? Or maybe one in particular, who mattered enough to turn you into a cynic?"

At the intensity of his tone she looked up. "Yeah. Something like that. After all, McCord, your reputation precedes you. You're not exactly shy with women. I'm sure you've used plenty of lines like that to get what you want."

His eyes, steady on hers, were hot and fierce.

His voice was equally fierce. "I'll admit that when I first saw you, my initial reaction was purely physical. A healthy combination of testosterone and lust. What guy could look at you and not feel what I felt? You're beautiful, and bright and independent. And did I mention beautiful?"

That brought a smile to her eyes.

"But the more I got to know you, the more I realized you weren't just a pretty package. I started learning that you were someone special. Someone I wanted to treat very carefully."

"And now?"

"I'm still battling lust."

There was that grin, sending an arrow straight through her heart.

"But there's more here. Much more." He stared at her mouth with naked hunger. "I've waited a long time for this, but now I'm going to have to kiss you. And when I do, I can't promise to stop."

She stood very still, heart pounding. "How do you know I'll ask you to?"

"Careful. Because unless you tell me to stop, you have to know where this is heading . . ."

In reply she stood on tiptoe to brush her mouth to his, stopping his words. Stopping his heart.

He drew in a deep breath and drew her a little away to stare into her eyes. "I hope you meant that."

"With all my heart."

"Thank God." He dragged her against him and covered her lips with his. Inside her mouth he whispered, "Because, baby, I mean this."

She'd waited so long. So long. And it was worth all the time she'd spent waiting and wondering. Here was a man who knew how to kiss a woman and make her feel like the only one in the universe.

This kiss was so hot, so hungry, she felt the rush of desire from the top of her head all the way to her toes. And still it spun on and on until she became lost in it.

He changed the angle of the kiss and took it deeper until Marilee could feel her flesh heating, her bones melting like hot wax.

She wanted to be sensible, to move slowly, but her mind refused to cooperate. With a single kiss her brain had been wiped clear of every thought but one. She wanted this man. Wanted him now. Desperately.

When at last they came up for air, she put a hand to his chest. "I need a minute to catch my breath."

"Okay." A second later he dragged her close. "Time's up."

Her laughter turned into a sigh as he ran nibbling kisses down her throat until the blood was drumming in her temples.

When his lips moved lower she gasped and clutched

his waist and gave herself up to the most amazing rush of
heat that had the ground tilting beneath her feet.

Wyatt savored the taste of her, the feel of her flesh
beneath his touch. Hadn't he known it would be like this?
It was why he'd put off this moment. He'd sensed instinctively that the instant he kissed her, everything would
change. Nothing less than everything she had to give
would satisfy the need in him.

And what a need. It clawed at his insides, a beast fighting to be free.

His hands moved to the buttons of her shirt and he
slid it from her shoulders before unfastening the wisp of
lace that covered her breasts. The look in his eyes spoke
volumes.

"Oh, baby." His words, whispered like a prayer, had her
shivering. "You're even more beautiful than I'd thought.
All this pale white flesh dotted with"—he trailed kisses
across her shoulder to the sensitive hollow of her throat—
"freckles. Have I told you how much I love freckles?"

In spite of the heat of his kisses, she managed a weak
laugh. "That's good, because they're everywhere . . ."

"Shh. A very dangerous admission. Now you just know
I'll have to count every single one." His hands slid beneath
the denim miniskirt. "Ever since I saw you in this, I've
thought of nothing but getting you out of it."

Her skirt drifted to the ground, followed by her lace
bikini.

With his mouth feasting on hers, and his clever fingers
working their magic, she gave herself up to all the pleasure he was offering.

Such exquisite pleasure. He knew exactly how to touch
her. Where to touch her. How to please her. How to bring

her to her knees with a desperate need that bordered on pain.

Wyatt drove her up and over. She was wonderful to watch. The way her eyes widened as she rode the first crest. The possessive way her arms circled his neck and drew his head down when he shifted his weight.

"Wyatt." Her sigh filled his mouth. "We need a moment."

"All I need is you," he growled. "Now."

"Not yet." And then her hands were at his shirt, tugging it over his head before reaching for the fasteners at his waist. When his clothes joined hers on the ground, she was finally free to touch him the way he was touching her. And to marvel at the beauty of his body, all corded muscles and sinew.

"Oh, yes, Wyatt." She ran hot, wet kisses down his throat while her hands moved over the flat planes of his stomach, and then lower, until his breathing was as ragged as hers.

His tongue traced the curve of her ear, nipping and tugging on the lobe before darting inside, sending shivers along her spine.

Against his chest he could feel the wild, erratic rhythm of her heartbeat, as ragged as his own. From deep in her throat her breath hitched on a sob.

Wyatt knew he could take her now. It was what she wanted. What they both wanted. They could be free of this terrible tension that was raging through them now like an unchained beast.

But he'd fantasized about this for so long now. From the first time he'd seen her, he'd known that one day he would have to have her. Now, finally, he was free to do all the things he'd only dreamed of. Now, at last, he would have it all.

But not just yet.

With sheer force of will, he banked his needs and ran butterfly kisses over her cheeks, her eyelids, the tip of her nose.

He felt her relax in his arms and brought his mouth to hers in a kiss so sweet, so tender, it brought a sigh from her lips.

"Here." He caught her hands and together they knelt in the grass, littered with their clothes.

With his eyes steady on hers he leaned close, touching her lips with his.

His arms came around her and he drew her down until they were lying together, flesh to flesh, heartbeat to heartbeat. He heard the purr of pleasure deep in her throat as he ran kisses down her neck, across her collarbone, over her breasts, then lower.

Her body convulsed when he moved lower still and another climax ripped through her. Stunned and reeling, she had no time to recover as, with lips and teeth and tongue, he took her on a wild roller-coaster ride that left her staggered and hungering for more.

He felt the madness taking over. A sense of desperation that had him driving her high, then higher still, until they were both beyond reason, beyond control.

"Marilee." Blinded by a hard, driving need, he knew he could wait no longer. His eyes steady on hers, he entered her.

She wrapped herself around him, opening to him, whispering his name like a prayer.

"Come with me, baby. Stay with me."

With hearts thundering, they began moving, climbing.

Lungs straining, bodies hot and wet, they reached the very crest of a high, sheer mountain.

For one heart-stopping moment they paused, taking in deep breaths.

On a shuddering sigh, they stepped off the edge.

And flew.

CHAPTER TEN

$\longrightarrow \diamond \longleftarrow$

Marilee lay perfectly still, waiting for her world to settle. She had to fight the unreasonable urge to weep.

Wyatt's face was pressed to the hollow of her throat, his breathing rough, his damp body plastered to hers.

He nuzzled her neck. "Am I too heavy?"

"Umm." It was all she could manage.

"You all right?"

"Umm."

"Did anybody ever tell you that you talk too much?"

"Umm."

He brushed his mouth over hers. "If you hum a bit more, I might be able to name that tune."

That broke the spell of tears that had been threatening and caused her to laugh.

She wrapped her arms around his neck and kissed him back. "Have I told you how much I like your silly sense of humor?"

"No, you haven't." He rolled to his side and gathered

her into his arms, nuzzling her cheek, while his big hands moved over her hip, her back, her waist, as though measuring every inch of her. "What else do you like about me?"

"You fishing for compliments?"

"Of course I am."

"Glutton. Your sense of humor isn't enough?"

"Not nearly enough. How about my looks?"

"They're okay, for a footloose rebel."

"Stop. All these mushy remarks will inflate my ego." He gave a mock frown. "How about the way I kiss?"

"You're not bad."

"Not bad?" His hands stopped their movement. He drew a little away. "That's all you can say?"

"If you recall, tonight was the first time we've kissed. I haven't had nearly enough practice to be a really good judge of your talent."

"Then we'd better take care of that right now." He framed her face. With his eyes steady on hers, he lowered his mouth to claim her lips.

Marilee's eyelids fluttered and she felt an explosion of color behind them. As though the moon and stars had collided while she rocketed through space. It was the most amazing sensation, and, as his lips continued moving over hers, she found herself wishing it could go on forever.

When at last they came up for air, she took in a long, deep breath before opening her eyes. "Oh, yes, rebel. I have to say, I do like the way you kiss."

"That's good, because I intend to do a whole lot more of it." He lay back in the grass, one hand beneath his head. "Now it's my turn. Want to know all the things I like about you?"

"I'm afraid to hear it." Marilee lay on her side, her hand splayed across his chest.

"Besides your freckles, which I've already mentioned, the thing about you I like best is your take-charge attitude."

She chuckled. "A lot of guys feel intimidated by that."

"They're idiots. Don't they know there's something sexy about a woman who knows what to do and how to do it? I've watched you as a medic and as a pilot, and I haven't decided which one turns me on more."

"Really?" She sat up. "Want me to fetch my first-aid kit from the plane? I could always splint your arm or leg and really turn you on."

He dragged her down into his arms and growled against her mouth, "You don't need to do a single thing to turn me on. All I need to do is look at you and I want you."

"You mean now? Again? So soon?"

"Oh, yeah."

"Liar. I don't believe it's possible."

"You ought to know by now that I never say anything I can't back up with action."

"Prove it, rebel."

"My pleasure."

There was a wicked smile on his lips as he rolled over her and began to kiss her breathless, all the while taking her on a slow, delicious ride to paradise.

"Cold?"

Marilee's eyes opened and she found Wyatt watching her by the light of the moon. Nearby, the fire had burned to embers, occasionally sending up sparks that hissed and snapped in the darkness.

"You give off enough body heat for both of us." She drew her arms around his waist. "But your back's cold. I have blankets in the plane."

"I'll get them." He stood and slipped into his jeans, leaving the waist unsnapped as he made his way to the plane in that loose, lanky stride that had her mouth watering. She loved the look of him, like a cowboy in some Madison Avenue ad. Except that he was the real thing, with big, work-roughened hands and scuffed boots and a high-voltage smile that could reduce her to puddles when it was directed her way.

Minutes later he returned and shook out a quilt, which he spread out on the grass. Then he knelt beside her and draped a blanket around her shoulders before striding away to gather more wood for the fire.

A short time later, with the fire blazing, he dropped down beside Marilee, who had settled herself on the quilt.

She held out her arms and he moved in close before she wrapped herself and the blanket around him.

"Now this is what I call cozy and comfortable." He nibbled her lips and she sighed in contentment.

He offered her an apple he'd found amid the supplies. She took a bite before handing it back to him. Together they shared the fruit, then washed it down with a bottle of water.

He passed her the water. "What do you think about when you're flying?"

"Always happy thoughts. Sometimes I'm a kid again, riding on my father's shoulders. Sometimes I'm a pioneer, the first to fly to the moon or Mars. There's something freeing about being high above the ground and knowing I'm in control."

He glanced over. "How about when things go wrong and you have no control? How did you feel when you realized we had to land in the middle of nowhere?"

She shook her head. "It's hard to explain, Wyatt. I felt a flash of fear, but never any paralyzing panic. Even when we were heading toward rough terrain, I felt certain I could land without trashing the plane."

"What if you hadn't?"

She shrugged. "There wasn't time to play that game in my mind. I suppose it was the same for you when you decided to fall off that bull and land at my feet."

He chuckled. "Okay. I get it. Yeah. No time to worry. Just do the deed and live with the consequences. Looks like we're two of a kind."

"Exactly. Only you prefer to risk your life in the bull-ring, and I'd rather risk mine in the sky."

"I guess it proves we're a perfect fit. And both perfectly crazy."

She saw the way his eyes narrowed on her and recognized the same quick rush of desire that had suddenly come over her.

How was it possible that she could want him again?

There was no time to analyze her feelings as he gathered her close and kissed her until they were both trembling with need.

A spark from the fire shot into the air and blazed a fiery trail in the darkness. Neither of them took notice. They were too busy starting a blaze of their own.

"What are you thinking?" Marilee touched a finger to the smile that curved Wyatt's lips.

"That life doesn't get much better'n this." He stretched

out his long legs toward the blazing logs he'd added to the fire.

With one arm behind his head, he kept the other around Marilee, holding her close.

They'd spent the night alternately loving and sleeping. At times their lovemaking had been as soothing and gentle as a breeze blowing across a meadow, all soft kisses and easy sighs. At other times they'd been seized by a sort of madness that had taken them down, down into a deep abyss, where nothing had mattered except to feed the passion that drove them to the very edge of reason.

Now, as ribbons of dawn light began to streak the sky, they lay together, for the moment pleasantly sated, as cozy as old lovers.

"What took you so long?" Marilee played with the hair on his chest.

"So long?" He looked over.

"To make a move on me." She felt her cheeks grow hot at the way he was staring. "Most guys don't even give me time to learn their last name."

"I'm not most guys."

"I've noticed." It was one of the things that set him apart from every other man she'd ever known.

"You sorry we waited?"

"Oh, Wyatt." She lifted a hand to his cheek. "I'm not sorry about anything."

"Good." He leaned up on one elbow and kissed her. "It nearly killed me to walk away from you each time without so much as a kiss. But I knew the minute I tasted you, it was all over."

She laughed. "You make it sound like a death sentence."

"If so"—he gathered her close and kissed her until they were both sighing—"I can't think of a better way to die than this."

The need, sharp and swift, caught them both by surprise. With a blaze of passion they took each other into the very heart of their storm. A storm that, when finally spent, left them both shaking and craving more.

"Is that a plane?" Marilee awoke with a start, surprised to find the sun already high.

Wyatt shaded the sun from his eyes to scan the sky.

As the sound grew louder they both sat up at the same moment.

"A truck." Wyatt pointed. "Coming from that direction. Probably Jesse and Zane with that flatbed they promised."

"Oh, no. Look at me. What was I thinking?" With a cry Marilee grabbed up her discarded clothes and started dressing.

When she finished she tossed Wyatt's clothing at him. "Aren't you going to put these on?"

"Yeah. No rush."

"No rush?" She was already climbing into the cockpit of the plane to retrieve her gear.

Men, she thought. If they were standing naked in Grand Central Station, they would probably take their sweet time finding something with which to cover themselves.

While she ran a brush through her tangled hair, she watched as Wyatt calmly slipped into his clothes just as a ranch truck came into view over a hill. She let out a sigh of relief that at least they were both dressed.

As the truck roared to a halt and Jesse, Amy, and Zane

stepped out, Marilee rushed forward to greet them. "You made good time."

"We started at dawn." Jesse grinned at his wife. "If Amy had her way, we'd have started even earlier."

"I was worried sick." Amy grabbed her friend in a fierce embrace and held on. "Are you sure you're all right?"

"I'm fine." Marilee glanced over at Wyatt and the two exchanged a long, knowing look. "We're both fine."

"You look none the worse for it." Amy clutched her hand. "Lee, I was so relieved to hear that you two weren't hurt in the landing."

"Not as relieved as we were." Marilee gave her another quick, hard hug, and the two women clung for a moment before stepping apart.

"You had to be terrified."

Marilee managed a smile. "There was no time for terror, or any other emotion. But when it was over, I have to admit that my knees were quaking."

"Mine, too." Amy looked at her husband for confirmation. "When Jesse gave me the news, I thought for a moment I'd be sick. But then he said you were both fine, and I was so relieved."

Wyatt strolled closer to his cousins and indicated the ranch truck. "You promised a flatbed."

"It's on the way. Since it has to move at a snail's pace over this terrain, we decided to come ahead." Jesse gave him a slap on the arm. "How'd you two survive the night?"

"Fine." Wyatt smiled at Marilee, who returned his smile. "We had enough food and water and blankets. Since it didn't rain, we just made a fire and slept under the stars."

Zane glanced toward the ashes of the campfire, then at the bedroll beside it. "At least the plane's intact. If it had rained, you would have had shelter. Looks like you had all the comforts of home."

Wyatt crossed the distance to drop an arm around Marilee. "I don't think either of us would like to make a habit of this, unless we had all the provisions that Aunt Cora packs for her wilderness trips. And even then, I'm not sure it's something I'd do on a regular basis the way she does."

That had all of them laughing.

It was, Marilee thought, good to hear the sound of laughter.

Amy glanced toward the plane, noting the damage to the tail and wing. "That had to be some hard landing. You going to tell us all the details?"

"In time." Wyatt pointed to the cloud of dust coming up over the rise. "It looks like this is the flatbed truck."

Though they had dozens of questions, they managed to put them aside.

Within minutes the three cousins were working together, along with the crew from the ranch, to secure the plane for the long, tedious trip back to the airport.

CHAPTER ELEVEN

———◆———

As they crowded into the ranch truck, Amy passed a foil-wrapped container to Marilee, who'd climbed into the backseat with Wyatt.

She arched a brow. "What's this?"

"Breakfast. Dandy figured the two of you would be starving."

"Bless him." Marilee removed the foil wrapper and stared at the tray of deviled eggs, sliced ham and turkey, freshly baked rolls, and an array of fruit. Pineapple slices, grapes, strawberries, melon. "Was he planning on feeding an army?"

"Yeah. That's Dandy." Amy closed a hand over Jesse's. "That's why we all love him."

Marilee tasted the fruit, then offered a strawberry to Wyatt. As his lips closed around the tips of her fingers, she absorbed a jolt to the heart.

"After last night's cold burgers," she said, shooting a meaningful glance at Wyatt, "this is an absolute feast."

"Add this to the feast." Jesse handed Wyatt a thermos of coffee and some travel mugs. "There's nothing like really hot coffee to warm the soul."

While they bumped over rocky hills and dry washes, Marilee and Wyatt sat back enjoying Dandy's unexpected gift. And because they weren't able to eat everything, the others offered to help them out, since they'd eaten their own breakfast several hours earlier.

When they'd had their fill, Zane asked the question they all wanted answered. "Okay. Now that breakfast is out of the way, tell us. What happened to force a landing in the middle of the wilderness?"

"I'm not sure yet." Marilee set aside her mug. "The fuel gauge read empty. But I had the plane fueled in Razor-back while Harding's supplies were being unloaded."

"Is it common to spring a leak?"

At Amy's question Marilee couldn't help laughing. "If it were common, you wouldn't find too many people willing to be pilots. We may like flying with the birds, but we're not willing to drop to earth like wounded elephants."

The others joined in the laughter.

Wyatt sat back, letting the laughter wash over him. It felt good to see Marilee interacting so easily with his cousins. Though he hadn't meant for it to happen, they'd become a family again. After their years of separation, Zane and Jesse meant a great deal to him, as did Amy. But this woman had begun to mean as much or more. It mattered to him that they were accepting of her. Though he hadn't planned on this happening, Marilee mattered.

He looked up to see Zane watching him in the rearview

mirror. It occurred to him that he was probably wearing a stupid grin. Not that it bothered him. Right now he didn't care if the whole world saw him grinning like a fool. He felt wildly, foolishly happy, and so glad to be returning to civilization, even though he'd thoroughly enjoyed his night in the wilderness. His time alone with Marilee had been like a special gift from the gods. One he would cherish for a long time to come. Now, he was more than ready to get back to reality.

Daylight had faded to dusk by the time the plane had been unloaded from the flatbed truck and towed to a hangar at the Gold Fever airport.

Jesse, Amy, and Zane had long ago returned to the ranch.

The airport's trusted mechanic, Craig Matson, was busy overseeing every step of the operation. By the time Marilee had filled out the necessary paperwork, Craig had already completed a preliminary check of the plane's exterior.

He looked up as she and Wyatt strolled toward the plane. "You really did a number on this wing." He ran a hand over the damage. "And the tail. Just how many boulders did you manage to crush in that landing?"

"I'm sure we left a trail of gravel." Marilee moved in beside him. "How long will it take to repair?"

He shrugged. "Not my area of expertise. That's up to the manufacturer. But I'd say you're out of commission for a couple of weeks, until the company can fly in the parts and put it all back together."

"What about the fuel line?"

He squinted in the artificial light of the hangar.

"Won't be able to give it a thorough going-over until morning, with the door open and enough sunlight to really see every little piece of it. Here's what I've checked so far." He pointed to an initial he'd scribbled with Magic Marker. "That's as far as I can see tonight. But I'll tell you this much: There was nothing wrong with the fuel line when you left yesterday."

Wyatt stepped up. "You're sure?"

The man met his look. "I make it my business to be sure. My pilots' lives are on the line every time."

"Thanks, Craig. This pilot is grateful for all you do." Marilee patted his arm. "I'll be here first thing in the morning."

"I'll add my thanks to hers." Wyatt shook Craig's hand before turning to follow her.

Craig picked up his cold coffee and made another turn around the plane before heading for his car. Marilee and Wyatt had already climbed into their vehicles. He watched their taillights as they sped off in the darkness. Then he turned his truck toward the Fortune Saloon. There was still time to join the sheriff, the mayor, and a few of his cronies for a beer before heading home.

On his Harley, Wyatt trailed Marilee's truck to her apartment and into the garage where she kept the emergency vehicle. By the time she turned off the ignition, he was holding her door.

"Thanks, rebel." She led the way up the stairs to her apartment. When she'd unlocked the door she paused, unsure of where the night was heading. "Want to come in?"

He stepped inside and closed the door before leaning against it.

Marilee walked around, turning on lights before heading toward the kitchen, where she filled the teakettle and placed it on a burner.

She could feel his dark gaze watching her every move.

"Want some tea? Or would you rather have a beer?"

"I'll take a beer."

He remained where he was as she removed a cold longneck from the refrigerator and twisted the top.

She glanced over with equal parts annoyance and fear. Annoyance that she couldn't read his emotions. His face was perfectly expressionless. Fear that he was about to live up to his playboy image and, having enjoyed his latest conquest, was getting ready to move on to someone new. He looked ready to bolt out the door the first chance he got.

There was a trace of anger in her voice. "Are you coming in, or do you intend to just stand there, guarding the door?"

He managed a half-smile. "I'm having a hell of an argument with myself."

"Want to let me in on it? Or is it a big, dark secret?"

"The truth?" He crossed the room and perched on a barstool before lifting the bottle to his mouth. After a long drink he set it down and met her questioning look. "I'm filthy. I haven't changed my clothes in twenty-four hours. And, except for Dandy's breakfast, I haven't had another thing to eat all day."

"If you'd like to go, I'll understand. Or, if you'd like, you could shower while I make . . ." She half turned before he sprang up and caught her arm, startling her. Her mouth went dry as dust. "I was just going to offer you the use of my shower while I fix some supper."

"It's not food I want. Or a shower. Or a change of clothes. All I want . . . all I can think about, is taking you to bed."

She let out a long, deep sigh as relief flooded through her. "Is that all? I thought maybe you were looking for an excuse to leave."

"An excuse?" He stared at her in disbelief. "After what we've shared, is that what you think?"

"I didn't know what to think. You were hovering over there by the door like someone who couldn't wait to run."

He drew her close and framed her face with his hands. "Marilee, the only place I want to run is here, into your arms." He lowered his face and captured her mouth with his.

She returned his kisses with such eagerness, they soon were both moaning with need.

In a rush they tore off each other's clothes before he backed her against the wall and lifted her. With hearts pounding and breathing labored, they took each other with all the fever of a raging wildfire.

Spent, he sank into her, heartbeat to heartbeat, and rested his forehead against hers.

He touched a hand to her cheek. "Sorry. I was rough. I didn't mean . . ."

"Wyatt." She placed a finger to his lips to still his words. "I'm not fragile."

"No. You're not." He stared deeply into her eyes. "You're amazing."

"You're not bad yourself, rebel."

He took a breath. "I guess I could use that shower now."

"We both could."

He smiled. "I like the way you think."

She returned his smile. "Good. Because I'm thinking that after we shower, I'll toss our clothes in the washer and you can make me some supper. I've always wanted my very own naked chef."

She caught his hand and led the way to the bathroom. As the door closed, they were still laughing. When the water began flowing, their laughter turned to muffled sighs.

"This is good." Marilee perched on a barstool, wearing a green silk knee-length kimono she'd snagged from the closet.

"You sound surprised." Beside her, Wyatt speared a broccoli floret.

With his clothes in the washer, he'd opted for a pair of discarded scrubs he'd salvaged from a box of hospital supplies.

"You continue to surprise me. But I have to admit, I like a man who can cook for himself." She took another bite of grilled chicken that topped their salads. "And cook for me, in the bargain."

"You want a cook, I'm your man."

She glanced over. "Yes, you are. And though you're not naked as I'd hoped, being shirtless is close enough."

"For now." He sent her one of those heart-stopping grins. "After I clean up the kitchen, I'd be happy to get naked for you, ma'am. After all, a personal chef has to please the boss."

She set aside her empty salad bowl and sipped her tea. "Are you thinking about spending the night?"

He met her questioning look. "I'd say that's up to you. I'd like to, but I don't want to get in the way of your routine."

"My routine is pretty undemanding. With my plane out of commission, I only have my emergency medical services to see to. What about your routine?"

He shrugged. "I'll have to drive out to the ranch. When Zane and I agreed to stay on, we also agreed to take on whatever chores are needed around the Lost Nugget. It could be tending a herd, minding a sick heifer, or tearing apart the engine of one of our fleet of trucks."

"A man of many talents, I see."

He chuckled. "Zane and I are finding out just what our talents are. I thought I'd done enough in my travels to prepare me for anything, but I'm constantly learning something new."

"And from the smile on your face, I'd say you're loving every minute of it."

"I am. And so is Zane. I really misjudged him. I figured, because he did his growing up in Hollywood, that he'd be lost on a ranch. But he dives into every chore with more energy than any of us."

"And you love him for it."

That had Wyatt going very still, mulling it over, before nodding his head. "I never thought about it before, but yeah. I do love him for it. When we were kids, he was always pedaling faster, running harder, just to keep up with Jesse and me. But now the years have evened things up. He's our equal. More than equal, in fact. There are a lot of things he can do better than the rest of us."

"Like what?"

"He has a way of mingling with the wranglers, like he's always been there. And Jimmy Eagle, who oversees all the herds and wranglers, has begun trusting Zane with more and more responsibility."

"And you?"

"I was born responsible." He said it so straight-faced, she found herself almost believing him before he sent her that famous grin.

"I should have known you were teasing me."

"Hey. How can you doubt the guy who just made you supper?"

"Why would I believe a guy who's wearing a pair of cast-off scrubs that don't even reach his ankles?"

He lifted his leg. "I thought they made me look like a surgeon."

"Or a comedian pretending to be a doctor."

He wiggled his brows. "You keep this up, woman, and I may have to forget about washing the dishes so I can operate on you."

"Only if you have a license."

"Baby, I don't need a license for what I want to do to you."

That had her laughing harder. "I can hardly wait to see what you have in mind. Could we hurry up in here, so you can show me everything?"

He brushed a kiss over her lips that had her toes curling. "All in good time. Now sit there and drink your tea while I finish what I started here. Any chef worth his salary cleans up his own messes."

She drained her cup and picked up a towel. At his arched look she said, "I thought I'd hurry you along."

"You're turning into a very greedy woman."

"Are you complaining?"

"Hardly." He laughed. "In fact, it's a real turn-on."

She joined in the laughter. "Oh, I think right about now, anything, including a sneeze, would be a turn-on."

"You got that right, woman." He lifted his hands from the soapy water to drag her close. "Let's leave the dishes to dry on the counter. I don't think I can wait another minute."

She tossed aside the towel and grabbed his hand.

Laughing, they ran to the bedroom. And lost themselves in pure bliss.

The ringing of a phone shattered the silence. Before the second ring Marilee sat up, shoving hair from her eyes, and snatched up the receiver.

"Emergency One. What's the problem?"

Beside her, Wyatt snapped on a light on a bedside table and noted the time. Almost four in the morning.

Marilee listened in silence before saying, "Okay. I'm on it." She replaced the receiver and looked over at Wyatt. "Lucas Sandler. His wife thinks it's his heart. Doc Wheeler's meeting me out at their ranch."

As she began dressing, Wyatt climbed out of bed and did the same.

She arched a brow. "I don't need help."

He merely smiled. "My cousins do. By the time I drive to the ranch, they'll be up and ready for morning chores. I wouldn't want to miss out on the work assignments."

"Not to mention Dandy's famous breakfast."

He upped the wattage on the smile. "Yeah. There's that, too."

Minutes later they both walked from her apartment down the stairs to the garage. With a quick kiss, Marilee headed out, sirens blaring, while Wyatt turned his motorcycle in the opposite direction toward the Lost Nugget Ranch.

CHAPTER TWELVE

———◆◆◆———

Wyatt strolled into the kitchen just as Dandy was removing a pan from the oven. The entire room was perfumed with the fragrance of freshly baked cinnamon buns.

Wyatt snagged a glass of just-squeezed orange juice from a tray on the counter. "'Morning, Dandy. Marilee and I thank you for that care package you made us yesterday."

The ranch cook, sleeves of his crisp plaid shirt carefully rolled above the elbows, jeans looking like they'd just come from the store, sent him a warm smile. "Glad you enjoyed it. I figured after a night in the wilderness, you'd be ready for some real food."

He looked up as Cora stepped through the doorway. "'Morning, Miss Cora."

"Good morning, Dandy." She opened her arms wide to welcome her grandnephew. "Oh, Wyatt. I'm so happy to see you."

He gave her a warm hug. "It's good to be home."

Home. She felt a rush of pure joy at his easy use of the term. When he and Zane had first arrived at the ranch for Coot's funeral after years of separation, she'd feared that they would never be able to fully embrace their former home. But now, though there were still times when they butted heads with Jesse, who had never left, they had begun to bond like brothers.

She caught Wyatt's hand and led him toward the table. "I want to hear everything about the crash."

"Is that the reason for your early return?"

She nodded. "How could I stay away after such worrisome news? Even when Cal assured me that both you and Marilee weren't hurt, I had to come home and see for myself."

While Dandy poured her a fresh cup of coffee, Wyatt sat beside her. "It wasn't really a crash. I mean, we were forced to land in the wilderness, but except for some exterior damage to the plane, we weren't hurt."

"Thank heavens." She touched a hand to her heart. "When I heard, I was so afraid for you both. Considering the way you lost your parents, this had to be especially hard for you to endure. You're sure you're all right?"

He patted her hand. "Not a scratch."

"Maybe not on the outside." Jesse and Amy came in together and overheard the last of Wyatt's remarks. "But I think if you check his heart, Aunt Cora, you may find it changed."

Cora glanced from Jesse to Wyatt. "Your heart?"

Zane walked in and picked up a glass of orange juice. "Yeah, his heart. We're thinking it'll never be the same. Our world-traveler, old love-'em-and-leave-'em, man-of-the-world Wyatt may have finally met his match."

As she caught on to their little joke, Cora chuckled. "Ah. I see. You and Marilee?"

"Careful, Aunt Cora." Jesse devoured a cinnamon bun in three bites. "The mere mention of Wyatt and Lee in the same breath will probably jinx any chance they have for a real relationship. It's bound to tarnish his playboy image."

She looked over. "I really like Lee Trainor. I'm glad to learn that you like her, too."

"Thanks, Aunt Cora. That makes two of us." Wyatt sat back with a smile of pure contentment that had Jesse and Zane looking at each other with confusion.

"Uh-oh." Jesse squeezed Amy's hand and winked. "I'd say our cousin has fallen hard."

"Either that or he hit his head in that rough landing, and we ought to get him to the hospital for some tests."

"Are you guys through having fun yet?" Wyatt calmly picked up an empty plate and walked to the stove, where bacon sizzled and light-as-air flapjacks were stacked on a platter.

Filling his plate, he returned to the table and began to eat.

"It's even worse than I'd thought." Jesse kissed Amy's cheek before helping himself to a similar breakfast. "Our man's down for the count, and he's about to be declared out."

"You won't hear me complaining." Zane was grinning as he filled his plate. "That just leaves more unattached females for me."

"There are plenty of females looking your way, but they're all afraid of those damned cameras you carry with you everywhere." Jesse looked over. "If you want my advice, you should ditch the Hollywood filmmaker routine and concentrate on looking like a cowboy. That's what the ladies really like."

Amy playfully smacked his arm. "A lot you know about women."

"Hey. I married the prettiest girl in town. That makes me something of an expert."

"Well, Mr. Expert, consider this." Amy winked at Zane. "All women love to think they're just one step away from being discovered as the next big movie star."

Jesse roared with laughter. "Yeah, that's why they duck and run whenever they see our cousin walking toward them with his camera in hand."

"Well," she admitted, "only if they don't have any makeup on, or it's a bad-hair day."

Wyatt set down his cup. "Some women look gorgeous even without makeup and never have bad-hair days."

"I assume you're thinking about a certain drop-dead gorgeous redhead." Zane exchanged a grin with Jesse.

Instead of the expected defensive outburst, Wyatt merely shrugged. "I'm only speaking the truth. The woman doesn't have a flaw."

That had all of them, including Cora, laughing.

Dandy, busy at the stove, kept his face averted. But the shaking of his shoulders was a dead giveaway that he was enjoying this as much as the others.

All day, as he tended ranch chores, Wyatt was forced to endure the jokes about his time spent in the wilderness with Marilee. It had become the favorite topic of conversation.

At some other time he might have grown weary of the

teasing, and would have resorted to his temper to stop some of the wranglers from their endless comments, but this day, it all rolled off his back like rain off the ducks in the ranch ponds. He simply wasn't capable of anger on this perfect day.

By dinnertime, his family and fellow wranglers had given up ribbing him, recognizing that he was far too mellow to rise to the bait.

He emerged from his room freshly showered and wearing clean clothes, his dark hair still sporting droplets of water.

"Looking good, cuz. Off to see your lady?" Jesse looked up from the map, where he and Amy, Zane, and Cora were gathered around, checking their latest route.

New flags marked the trail they'd begun charting, along with sticky notes. The sight of the map jolted Wyatt's memory.

"In the excitement of the crash I almost forgot something I spotted from the air." He walked over to the map and drew a finger along the trail they'd been mapping for the past months. His eyes narrowed. "I only caught a glimpse of it, but I'd swear I saw this same path as we flew over. It appeared to be the width of a crude horse-drawn wagon trail, and it stretched from the river to Treasure Chest Mountain."

"You're sure?" Jesse walked up beside him and moved his finger along the flag-marked trail. "From Grasshopper Creek to Treasure Chest?"

"Yeah." Wyatt glanced around. "Do you think Coot left a trail?"

They all turned to Cora.

She shook her head. "It's hard to say. Coot searched

alone. And spent a lifetime looking for the gold. But he rarely ever went out on horseback. These past few years he always used a truck or an all-terrain vehicle, especially if he was traveling through the more rugged stretches of our land."

"So how do we explain the trail I spotted?" Wyatt continued studying the map.

"I don't know." Jesse's mind was awhirl with ideas. "But I think we ought to take another flyover and see if we can pin it down more accurately."

Zane and Wyatt nodded in agreement.

"Let's see how soon Marilee's plane can be airborne." Wyatt pulled his cell phone from his shirt pocket and dialed Marilee's number. Instead of her voice he got her voice mail and left her a message. Knowing the others were listening, he kept it short: "Hey, I bet you're out on another emergency. Give me a call when you get this. I thought I'd head into town and treat you to one of the Fortune Saloon's famous greasy burgers."

He dropped the phone into his pocket and glanced around. "Anybody feel like tagging along to town?"

Jesse and Amy were the first to refuse. "Sorry. We're bringing supper to Amy's father."

"How is Otis feeling?" Cora asked.

"Dad claims, now that the treatments are finished, he's as good as new." Amy gave a sigh of relief. She had returned to Gold Fever to nurse her father through a serious illness. Now in remission, Otis Parrish had been transformed from an angry, grudge-holding man to a kindly, grateful neighbor who looked forward to visits with his daughter and her new husband. "He's been handling all his own ranch chores lately without outside help, so that's a very good sign."

"Indeed it is." Cora turned to Wyatt. "I'm off to my studio for at least another hour. Then I promised Cal I'd have dinner with him here at the ranch. We have a lot of business to catch up on."

Zane gave a quick shake of his head. "I can't go either, cuz. I'm joining Jimmy Eagle and some of the crew in the bunkhouse for an evening of Texas Hold 'em."

"Drinking. Gambling. Next thing you know," Wyatt said with a grin, "you'll be chewing tobacco and looking for loose women."

"It can't be soon enough for me," Zane added with a laugh.

That had the others laughing, as well.

Wyatt kissed his aunt's cheek before heading out the door.

All the way to town his heart was light. It wasn't the thought of Violet's burgers, or Daffy's bawdy jokes. He was feeling like a randy high school boy with his first crush.

And truth be told, he didn't care if the whole world knew it.

"Hey, rebel." Marilee yanked open the door of her apartment before Wyatt had a chance to knock.

"Ahhh." He breathed the word while he studied the way she looked in her faded jeans and tee that showed every line and curve of that fabulous body. "Now this is what I call perfection."

She felt the heat stain her cheeks and was surprised by it. How could she be blushing after all they'd shared?

She shot him a dimpled smile. "You're not bad yourself."

"Not bad? I bet you can do better'n that." He dragged her close and kissed her until she clutched at his shirt-front.

When he lifted his head she sucked in a breath. "I meant to say you look so good to me I could drink you up in one big gulp."

He chuckled. "Much better. And I have to say, I feel the same way about you. Ready for some of Vi and Daffy's beer and burgers?"

"As long as I don't have to cook, I'm ready for anything."

He caught her hand and led her down the stairs. In her garage he paused. "My Harley or your truck?"

She shrugged. "I think I like the idea of having the wind in my hair."

He climbed on his motorcycle and she settled in behind him.

While he revved the engine and started forward she rested her cheek on his back, loving the strong, solid feel of him.

They rode in silence, unable to carry on a conversation over the roar of the engine. He pulled up outside the saloon.

In the sudden silence he pocketed the keys and caught her hand. "Long day?"

"Yeah." She sighed.

Hearing it he paused. "Is Lucas Sandler okay?"

"He's fine. Doc said it was heartburn. Wrote him a prescription for acid-reflux medication and we were on our way."

"Were you out on another emergency run this afternoon?"

She shook her head.

"I tried calling you and got your voice mail."

"Yeah. I turned off my phone after meeting with Craig. I wanted some time to absorb the news."

"News?" He was suddenly alert. "About the fuel line?"

She nodded.

"Did he find something?"

"He did. But not what we were expecting." She took a breath. "Do you remember how Craig explained that he'd examined part of the line, but that he would have to wait until today for a thorough examination?"

"I remember."

"He initialed the portion that he'd already examined, so he could begin from there." She looked over. Met Wyatt's steady gaze. "Today he couldn't find his initials."

Wyatt's brow furrowed. "I don't get it."

"Neither did Craig for a while. Then he figured it out. Overnight, somebody must have switched fuel lines."

When he realized the implication, Wyatt's eyes narrowed. "Somebody would have to be really worried about what Craig would find. Especially if the fuel line had been tampered with. The only way to get rid of the evidence of their crime would be to replace the entire fuel line with a new one before morning."

"Exactly. And whoever did it had no idea that Craig had left his mark on the existing one."

"Did Craig report this to Sheriff Wycliff?"

"He called and left word that we wanted to meet with him. Deputy Atkins took the message and said he'd get back with him."

"Good. It's time to bring the law into this." Wyatt

squeezed her hand. "We need to know who has access to the hangar after hours. And who Craig might have talked to last night. Where can we find him?"

She nodded toward a rusty old truck parked outside the saloon. "That's Craig's. I'd say the odds are pretty good that he's inside right now."

Keeping her hand firmly in his, Wyatt made his way into the Fortune Saloon with blood in his eyes.

Daffy was the first to spot the couple stepping through the door. With a tray full of drinks she swooped down on them.

"Aren't you the pair? The whole town's talking about the fact that you survived a plane crash and spent a romantic night out in the wilderness."

She managed to balance the heavy tray in one hand while patting Wyatt's cheek with the other. "Leave it to a McCord to come through it all smelling like a rose."

She turned to Marilee and dropped a hand to her shoulder. "Girlfriend, I hope you realize that the minute you become romantically involved with a McCord, the whole town considers you fair game to suffer the curse of the lost fortune."

"You know better than to believe in urban legends, Daffy."

"Hey, tell it to all these folks. I'm just the messenger." She leaned close. "I expect to hear every yummy little detail of your hot new romance the next time you come in here"—she stared pointedly at Wyatt—"without your copilot."

By the time she'd turned away and strolled over to a nearby table to deliver drinks, it seemed as though half the patrons had paused to watch as Wyatt and Marilee made their way to an empty table in the corner.

Once they were seated, the buzz of conversation resumed.

Wyatt leaned his face close to Marilee's ear. "So much for having a private conversation with Craig. By now, half the town knows our business, or thinks they do. And the other half wants to."

Marilee nodded. "We both know that there are no secrets in Gold Fever."

"Unless you're a bad guy." Wyatt held up two fingers, and minutes later Daffy brought them two frosty longnecks.

"You two want the special?" She stood, pad and pencil in hand.

"What is it?" Wyatt asked.

"Vi calls it Bull on a Bun. Ground Angus, grilled onions, tomato, cheese, and Vi's secret hot sauce that gives it a kick."

Marilee couldn't help grinning.

"We'll have two of those. And some of Vi's fried potatoes." Wyatt lowered his voice. "I'd like to buy Craig a beer. When you deliver it, ask him if he'd mind coming over to join us."

"Sorry, honey." Daffy finished making notes on her pad before looking up. "He got a phone call about a minute ago and said he had to go."

Wyatt looked over to the empty stool where Craig had been seated just minutes earlier. "Did he say where?"

She shook her head. "Just bolted out of here like he had a bee in his britches." She shrugged. "He'll be back tomorrow. Old Craig hasn't missed a night at our place since we opened."

She maneuvered her way through the smoky room and

shouted her order to her sister, who was sweating over the grill.

Seeing Wyatt's thoughtful look, Marilee touched a hand to his. "What are you thinking?"

He took her hand between both of his. "I don't like it. We walk in and Craig takes off."

"It isn't as though he's ducking us. Craig has been a fixture out at the airport for as long as I've been flying. Every time I go up in my plane, I trust that Craig has gone over every inch of it with a critical eye. I put my life in his capable hands."

"I get that. And I appreciate what he does. But . . ."

She shook her head. "You heard Daffy. He'll be here again tomorrow. Besides, talking here isn't such a good idea. Too many ears. Tomorrow we can catch him alone in the hangar, where we can have some privacy. And hopefully, Sheriff Wycliff will be there, too."

He willed himself to relax. When Marilee picked up her bottle and took a long drink, he did the same.

By the time Daffy returned with their order, Wyatt was able to put aside his concern and concentrate all his energy on the strong, funny, vibrant woman seated across from him.

But in the deep, dark recesses of his mind, a nagging little fear remained. Somebody knew something important about Marilee's plane. Something important and perhaps critical. Something they didn't want anybody else to learn.

And he wouldn't be satisfied until he had a chance to quiz Craig Matson and be assured that the sheriff was on the case, because there were pieces of the puzzle that didn't fit.

CHAPTER THIRTEEN

❦

W ell?" Daffy paused beside their table. "What'd you two think of Vi's bull on a bun?"

Wyatt drained his beer. "Tell Vi we give it two thumbs-up."

"Want another round?" Daffy slid their empty plates onto her tray.

Wyatt glanced across the table at Marilee before shaking his head. "I think we'll head home now. Thanks, Daffy."

"Sure, honey. Anytime." In an aside to Marilee she added in her smoke-fogged voice, "If I had a cowboy who looked like this, I'd be in a hurry to get him back to my place, too."

With a loud cackle that caused heads to turn, she strolled away.

Wyatt caught Marilee's hand and the two walked out of the saloon after waving good-bye to Vi, still at her post at the grill.

Outside it had begun to rain. A soft, misty rain, which, after the heat of the day, felt as soothing as a shower.

They rode in silence, enjoying the mist on their faces. They had just pulled into Marilee's garage when her cell phone rang.

She answered it, listened in silence, then gave her usual response. "Thanks. I'm on it."

She looked up. "Got an emergency run to Highway Six. Accident and injuries."

Wyatt helped her from the back of his Harley before walking with her to her emergency vehicle.

She arched a brow. "Thinking of going somewhere?"

"Yeah. With you. I figure you might need an extra pair of hands."

"Suit yourself." She grinned as she fastened her seat belt and put the vehicle in gear. With lights flashing she headed out of town.

Once they hit Highway Six she gunned the engine. "You're a sly one, rebel. Tell me the truth. You just didn't want to be cheated out of a good-night kiss."

Laughing, he held up both hands. "Guilty. In fact, I'm hoping, if I play my cards right and prove to be really helpful, I may even be invited to spend the night again."

"I think I could be persuad . . ."

They heard the sound of a blowout at the same instant the vehicle fishtailed.

Gripping the wheel, Marilee struggled for control as they swerved from one side of the rain-slicked highway to the other. As the wheels encountered the gravel shoulder, they stuck, and the ambulance gave a sudden lurch before tumbling end-over-end, finally landing in a field alongside the highway.

The passenger-side air bag had exploded, cushioning Wyatt. When he managed to release his seat belt he turned to Marilee, slumped over the wheel.

"Oh, baby. Hang on." He released her seat belt, noting idly that it had almost torn free and was holding on by a thread. He helped her lean back.

There was a gash on her forehead where she'd come in contact with the steering wheel. Heart racing, he pressed a handkerchief to the spot while he looked for other injuries.

With a moan, she opened her eyes. "You all right?"

"Fine. It's you I'm worried about. Thank heaven your seat belt held. You'd've been really tossed around without it, because your air bag didn't inflate."

"Umm." She struggled to clear her head, but there were butterflies fluttering and bees droning. Not to mention pain radiating from her head to her neck and across her shoulders. "Just had the safety inspection last month."

"They did a lousy job." He reached for his cell phone and pressed Zane's number.

"Hold on," came Zane's excited voice. "Four aces. I win it all."

"Collect later." Nerves had Wyatt's tone sharpening. "There's been an accident. Highway Six, a couple miles out of Gold Fever. I need you, cuz. Now."

"I'm there." The line went dead.

Wyatt drew Marilee into his arms and leaned back, willing his nerves to steady.

"Hold on, baby. The cavalry's on its way."

A fleet of ranch trucks formed a convoy of lights looming out of the darkness. From the number of headlights,

Wyatt decided that Zane must have alerted the entire bunkhouse about the news of the accident.

Arriving on their heels was a police car, siren wailing, lights flashing.

Zane, Jesse, and Amy were the first to race up to the emergency vehicle, where Wyatt sat holding Marilee.

"What happened?" Jesse demanded.

"Blowout." Marilee's tone was still dazed. "Lost control."

"What's the damage?" Zane demanded. "Can you two stand?"

"Yeah." Wyatt lowered the driver's-side window. "Marilee hit the wheel pretty hard. I'm pretty sure she'll need stitches."

Blood oozed through the gauze dressing Wyatt had found among the supplies. He was pressing it firmly to the wound on her forehead.

Deputy Harrison Atkins hurried over.

Zane seemed surprised to see him. "How'd you make it here so soon?"

The lawman shrugged. "I was in the area. Checking out an accident on Highway Six. No serious injuries, so when I got your call, I sent them on their way and raced over here." Seeing Marilee's injury he pointed to his car. "I'll take you to Doc."

"We'll drive." Zane took hold of the door. "Let's get you out of there."

The door didn't budge. It took both Zane and Jesse working together to pry the badly damaged door open.

They helped Marilee from the wrecked vehicle and walked on either side of her as they made their way to their waiting truck.

Wyatt held back. Turning to the deputy, he kept his voice low. "You'll want to have this vehicle towed and looked at by a mechanic you trust. Maybe you ought to use one from the state police."

The lawman shot him a startled look. "And just what'll he be looking for?"

"Any sign of deliberate damage to either the tire or the air bag."

"You mind telling me what's going on here, McCord?"

Wyatt could feel the deputy's obvious annoyance. "Look, Harrison, most nights, Marilee would have been making this run alone. It was an accident that I happened to be along. All I'm saying is that it bothers me that the passenger side air bag worked perfectly, and the driver's-side air bag didn't."

"Okay." The lawman looked from the battered vehicle to Marilee's pale face as she climbed into the ranch truck. "I know you two have a thing going on. Hell, the whole town knows it. I'll get somebody on it. But I think you're seeing bad guys where none exist."

"I hope you're right." Wyatt shook the deputy's hand before walking to the truck.

In the backseat he drew Marilee close, needing to assure himself that she was all right.

They rode the entire distance back to town in silence.

"That's a nasty cut," Dr. Wheeler said as he tied off the last stitch. "But it could have been a whole lot worse."

"Yeah. Thanks, Doc." Marilee sat up and waited until her head cleared. She was grateful for Wyatt's strong arm around her shoulders.

"Take this." The doctor handed her a pill and a glass of water and waited until she'd swallowed. "Just a mild sedative to help you sleep. You probably shouldn't be alone tonight."

Wyatt's voice was firm. "She won't be."

Dr. Wheeler smiled. "Good. It's just a precaution. If she complains of a severe headache, I want you to call me."

"Thanks, Doc, for everything." Wyatt eased Marilee off the examining table and kept his arm firmly around her as he led her out the door of the clinic.

In the waiting room, Amy, Jesse, and Zane stopped their pacing to look up. Though Wyatt knew they probably had a million questions, they remained silent out of respect for the pale young woman who appeared absolutely drained.

"You can drop us both at Marilee's place."

"I'll get the truck." Zane raced out the door while the others stepped out into the rainy night and waited.

Within minutes Zane drove right up over the sidewalk to the door of the clinic.

Wyatt helped Marilee into the backseat, while Amy and Jesse climbed in beside Zane.

Once again they drove in silence.

When they arrived at her apartment, Zane called over his shoulder, "You'll call us in the morning?"

"Yeah. Thanks. For everything."

"Hey, that's what family's for." Jesse jumped down and raced ahead to hold open the door of her apartment.

Wyatt helped Marilee up the stairs. "Thanks, cuz."

When the truck backed away, Wyatt closed the door and led her into the bedroom.

As she sat down on the edge of her bed, she looked up

with a weak smile. "It's a cut, Wyatt. It'll heal. I'm not an invalid."

"I know. But I want to take care of you, so humor me." He rummaged through her closet until he found a night-shirt. He slipped off her shoes, then ever-so-gently slid the blood-spattered T-shirt over her head, careful not to disturb the dressing that covered her stitches. When he'd helped her remove her jeans, she pulled on the nightshirt. Even that simple task left her drained.

Noting her pallor, he pulled back the bed linens and tucked her in as gently as possible.

"Want some tea?"

"Mmm. That would be nice."

He made his way to the kitchen and filled the kettle. A short time later he returned to the bedroom. Marilee was fast asleep.

He set the tea on a night table and kicked off his boots. Crawling into bed beside her, he propped up some pillows and sipped the tea, all the while watching the gentle rise and fall of her chest.

He knew he was too wired to sleep for several more hours. But right now, this moment, it was enough just to sit here by her side, content in the knowledge that she was safe.

In her dream, Marilee was flying above Treasure Chest. The sky was a clear, cloudless blue. Her father, frowning, was seated beside her, wearing a parachute. She didn't think it odd because, after all, he was always angry, and always flying in and out of her life. Before she could speak he was gone, and in his place was Wyatt McCord, smiling at her with that magical, heart-stopping smile. He started to tell her something very important, but just then the plane was diving, falling, spinning. And then the plane turned into her rescue vehicle, and it was swerving back and forth across a rain-slicked highway and she realized she couldn't control it. There was a sickening sound, like breaking glass, and the vehicle suddenly broke apart and she was flying, falling . . .

She woke with a start, thrashing about, sweating, disoriented.

"It's okay, baby. I'm here." Wyatt's deep, soothing voice in the darkness, and his lips pressed to her cheek as he gathered her close, helped her settle.

"I . . ." She moistened her dry lips. "Bad dream."

"Yeah. I've had a few of those. Hold on."

And she did. She clung to him like a lifeline, loving the strength of him. His strong, steady heartbeat soothed her own rapidly beating tattoo until it began to slow, keeping time to his. Her breathing slowed, as well, until she was no longer sucking air into starved lungs.

"Did you sleep at all?" She whispered the words against his throat, causing a rush of heat that had him sweating.

"Some."

"You need to sleep."

"I will. Right now, I'm more concerned with what you need."

She touched a hand to his cheek. Just a touch, but it brought a smile to his lips. "I'm so glad you're here, Wyatt."

He pressed his lips to her forehead. "Me, too."

"You were going to bring me some tea."

"I did. You were asleep, so I drank it."

She chuckled.

"I could make you some more if you'd . . ." He looked down.

Her eyes were closed, her breathing soft and rhythmic.

He kept his arms around her and lay perfectly still, listening to the sound of her breathing, loving the fact that her fears were gone. At least for the moment. And if the demons should return, he would be here to help her fight them.

To keep her safe. It was all that mattered.

To keep her safe. It became a litany in his mind.

He would do whatever it took, pay whatever price necessary, to keep her safe.

How had it happened that this woman in his arms had begun to mean so very much to him?

He hadn't meant for this to happen. But now that it had, there was no denying the truth.

He loved her. Loved her so much, he'd willingly lay down his life to keep her safe.

Chapter Fourteen

A rchie." Wyatt stood in the shadows of Marilee's garage, speaking softly into his cell phone to the mysterious man he'd met in his world travels who was not only a private detective, but also a bounty hunter. Archie had spent a lifetime learning things about elusive figures who managed to stay below the radar of police agencies. "I'm in need of your special services."

The Cockney voice on the other end had him smiling. "In trouble with the law, are you, boyo?"

"Not that kind of trouble. But there have been some strange things happening that have me concerned. First there was a leak in the fuel line of a friend's plane, forcing us to make an unexpected landing in a wilderness area. The airport mechanic who examined the fuel line has suddenly gone missing. When I tried phoning him this morning, I got his message machine. And when I phoned the airport, I was told that he had to leave town suddenly to help with an emergency at his sister's place in Wyoming. Nobody knows when he'll be back."

"Emergencies happen, my friend. This doesn't sound ominous to me."

Wyatt added, "Yeah. That in itself doesn't sound ominous. I'm hoping by tomorrow the mechanic will be calling with news of when he'll be able to return to work. But now, on the heels of the forced landing, this same friend and I had a blowout on the tire of her emergency vehicle, and when it flipped, the driver's air bag didn't inflate, even though the vehicle had just passed its annual safety inspection."

"*Her* emergency vehicle. Why am I not surprised that there's a female involved? I take it she's worth all this concern on your part?"

Archie's words had him chuckling. "I guess I should have mentioned that up front. As you guessed, she's a gorgeous female, and she's special to me."

"I hope you haven't withheld your suspicions from the local constabulary."

"I already told the local deputy my concerns. But he's a lawman, Archie. His job is to deal with facts. Right now, he knows only that the plane ran out of fuel, even though it had just been refueled before takeoff, and that an air bag didn't inflate, even though the vehicle had recently passed a safety inspection. None of which, he insists, has him considering them to be anything more than a series of accidents."

Archie's voice grew louder. "You know I don't believe in that many coincidences."

Wyatt paused before adding, "My thoughts exactly. Now this is what I'd like you to do."

For several minutes more they talked, while Wyatt gave Archie the information he wanted checked out.

"Thanks, my friend. If anybody can untangle this mess, it's you. I leave it in your capable hands."

After ringing off he stood a moment, staring at the peaks of Treasure Chest in the distance. He'd been willing to write off one incident as an accident. But two dangerous incidents happening in such a short time felt like much more than mere coincidence.

And there was one other thing that tugged on his conscience. He'd had a lot of time to think during his long, sleepless night. And he was feeling guilty.

What if these things that had begun happening were aimed at Marilee because of her association with him and his search for the treasure? It had happened to his cousin Jesse and his wife, Amy. Even though the one responsible for those attacks was now dead, there could be others who had more than a passing interest in the fabled lost fortune. Money, or the desire for it, often caused people to do strange and desperate things.

This was why he'd phoned Archie.

Now that Archie was on the case, Wyatt felt a whole lot better. If he had to put his money on Archie or the sheriff, it wasn't even a contest. Ernie Wycliff was bound by the rules of fair play. Archie played by his own rules.

Satisfied, Wyatt climbed the stairs to Marilee's apartment above the garage.

"Hey." He found Marilee in the kitchen, whipping up some scrambled eggs. "Aren't you supposed to be resting?"

"I can't just stay in bed all day." She fed bread into the toaster and turned bacon sizzling in a pan.

He caught her hand and led her toward the barstools. "Sit. I'll finish this."

Grateful for his quiet strength, she sipped her tea and watched as he smoothly slid the eggs onto a plate, drained the bacon, and popped up two slices of perfect toast. "When I found you gone, I figured you were headed back to your ranch. You must have dozens of chores piling up while you're here playing nursemaid."

"Don't worry about my chores. They'll keep. The most important thing in my life right now is seeing that you rest and recover."

"Wyatt . . ."

He touched a finger to her lips. "Eat. I'll clean up the mess you made. You really are a messy cook."

She laughed as he moved about the tiny kitchen, scrubbing the skillets, wiping the stove and countertops until they gleamed.

He wasn't fooling her. She recognized that underneath his charming pose, he was as concerned as she was about these troubling accidents. She understood his need to do something, anything, while he worked through his thoughts. She'd been dealing with similar thoughts, until, too agitated to rest, she'd been forced to get up and get moving.

She had to admit that the thing she found most troubling of all was the sudden disappearance of Craig Matson. In all the years she'd been here, Craig had been a fixture at the airport. Never once had he ever spoken about family. Now he was gone, claiming a family emergency.

Still, she wanted to believe that there was a reasonable explanation.

Wyatt picked up her empty plate and helped her to her feet. "Come on. You're going back to bed."

"Wyatt, I'm fine."

"Yes, you are. But you're going to do what the doctor ordered."

"And if I don't?"

He gave her one of those dangerous, heart-stopping grins. "I'm thinking, if I really apply myself, I can probably find several clever ways to keep you in bed all day, Ms. Trainor."

She was laughing as she allowed him to lead her to her bed. But as he lay beside her and drew her into his arms, her laughter faded, replaced by a series of soft, gentle sighs.

"All right. I'll let you persuade me. But only because the doctor ordered it."

Her words were followed by muffled laughter as they found the perfect way to leave the cares of the world behind.

"Well, my friend." Archie's voice on the cell phone had Wyatt stepping out of Marilee's bedroom and closing the door behind him. "You've got quite a cast of characters in that charming little town you currently call home."

"What's that supposed to mean?"

"Let me begin with the Cowling family."

"Ledge and Delia?"

"Brother and sister." The Cockney accent thickened. "Did you know that there was an . . . interesting connection between the sister, Delia, and your grandfather?"

Wyatt stopped in mid-stride. "What?"

"I see that got your attention." Archie's booming laughter carried over the cell phone. "It seems that once upon a time, in their younger days, they had a hot little romance. Rumors are that it was Delia's bully of a brother, Ledge, who caused their breakup."

"Ledge? Ledge Cowling?" Wyatt had an image of the prissy, suit-and-tie banker balking at getting his hands dirty. "What did he do to break them up?"

"There are several versions of the story. Nobody knows the truth except those intimately involved. But the bottom line is, after a knock-down, drag-out fight with Ledge Cowling, Coot took off on his horse for parts unknown. He was gone for quite some time. When he returned, he was accompanied by a brand-new wife, pretty little Annie Moffitt."

Wyatt chuckled. "Thank heavens for sweet little Annie. She and my grandfather were devoted to one another for more than thirty-five years."

"According to my information, Delia Cowling never married. It would seem she carried the torch for your grandfather until the day he died."

"Who knew?" Wyatt gave a mock shudder. "I'm trying to imagine life on the ranch with the town grouch Delia as my grandmother." By way of explanation he added, "I'm sure you wouldn't understand, Archie, but I can assure you that Coot was one lucky man to have dodged that bullet."

The two men shared a laugh until Archie said, "Just a thought, since you know the parties involved more than I do. Could Delia be holding a grudge against Coot's family for all these years?"

Wyatt was reminded of a long-forgotten incident from his childhood. He was seven years old and had gone into town with his father. He'd been standing outside the feed and grain store when Delia Cowling had walked past. She'd paused, looked back, then retraced her steps until she stood towering over him. "Aren't you Benjamin McCord's boy?"

"Yes'm." He'd given the woman his best smile.

Instead of the charmed reaction he usually got for such efforts, she merely glowered at him. "Are you chewing gum?"

He blinked. "No, ma'am."

"But you were. And you spit it out, didn't you?"

Before he could deny the accusation, she rounded on his father as he stepped through the doorway. "Benjamin McCord, your boy has the manners of a sow. His chewing gum is now stuck to the bottom of my shoe."

Ben glanced at his son, then back at the furious scowl on Delia's face. "Sorry about that, Miss Cowling. I'll have a talk with my boy."

"See that you do. And see that this never happens again." She turned the full volume of her temper on the boy. "Do you understand me?"

Wide-eyed, he stammered, "Ye . . . yes'm."

As she walked away, his father got eye-level with him. "Was it your gum, son?"

"No, sir."

"I didn't think so." Ben grinned as he watched the older woman's progress. "She surely blows like a Texas norther, doesn't she?" He laughed. "That's Delia Cowling. Got the meanest mouth in town. Though I don't understand it, she seems to have a special grudge against the McCords. Remember to steer clear of her, Wyatt."

"Yes, sir."

Hearing Archie's voice on the other end of the phone, Wyatt sobered. "If she carried a torch for Coot, that would explain why she might hold a grudge against our family. But to think that one old woman could cause the incidents I described to you is just too much of a stretch. I can't picture Delia Cowling going so far as to cause real physical harm to anyone. Most of her damage is inflicted by that mean mouth."

"You'd know better than I." Archie paused for emphasis. "But what about her brother, Ledge?"

What about Ledge?

The question worried the edges of Wyatt's mind days later as he and Marilee pulled up on his motorcycle outside Delia's tidy little house.

Marilee shot him a quick glance. "You sure we're doing the right thing?"

"No." He took a deep breath and slid off his helmet before taking her hand. "But I think the time for misunderstandings and unanswered questions is over. Now it's time for some straight talk."

Marilee paused beside him on the little front porch as he lifted a hand to knock. "She could order us to leave."

"She could. She certainly has the right to."

The door opened and Delia peered at the two of them in surprise. "Marilee. Wyatt. What can I do for you?"

Wyatt offered his most charming smile. "We have some questions, if you don't mind."

"I don't know. I'm not in the mood for company." She started to close the door.

"Please." Wyatt lifted a hand to the door to halt its motion. "Just for a moment."

Grudgingly the old woman stood aside and held the door as they walked past her into the neat little parlor.

She looked around as though searching for an escape. "Why don't we go to the kitchen?"

Marilee shot Wyatt a guilty look. "We don't want you to go to any trouble, Delia."

"It's no trouble. Really." She led the way. "I don't know about you, but I always prefer a nice cup of tea whenever visitors come calling."

She indicated two chairs at the table before she busied herself filling the teakettle and setting it on the stove.

Watching her, Wyatt and Marilee could see that she was actually relieved to have something to do. It was obvious that she entertained few visitors.

While the kettle heated she placed tea bags in a floral pot and set out dainty cups and napkins.

She smiled at Marilee. "I'm grateful for the professional way you handled my fall, Lee. I was feeling really frightened, and more than a little embarrassed. And I know my neighbor, Frances, was feeling helpless until you came along."

When the kettle began whistling she filled the teapot and set it on a tray with cream and sugar and some raspberry-filled cookies before settling herself at the table.

"I'll let you pour, Lee." The old woman held out her cup.

Marilee filled it, then filled Wyatt's cup and her own.

"Oh. My." Delia stared at the stitches on Marilee's forehead, and the bruise that spread down to her cheek. "I heard about your accident. I had no idea you'd been so badly injured."

Marilee flushed. "It looks worse than it feels. Really."

"That's a relief to hear." Delia passed around the plate of cookies before helping herself to one and nibbling. "I'm afraid I'm not very good at entertaining company, especially young people. I so rarely have any visitors. Oh, not that I'm complaining. I keep myself busy. But this is rather . . . pleasant." She studied Wyatt and the words tumbled out before she could stop herself. "You're the image of your grandfather, you know."

"Speaking of my grandfather . . ." Wyatt found himself sweating. He'd come here hoping to bully a meddling old gossip into telling him the truth about what she knew. Now she'd turned into some lonely, neglected old woman who looked like everybody's sweet grandmother, complete with tea and cookies. He didn't know how to handle the situation.

"Yes?" Delia sipped her tea. "I believe you said you had some questions."

Wyatt shifted, avoiding Marilee's eyes. "I wondered . . . That is, I heard that you and my grandfather were once close."

The old woman went very still, but a look crossed her face that had Wyatt mentally cursing himself.

Delia chose her words carefully. "My brother and I were once friendly with Coot. That was a long time ago, when we were all young and carefree."

"Did something happen to end the friendship?"

"Did I say it ended?"

He shook his head. "You said you were once friendly. That suggests it didn't last."

She looked away. "As you know, Coot's strange behavior made it difficult for anyone to be his friend."

"In what way?"

She picked up her cup. Sipped. Set it down. "He was a tortured soul. Obsessed with his family's lost fortune. Those of us who . . . cared for him realized that he was slipping further and further into some sort of dangerous fantasy."

"Did you point that out to him?"

She nodded. "Many times. But he was beyond listening."

"Did my grandmother share that view?"

Delia shrugged. "I couldn't say. Annie Moffitt and I were never close."

"But you knew her?"

She avoided Wyatt's eyes. "I knew of her." She lifted her chin. "Once Coot married, he stopped seeing old friends." She glanced pointedly at her kitchen clock. "I suppose I should be thinking about fixing something for supper. Is there anything else?"

Wyatt drained his tea. "I know you once said that you wouldn't be comfortable allowing us to look at your brother's old keepsakes without his permission. But since we're here, and we're still missing a lot of my grandfather's papers, I was hoping that you might have had a change of heart."

"I'm afraid that's not possible." She looked up with an odd little smile. "As soon as Ledge returned home from his latest business trip, he stopped over and retrieved all his belongings."

"He emptied the basement?"

"Completely. He knew the clutter bothered me. It's such a relief to have all those old boxes and plastic bins gone. I was able to find my mother's recipe box, and even managed to locate some of our old family albums." She got to her feet. "Would you like to see them?"

Wyatt glanced at Marilee, who gave a slight shake of her head.

"I'm sorry. There's no time. But maybe we could stop by another day."

"Of course." Her smile faded and she became once again stiff and formal. "Another time."

They made their way to the front door.

Marilee took Delia's hand in hers. "Thank you for the tea and cookies."

"You're welcome."

"Thank you." Wyatt surprised himself by pressing a kiss to her cheek. "I enjoyed it, too."

Delia was completely caught off-guard.

She was still standing stiffly at the front door watching as they climbed aboard Wyatt's motorcycle and took their leave.

Marilee wrapped her arms around Wyatt's waist and pressed her cheek to his back. She'd made this trip half fearing a confrontation with the feisty old woman. She was leaving with the realization that Delia Cowling was much more than the nosy old biddy she showed the town.

What would it be like, Marilee wondered, to be Delia's age and look back on a life with very few family and friends?

Did she also live with regrets?

Marilee had a flash of her own future. With her mother gone, she now had no family.

Regrets? She could probably list hundreds.

She decided not to dwell on the past.

For now, for today, she felt perfectly content.

She would worry about her future tomorrow.

CHAPTER FIFTEEN

———◆———

Wyatt broke the news of Delia's empty basement the following morning over breakfast. Jesse and Zane were both frowning.

"I say we go to Ledge and demand to see anything that may have belonged to Coot." Jesse, too pumped to sit, paced the kitchen.

"I'm with you, Jess." Zane nervously tapped his fork against the edge of the plate, Dandy's perfect French toast forgotten. "He knew we wanted to look through those papers. That's got to be the reason he took them away."

"I agree." Wyatt glanced at their aunt, who had remained silent throughout his narrative. "Did you know about Coot and Delia?"

She nodded. "It wasn't a secret. We all knew that they were sweet on each other. Delia's family wasn't happy about it. They considered my brother beneath them." She sighed. "When Coot came home with a bride, Delia's family was relieved. I was a bit puzzled by how quickly it all happened, but I was soon completely convinced that Coot and Annie were a perfect fit. Annie was content to raise her family. In all the years they were married, I never heard her complain about the time he spent on his all-consuming search for the family treasure. In fact, she believed in the lost treasure as deeply as Coot."

Cora looked down at her hands. "But I've always felt sorry for Delia. I believe she really loved Coot. I saw the gradual change in her. She went from being a sweet, sunny young woman to a lonely, bitter gossip who seemed to take joy in learning anything unpleasant about anybody around her."

Wyatt gave Cora's hand a squeeze. "She may have been caught by surprise when Marilee and I came calling, but after her initial shock, she was more than civil. She even made us tea."

Cora gave him a gentle smile. "And why not? Look at you." She glanced around the table at her nephews. "There's no denying that the three of you carry Coot's blood. The look of him is there in your faces." She lifted a hand to Wyatt's cheek. "Maybe, for just a little while, Delia felt the way she had when she was young and happy and wildly in love with your grandfather."

Her words had the three of them falling silent.

Later, when Cora headed to her studio, the three walked to the fleet of trucks in the main barn.

Wyatt tossed the keys to Jesse. "I say we follow your suggestion and pay a call on Ledge Cowling."

"Good. If you hadn't said that, I was planning on paying a visit alone." Jesse yanked open the truck door, only too happy to oblige.

Zane and Wyatt quickly crowded into the front seat, eager for the challenge.

"Ledge will see you now." Paula Henning held open the door to Ledge's office at the bank, closing it behind the three McCord cousins after they'd stepped inside.

"Well." Ledge gave them his best professional smile and handshake before inviting them to sit. "You three in need of a loan? Or maybe, in your case, you're here to see if I need one."

They smiled pleasantly at his joke.

He sat back, looking pleased and relaxed. "Tell me what I can do for you."

Wyatt spoke for them. "Your sister told me that you'd picked up all your belongings from her basement."

"Did she happen to mention how happy that made her?" He chuckled. "She's been after me for years to clean up that mess. Our parents were pack rats. I think they saved everything, from our nursery rhymes to my college awards. I've finally given Delia the space she wanted."

"My cousins and I were hoping you would give us a chance to look through the boxes in case there were more of Coot's notes or scraps."

Because Wyatt was bracing for a vague rejection, or even an outright refusal, he was surprised when Ledge's smile grew.

"Well now. I wish you'd come to me sooner. I would have been happy to let you rummage through that old junk. Unfortunately, it's not possible now."

"Why is that?" Wyatt's uneasiness grew in direct proportion to Ledge's easy affability.

"I shredded everything." Ledge tipped his chair back, lacing his fingers over his substantial middle. "Ten boxes in all."

"Shredded everything?" Wyatt glanced at Zane, who looked thunderstruck, and then at Jesse, who wore a look of disbelief. "Must have taken you hours."

"Yes, indeed. Kept me here long after everyone else had gone home for the night. But I considered it my patriotic duty." He was positively beaming. "I certainly didn't want all those old papers and documents to clog a landfill."

"That lying . . ." Jesse turned the key in the ignition before exploding. "Destroying papers that don't belong to him and acting as though he was doing his sister a favor."

"And having a good laugh at our expense." Zane swore under his breath.

"With that smile in place, he completely transformed himself from Scrooge to jovial Old Saint Nick." Wyatt grew thoughtful. "You have to admit that he made a smart move. We'll never know how many pages of Nathanial's journal or how many of Coot's notes and maps were in those boxes."

Jesse drove the truck along the main street. "Now what?"

Wyatt shrugged. "Ledge won this round. We'll just have to come up with another way to entice him back into the ring."

Zane stared at the sunlight glinting off the peaks of Treasure Chest in the distance. "Maybe he's already won the fight and we just don't know it." When Jesse and Wyatt turned to him he added, "Who's to say he didn't shred important papers that could lead him right to the treasure? He could be waiting for us to lose interest in the search, and then he'll step in and quietly claim the prize."

"Just as Vernon McVicker had hoped." Wyatt digested his words before nodding. "All right. And maybe all these things that have been happening were designed to distract us from our original goal. If so, my pal Archie will fill me in with whatever details he can learn. And since there's nothing we can do until we have more facts, I say it's time for us to get serious and step up our game."

As the others turned to him he mused aloud, "It's time to put down everything we know, from the trail we've drawn of Coot's wanderings, from the places he searched and discarded, to the places we believe are unlikely to be good hiding places. And then, taking it all into account, I say we chart our own course. And that means using modern technology to aid in our search." He turned to Jesse, then to Zane. "Do you agree?"

Jesse nodded.

Zane shrugged. "Why not? I say we go for it full-steam ahead."

The three solemnly shook hands.

Wyatt suddenly burst into gales of laughter.

At their matching looks of concern he explained, "I was thinking about the time we took a solemn vow to not let anybody know about where we found that nugget."

Jesse thought a moment. "The one that turned out to be fool's gold?"

"That's the one. You realize, of course, that it's our duty to continue the family tradition of looking like crazy coots to everyone in this town?"

The other two joined him in laughter.

It was, Wyatt realized, good to find something to laugh about. And good to have a common goal with his two cousins.

Cora, Jesse, Amy, and Zane, seated in the great room enjoying the evening sunset, looked up as the roar of a motorcycle broke the calm that had settled over the land. Minutes later Wyatt and Marilee entered through the kitchen, greeting Dandy as they passed him. Entering the great room, they hurried over to greet the family.

"Miss Cora." Marilee brushed a kiss over the older woman's cheek.

"I'm so glad you're here, Lee. Did you and Wyatt have dinner?"

"Vi's burgers and fries."

As Marilee and Amy hugged, Cora thought how young and pretty they both looked. Amy, with her fair hair in a ponytail; Marilee wind-tossed and casual in denims and a gauzy shirt, her cheeks bright pink from the long ride on the back of Wyatt's bike.

Cora returned Wyatt's hug. "Dandy made apple cobbler."

Wyatt nodded. "He was just filling a tray with desserts and coffee. Our timing is perfect."

Within minutes Dandy entered and set the tray on a side table. Seeing that they had everything they needed, he walked away, eager to tidy the kitchen before retiring for the night.

Amy passed around the plates of cobbler while Marilee handed out cups of coffee.

While they enjoyed their dessert the three cousins

walked around the map with its parade of pins and sticky notes, examining it from every direction. By the time they'd set aside their empty plates and cups, they were ready to tackle the problem at hand.

"We can easily see where Coot was headed." Jesse ran a finger along the trail of red pins they'd used to indicate the land Coot had already studied and discarded as a possible hiding place for the treasure.

Zane pointed to the accumulation of paper scraps they'd pieced together. "And from his notes and drawings, we know that he continued moving toward Treasure Chest."

"What's more, Vernon McVicker admitted following Coot for years, hoping to take up the hunt if Coot should ever die or grow tired. When Vernon realized that Coot might outlive him, he decided to"—Wyatt glanced over at his aunt, knowing how painful it was for her to hear, even now—"get rid of Coot so that he could search by himself, without interruption." Wyatt sighed. "Gold has a way of bringing out the worst in some people."

"And bringing out the best in others." Cora set aside her coffee and glanced around at her grandnephews. "I know how much you yearn to find our family's treasure. But I want each of you to promise me that you'll never allow this search for the gold to tear apart the bond that we've been building here. No treasure is worth that."

Hearing the passion that caused her voice to tremble, they were quick to assure her.

"I give you my word, Aunt Cora." Jesse crossed the room to place a hand on her shoulder.

"You have my word, too." Zane nodded his head for emphasis.

"And mine." Wyatt met her steady look. "We've all been witnesses to just how fragile this bond is, and how easily it can unravel. That makes us more determined than ever to see that it doesn't happen again."

She gave a long, deep sigh before the smile returned to her eyes, and to her voice. "Now. Let's get down to the business of determining just where we want to take up the search." She closed a hand over Jesse's. "Why don't you begin?"

As he pointed out the place on Treasure Chest where his grandfather had been found after his fall, the others became animated and jumped in with their own suggestions.

Cora studied their faces and found herself once again thinking about how deeply ingrained her brother's influence had been in the lives of these three young men. In their boyhood he'd been their rock. It was Coot they had gone to with their questions and concerns, knowing he would always have time for them, unlike their fathers, who were often too busy with ranch chores. And even though Wyatt and Zane had been absent for much of their growing-up years, it was Coot who had continued to color their lives. Now they were here, taking up the cause that had consumed him, and making it their own.

"It's agreed then?" Jesse's voice broke through Cora's reverie. "We'll concentrate on the foothills around Treasure Chest?"

"It's the most sensible place to start." Zane, busy setting up his camera, brought Jesse and Wyatt into focus before joining them for the picture.

"Right." Wyatt stuck out his hand.

With Jesse on one side of him and Zane on the other, the three cousins clasped hands and smiled at the camera as the moment was recorded.

Then they drew Amy and Marilee over with them as they gathered around the map and added a red flag to the exact spot in the foothills where they intended to begin their search the following day.

Hours later, as the logs on the fire burned low, they shared a round of longnecks and reminisced about their childhood spent roaming free on the thousands of acres of ranchland that had been their playground.

Cora found herself laughing aloud as they revealed some of the adventures they'd shared and the trouble they'd gotten into.

"Do you remember the time we tied a lasso to a tree limb and decided to swing across the creek like Tarzan?" Wyatt tipped up his frosty bottle and took a long pull.

"Yeah." Zane was already laughing. "As usual, you two decided that I'd be the one to try it out first. That way, if it broke, I'd be the one tossed into the creek."

"It stands to reason." Jesse chuckled. "You were the youngest. That's just the price you had to pay to hang out with us."

"And," Wyatt added, "you were always willing to go along with whatever we decided."

"What choice did I have?" Zane set down his beer. "The few times I refused to try one of your crazy schemes, I was sent back to the ranch and had to hang out with the wranglers for the rest of the day, which usually meant that they'd dream up some chores for me to do, just to get me out of their hair."

"So?" Amy demanded. "Did the rope break?"

Zane shook his head. "Not when I used it to fly across the creek."

"And not when I followed him," Wyatt said with a laugh. "But Jesse, assured that it was safe, grabbed hold and was flying through the air when the branch snapped."

Amy looked over at her husband. "You landed in the creek?"

"Yeah. On the day after one of our biggest storms, with the water spilling over its banks and rushing so fast it carried me downstream half a mile or more."

She put a hand to her mouth to cover her shock and saw Cora do the same.

Wyatt laughed. "He was lucky Zane and I had our horses tethered nearby. We chased along the banks of the creek until we could get far enough ahead to toss him a tree branch to catch. By the time we hauled him out, he looked like a drowned rat and was spitting mad."

"I had a right to be. I swallowed half the creek."

Zane laughed. "But think how lucky we were that it happened to you instead of me. At least you could swim."

Marilee's eyes rounded. "They had you test the rope when they knew you couldn't swim?"

Wyatt was laughing even harder. "We figured it was one way for him to learn."

"How old were you?"

They thought a minute before Wyatt answered. "I was eight, so that would make Jesse ten and Zane seven."

"You could have all drowned."

"Yeah. Looking back, we were lucky to have survived so many foolish adventures. But," Wyatt added, "I wouldn't have missed a single one of them."

An hour later, as Cora made her way to her room, she listened to the roar of Wyatt's motorcycle fade into the distance. Zane had retired to his suite, where he routinely stayed awake until the wee hours of the morning reviewing film for his documentary project. The sound of muffled laughter drifted from Jesse and Amy as they made their way to their suite of rooms on the far side of the house.

Too wired to settle down, Cora stepped into her studio and cast a critical eye on her latest canvas. It was an extreme close-up of a bitterroot in full bloom. The pink blossom with its yellow center filled the entire canvas and seemed to explode with vibrant color.

She couldn't help smiling. Her creations always had that effect on her. But it was especially easy to feel joy tonight.

She'd spent such pleasant hours watching her nephews reliving their childhood pranks and reestablishing that invisible thread that held all of them together.

Oh, Coot. Did you see them? Did you hear the laughter? Did you feel the love?

She paused beside a window and stared at the full moon resting at the very tip of Treasure Chest, casting a pale glow over the entire mountain range. As though, she thought, in benediction.

She was still smiling as she made her way to her bedroom and prepared for bed.

Her nephews had confided their concerns about Ledge Cowling, and the papers he'd destroyed. But now, this night, she couldn't work up any emotion except happiness.

Her nephews had taken up Coot's lifelong odyssey. They were on the right course. She was convinced of it.

And at least for tonight, she was filled with a quiet sense of peace.

On this very special night, nothing could possibly go wrong.

All was right with the world.

Chapter Sixteen

———◆◆◆———

Chief Wycliff was beaming as he handed Marilee the keys to her restored emergency vehicle.

"Deputy Atkins made the round-trip to the state police post and back just to pick up this report. Their lab gave it a clean bill of health. They found a glitch in the driver's-side air bag, but they assure me it's been corrected."

"Thanks, Ernie." She opened the door and breathed deeply. "I wonder how they got that new-car smell in this old thing."

"Probably a combination of disinfectant and wax." He looked over her shoulder. "Clean as a whistle."

"Yeah." Her spirits lifted considerably. She couldn't wait to fill it with supplies and get on with her job.

Get on with her life.

"How about you, Lee?" The police chief studied the faded bruise on her forehead. "You nervous about getting that first call?"

She shook her head. "You know me, Ernie. I just want to get past this."

"Fearless. Good for you. When do you expect to get your plane ready to fly?"

"The manufacturer sent a crew with the parts. They're planning a test flight in the next day or so."

"Any word from Craig Matson?"

She shook her head.

The chief glanced past her to where Wyatt stood, watching and listening. And frowning. "I want you to know I'm looking into his sudden departure. I talked to Harding and Ledge to see if they knew anything. After all, they're the ones who pay his salary. They don't seem to know any more than we do. He left to see about a family emergency, and nobody's heard from him since. But I've got a couple of leads, and when I know more, I'll get back to you both."

"Thanks, Ernie. I'll let you worry about all that." Marilee ran a hand over the gleaming door of her vehicle. "Right now, I'm just happy to get back to work."

"Then I'll leave you to it." He turned away and climbed into his four-wheel-drive truck decked out with the town logo and sporting every bell and whistle the town could afford.

By the time Wyatt was headed toward the ranch for a day of chores, Marilee was happily loading medical supplies into the back of her vehicle before making a run to the clinic.

The ringing of her phone dragged Marilee out of a sound sleep. She reached for the receiver in the same instant that she glanced at the clock. Why did so many accidents occur at two in the morning?

"Emergency One. What's the problem?"

She listened in silence, aware of Wyatt sitting up in bed beside her.

"The Turner place? It'll take me half an hour at least."

She slipped out of bed and reached for a shirt, trying not to think about the long, dark ride ahead of her. But though she was outwardly calm and controlled, her heart was working overtime. This would be her first run since the accident. Her first real test of nerves. Though she was determined to be the victor in the battle for control, so far, nerves were winning.

She was still snapping the waist of her jeans when she walked from the bedroom. All her concentration was on the need to banish these fears that had come sneaking up on her like a thief in the night.

Wyatt fell into step beside her.

Surprised, she swiveled her head. "What are you doing?"

"Going with you."

A part of her felt a quick rush of relief. She wouldn't be alone. Another part of her deeply resented her reaction. She needed to be strong, not weak at a time like this.

She crossed her arms over her chest, determined to hold herself together. "Don't be silly. This is my job, not . . ."

He cut off her argument by opening the door of her apartment and stepping aside, forcing her to precede him.

Stiff-backed, she descended the stairs. She heard his footsteps behind her and knew that he was following. The knowledge was both a comfort and an annoyance.

She didn't want comfort. She wanted to stand up against her fear and conquer it. Alone.

She paused, hand on the waiting vehicle, and turned to him. "Go back to bed."

"Too late." He tried for a smile, but it lacked the warmth or humor that had become his trademark. Instead he appeared . . . watchful. Wary. "I'm wide awake. I'd never fall back asleep now."

Her tone lowered in direct contrast to her rising anger. "I don't care, Wyatt. I don't need you here."

"I know you don't. But I need to be with you."

"You know I work alone."

"Not tonight."

She heard the finality in his tone and realized that it was useless to argue this any further, especially since she needed to be on the road as quickly as possible.

Without a word she climbed into the driver's side and turned the key in the ignition.

He climbed into the passenger side and fastened his seat belt. "Where are we headed?"

She sighed before turning on the flashing lights. "Turner ranch. Ken's moaning in pain. Laura doesn't have a clue what's ailing him. Doc will drive to the clinic and wait for my report."

As they headed out of town, Marilee was grateful for the hot, dry weather. Would rain have spooked her? She hoped not, but she couldn't be certain.

When a truck's headlights crossed the median, appearing to be headed right toward her vehicle, she turned on the siren and swerved.

"Damned drunk." Her heart was thundering in her chest, and though she hated to admit it, she was suddenly glad for Wyatt's company. That thought had her frowning.

When she glanced over at him, he smiled and closed a hand over hers.

She drew her hand away and returned her attention to the road, waiting for her heart rate to return to normal.

She was so glad he was here beside her, and so frustrated with herself because of it. What the hell was happening to her? She needed to get a grip.

"We're heading into town, Doc." Marilee spoke quietly into her cell phone. "Ken's in the back, in a lot of pain. High fever. Lower abdomen and side very tender. My best guess is a ruptured appendix. Laura will stay home, since the little ones are asleep, and wait for your call."

She listened, before adding, "Right. I have the lights flashing, but will kill the siren. No sense waking half the town. I should have Ken there in less than half an hour. Do you have Elly there to assist you?"

His voice broke through the static. "She will be by the time you get Ken here."

Marilee tucked her cell phone into her pocket and pressed down on the accelerator. With no traffic at this hour, she would be back to town in record time.

It was, she thought, a relief to be busy once more. Though she'd enjoyed some time to herself, and loved being pampered by Wyatt, she'd missed this more than she cared to admit.

Now if she could just shake off the last of her nerves, her life could return to normal.

Marilee was feeling sluggish after a very long night. Instead of collapsing into sleep when she'd returned to her apartment, she'd tossed and turned, too wired to relax and turn off her brain. When she finally did sleep, it had been interrupted with strange, dark dreams.

Knowing that Wyatt was asleep beside her gave her no consolation. In fact, seeing him so completely relaxed only added to her discomfort. How had he adjusted so easily to sharing her bed? And why couldn't she do the same? Why did she have this prickly feeling along her scalp, as though everything she'd been building in her life was slowly unraveling?

Now, seeing the bed empty, she walked to the shower and stood under a steamy spray for long minutes, hoping it would revive her.

Once dry she dressed in a pair of cuffed shorts and a denim shirt tied at her midriff. Before she could slip into a pair of sandals the phone rang and she picked it up, talking as she made her way to the kitchen.

"Oh, Laura, thanks for the update. I'm so glad Doc has it all under control. How long will Ken have to stay at the clinic?"

While she listened, she was distracted by the wonderful fragrance of cinnamon French toast wafting from the griddle.

"I'm glad it wasn't anything more than his appendix. Tell him he'll be much happier without it."

She rang off and watched as Wyatt set a plate on the bar counter. "Something smells wonderful."

"Dandy's secret recipe for French toast stuffed with apples and drizzled with syrup and cinnamon."

"If it's a secret recipe, how did you get it?"

He wiggled his brows like a villain. "I could tell you,

but then I'd have to kill you. Now eat, woman. You need your strength."

"Yes, sir." She dug in and watched as he sat beside her and did the same.

At last she sat back, sipping strong, hot coffee. "Oh, that was wonderful. I didn't realize just how hungry I was. Thank you."

"You're welcome. But don't tell Dandy. This must remain our little secret."

Wyatt saw the smile that touched her lips and was grateful that he'd been able to lift her spirits, at least for the moment. She'd been so tense last night. So coldly, carefully controlled, as though holding herself together by sheer force of will.

It was natural enough to have to deal with nerves, especially so soon after the accident. Still, he was worried about her reaction. It seemed a bit extreme.

He shot her a sideways glance. "You were having quite a dream this morning."

"A dream?" She went very still, as bits and pieces of the bad dream began flashing through her mind. "Did I say anything?"

"You were saying lots of things, but nothing that made sense. My impression is that you were mad as hell, and somebody was going to feel the sting of Marilee's mighty temper."

"Is that all?" She started toward the sink with her empty plate.

Wyatt held out his hand. "I'll take that."

She held back. "You cooked. I'll clean up."

"I don't mind. You're still recovering from . . ."

She poked a finger at his chest. "You have to stop this."

He jerked back. "Stop what?"

"Coddling me."

"I'll coddle if I want . . ."

"Wyatt. I'm serious." She stepped around him and set her plate in the sink before taking his empty plate from his hands. "I'm warning you to stop. You're not only coddling me, you're crowding me."

"Crowding . . . ?"

"Suffocating me, in fact."

She saw the look in his eyes. As though she'd slapped him. And though it pained her to hurt him this way, she couldn't seem to stop. All the feelings that she'd kept bottled up now began to bubble to the surface. All her old fears erupted.

"Like you, I've been on my own for a long time now. I'm used to making my own decisions. Making my own mistakes. I had to fight long and hard to overcome the feeling that I'd never be smart enough, good enough, to please my father. I'd never be the son he wanted. And then there was my mother, who couldn't make a simple decision without first consulting him. I swear, she couldn't even decide which dress to wear without first getting his approval. I made myself a promise that I'd never let that happen. I'm my own person. I answer to nobody. I don't want anybody else directing my life."

"Directing . . . ?

"So as much as I love having you here, I can't allow this to continue. You can't keep up with your ranch chores during the day and then race all over the countryside at night every time I have an emergency run. Before long, you'll hate me for making such a mess of your life."

"That's nonsense. I could never hate you, Marilee. I love being with you. Taking care of you. Don't you think this should be my decision?"

Her voice rose a fraction. "What about me? What about what I want?"

"You have to know that I care about you and what you want."

"If that's so, then you'll listen to what I'm saying."

He went very still. "Are you saying you don't want me here?"

"It isn't about that. I love having you here." Frustrated, she could feel her temperature rising along with the tone of her voice. "Wyatt, you need to get your life back." She took a quick, steadying breath. "And so do I."

"You want your life back." He studied her, eyes narrowed in thought. "And so, for that reason, you're ordering me to leave?"

"Not to leave. Just to step back. You have to trust me . . ."

"Of course I trust you."

"You have to trust that I can take care of myself. Trust that I can decide what's best for me." Her voice trembled. "Do you know how wonderful it is to have someone care this much about me? Wyatt, I've waited a lifetime for someone like you. But you've started to make me your responsibility. Your . . . job. And I'm afraid that very soon your job will become your . . . burden."

He took a step back, studying her with eyes that had gone flat and cold. "I can't believe what I'm hearing. You can't be serious."

Not trusting her voice, she merely nodded.

At first, all he could see was the way she kept her spine rigid, her head high in that haughty, take-charge stance he so admired. Wasn't it the first thing he'd noticed, right after that lush body, that flaming hair, those kiss-me-until-my-heart-stops lips?

Now he saw more. He saw that she was stubborn and intractable and completely unreasonable. Every cliché he'd ever heard flew into his mind. She wasn't just take-charge, but bossy. Not just capable, but demanding. Not just independent, but selfish.

She blinked, and he could see the sudden trace of sorrow in her eyes. Could see the way her lower lip was trembling. Now she was going all female on him. God, he didn't think he could bear it if she started crying.

Though he could think of a dozen things he wanted to say, he turned away, needing to escape as much as she needed her privacy.

He retrieved the keys to his motorcycle and let himself out of her apartment without a word.

He gunned the engine and took off without a backward glance.

As his bike ate up the miles back to the Lost Nugget, he found himself fuming over all the things she'd said.

How could she believe that he'd been crowding her? Suffocating her? He swore. All he'd wanted was to keep her safe.

He'd never before felt the need to so completely take over someone else's life. But this was his beautiful, talented Marilee, and all he wanted was to keep her out of harm's way. Couldn't she see that?

When he arrived at the ranch he avoided the big house, choosing instead to storm into the barn and work alongside a couple of the wranglers who were mucking stalls. If they were surprised by his presence, they gave no indication.

By the time Jesse and Zane had finished breakfast and saw Wyatt's bike parked beside the barn, he had worked up a sweat, doing the job of three men, forking enough straw and dung to completely fill a wagon.

"Hey." Jesse leaned on a rail to watch as Wyatt bent to his task. "When did you get back?"

Wyatt barely paused. "Not sure. Time passes, you know?"

"Yeah." Jesse arched a brow. "Something eating you, cuz?"

"I'm fine."

"Yeah. I can see that." Jesse turned to Zane and rolled his eyes. "We're heading up to the north range. Want to ride along?"

"I'm fine here."

"Well, yeah, you're doing a great job on that stall. But when you're through shoveling manure, what're you planning on doing the rest of the day?"

Instead of the laugh he was expecting, Wyatt swore. Loudly. Fiercely.

"I guess that means you'd like to be alone." Jesse shoved his hands into his back pockets. "Speaking from experience as an old married man, I'd say this also means that you and the lovely Lee have had a lovers' spat."

In response Wyatt dug the pitchfork into a pile of dung and tossed it Jesse's way.

Jesse ducked, avoiding most of the mess, except for a few bits of straw that clung to his hair.

From a safe distance Zane gave a roar of laughter. "I think that means he isn't seeking your sage advice, O Ancient One."

"Your loss, cuz. I could have told you that what women really want is for you to admire their minds. Even when they don't make any sense at all." Jesse picked out the pieces of straw and tossed them aside before turning to Zane. "Come on. We've got a herd to deal with. Let's leave Mr. Happy to work out his problems in this pile of . . . horse manure."

Laughing, the two strolled out of the barn.

Wyatt swore again and continued shoveling until every stall sparkled. Then he moved on to the cow barns, working his way through a mountain of frustration.

CHAPTER SEVENTEEN

Hello, handsome." Daffy managed to press a kiss to Wyatt's cheek while balancing a tray filled with longnecks. "You want a table, or are you sitting at the bar?"

His gaze roamed the entire room and back before he shrugged away the quick wave of disappointment at not seeing the familiar flaming hair. "Guess I'll just sit at the bar."

"Zane is there, right next to Jimmy Eagle."

"Yeah. I see them. Thanks." Before he could turn away Daffy added, "You just missed Lee."

He paused, hating the way his heart stopped for the moment. He hoped Daffy would say more without forcing him to ask.

Daffy patted his hand. "She was here with Amy. It was good to see those two best friends making time for one another."

"Yeah." He forced a smile.

She gave him a long look. "You been busy up in the high country?"

At his arched brow she explained. "Delia Cowling was hovering over their table, and I overheard Lee saying something to that effect." She gave one of her throaty laughs. "The old busybody is never happy unless she knows everything about everybody. And that includes why two of the town's hottest couples aren't together every minute." There was another long look, followed by an even longer pause, before she walked away.

Frowning, Wyatt threaded his way between tables and made his way to the bar. So much for keeping this under wraps. Not in Gold Fever.

As soon as he was seated beside Zane, Vi slid a frosty bottle down the bar. Wyatt caught it and tipped it up, draining half the bottle in one long swallow.

Zane swiveled his barstool to study his cousin. "Didn't expect to see you here tonight."

"Didn't expect to be here."

"Did your date stand you up?"

"Didn't have a date."

"Too bad. There was quite the hot-looking babe in here just a few minutes ago."

Wyatt gave a sigh of disgust. "Okay, you're the second one to tell me that breaking news."

Zane winked at Jimmy Eagle. "My cousin's a little edgy these days. He's taken a real liking to mucking stalls, though, so the wranglers in the barn are mighty grateful for his new attitude."

Seeing Wyatt's scowl deepen, Jimmy bit back his grin. "Hard work's good for a troubled soul."

"Then I say more power to you, cuz." Zane touched his beer to Wyatt's. "I'll gladly leave the manure removal in your very capable hands."

He and Jimmy were still chuckling when Wyatt picked up his beer, slid from the barstool, and joined a table of wranglers in the rear of the saloon.

The afternoon sky was as dreary as Marilee's mood as she drove the rescue vehicle around to the rear of the medical clinic and parked in the designated space. Opening the back door, she began hauling fresh supplies from the clinic storeroom to the ambulance. When it was neatly stocked she made her way inside, where Elly Carson and Dr. Wheeler were talking quietly.

Elly looked over. "Hi, Lee. You just missed Wyatt. He was here on an emergency run and walked out the front door to his truck not five minutes ago."

Marilee's heart slammed against her ribs. "Was he hurt?"

"Not Wyatt. One of the wranglers. Got careless mending a fence and had a really nasty gash from the barbed wire. Wyatt drove him in for stitches."

"Oh." Marilee felt almost giddy with relief.

"I'm surprised he didn't tell you." Elly turned away to remove the disposable covering from the gurney. "He could have called you and saved himself that long drive from the ranch."

Doc peeled away his sterile gloves. "Just as well he didn't wait around for an ambulance. That wound was deep. Len had already lost a lot of blood. Wyatt did the right thing bringing him in immediately."

He handed Marilee a slip of paper. "Next time you're making a run to Helena, we'll be needing these supplies."

"Thanks." She pocketed the list and turned away. "See you soon."

Once in the emergency vehicle, she leaned her head back and closed her eyes for a moment.

Minutes sooner and she would have come face-to-face with Wyatt. Maybe he would have smiled, or talked, and she could have done the same. Maybe then they could break through this terrible wall that they'd built.

That she'd built.

Or maybe, she thought, struggling to ignore the stab of guilt, they would have merely added another layer of pain and deepened the wound.

She opened her eyes, lifted her head, and turned the ignition, determined to get on with the day.

To get on with her life.

She absorbed a fresh stab of pain. A life without Wyatt.

"Hey, Wyatt." Amy sat astride her mare and watched as Wyatt and a crew handled the backbreaking job of setting new fence posts.

He looked up, then, lifting his hat to wipe at the sweat, ambled over. "Hi, Amy. What brings you out this far?"

"Jesse and I are going to drive up in the hills tonight to look at the piece of land we've chosen for our home site. We thought you and Lee might like to come along."

Except for a slight narrowing of his eyes, he managed to keep a tight lid on his emotions. "Thanks for the offer, but by the time we finish here, I'm betting I'll be ready to fall into my bunk and zone out until morning."

"Okay." She bit her lip. "Maybe another time."

"Yeah." He replaced his hat while walking back to join the crew.

When Amy rode away he turned with a thoughtful expression. Was she trying to play matchmaker on her own, or had she and Jesse hatched this plan together, hoping to meddle?

For one quick moment he wondered whether Marilee had had a hand in it. Then he berated himself for wishful thinking. Marilee had made herself perfectly clear.

Whatever game Amy was playing, he had no intention of setting himself up for any more heartache.

Wyatt stood under the shower, hands braced on either side of the tiled wall, face lifted to the spray of hot water.

It had been the longest week of his life. And though he'd waited and wondered, and even picked up the phone a dozen or more times, in the end he'd decided that Marilee would have to make the first move. He wasn't going to call her. He wasn't even going to allow himself to think about her. She needed her space? Fine. He'd give it to her. In spades.

He'd made a good life for himself. Alone. He didn't need anybody calling the shots. Especially some female who blew hot and cold, loving his pampering one day and feeling crowded the next.

Crowded. The very thought had him frowning.

By the time he'd toweled himself dry and was pulling on a clean shirt, he was toying with the idea of driving into town. He was sick and tired of the looks he was getting from his aunt and cousins. This ranch may consist of thousands of acres of land and a hundred or more wranglers, but there was nowhere to hide from the rumors and gossip that floated around.

Everyone on the Lost Nugget Ranch, it seemed, knew that he and Marilee were no longer together.

Together. What a strange word that was. There were probably plenty of married couples who thought of themselves as more alone than together. And plenty of his friends who thought of themselves as so together they would never need a partner to add anything to their lives.

He paused. Marilee had added so much to his life. Everything had been more fun with her. Laughter had been more spontaneous with her. With Marilee, work had become play. And play had become pure joy.

He wadded the damp towel into a ball and slammed it into the corner of his room, determined to put her out of his mind once and for all.

Maybe he'd stop at the saloon and have a beer with the wranglers. Listen to Daffy's throaty laughs telling one of her stale jokes, and enjoy one of Vi's greasy burgers.

He stepped into clean denims and boots.

Maybe *she'd* be there. He'd be civil. Cool and civil. Let her make the first move. If there was a first move. Or not. It didn't matter to him. She didn't matter to him. Nothing mattered to him.

When he descended the stairs and walked past his aunt's studio, he was relieved to see the door closed. That meant she was still working on her latest canvas. He could leave without suffering the need to pause and make small talk. Doing that lately had begun to stick in his throat.

He made his way through the kitchen, where Dandy was chopping vegetables at the counter.

The cook looked over. "You staying for supper?"

"No thanks. Heading into town." He hurried out to his Harley and climbed aboard, eager for the wind to take his hair. And hopefully his dark thoughts.

Marilee finished polishing the last of her living room shelves and returned the baskets and masks to their former positions. She stepped back and looked around her apartment. In the past week, between ambulance runs, her floors had been scrubbed and waxed to a high shine. The kitchen tiles gleamed, looking as new as the day they'd been installed. The windows sparkled in the sunlight. The bed had been freshened with new linens. Her laundry was folded and put away. She'd even cleaned out her closets and drawers, and had filled a garbage bag with discarded clothing, which she would drop off at a local charity.

She set the kettle on the stove and sank down on a barstool to wait for the familiar whistle. She'd needed this time to work. Hard work had always been her refuge when she was troubled. But now, after scrubbing, polishing, and waxing, she ought to be feeling a sense of accomplishment. Instead, she felt only a vague sense of dread at the days and weeks and months looming ahead of her.

She'd hurt Wyatt. Had seen it in his eyes. Heard it in his voice. And even though she had no doubt that she'd needed to say what she was feeling, it didn't make it any easier. Being right didn't help much when it meant hurting the one you loved.

The one you loved.

Shocked, stunned, she put a hand to her heart to ease the sudden spear of pain.

She did love him. In a way she'd never loved anyone else. She loved his silly humor, his quick, sharp mind, his sense of fair play. She loved his interaction with his large, loud family. She especially loved his fierce independence.

Her beloved rebel.

What would she do if the tables were turned? What if she believed Wyatt was in some kind of danger? Wouldn't she move heaven and earth to keep him safe? And yet she'd asked him . . . no, she'd ordered him away. Had told him that he was suffocating her. Smothering her with his care and concern. She'd sent him away, angry and hurting, and all because of her damnable need to take care of herself.

What had she done? Oh, what had she done?

She grabbed up the bag of discarded clothing and went in search of her keys.

She had to get out of here. She had to escape her dark thoughts, her perfectly appointed apartment, her uncluttered life that was suddenly making her feel horribly, miserably alone.

As Wyatt's Harley danced along the open highway he mulled the things Marilee had said, playing them this way and that through his mind, turning them over and over, struggling to make some sense of them, as he had a hundred times in the past week.

She needed the freedom to live her life on her terms. To make her own mistakes. Well, wasn't that the same thing he'd wanted all these years? Hadn't he been the original rebel, letting his family know in no uncertain terms that he would live by his own code?

Didn't everybody have the right to that?

He slowed the bike. Stared around as though coming out of a fog. Had he been holding her too tightly? Afraid to let go, not only out of love, but also out of fear for her safety? If someone did that to him, no matter how noble the reasons, he'd clench his fists and fight until only one of them was still standing.

What had she said about her father? That she'd never been the son he'd wanted. And so she'd rebelled and fought and clawed her way to a life that satisfied her needs.

She had her own demons to fight. A distant father and a clinging mother, and Marilee struggling to find out where she fit into that equation. A classic contest of wills, and one that she had to fight every day for the sake of her battered self-esteem.

Maybe, Wyatt thought, the only way to keep from losing her would be to learn to let her go. Even if it meant knowing that she could be putting herself in harm's way.

Dear God, was he strong enough?

It went against everything he'd ever believed about love and family. Didn't a man have a duty to keep his loved ones safe, by any means possible?

The mere thought of stepping back, of letting go, of abdicating what he considered his right, had him shuddering. It would be harder than anything he'd ever done before, and he wasn't at all certain he was up to the task.

But, if it was really a test, not just of moral strength but a test of love, how could he do otherwise?

Suddenly, this was all too much to take in. It was too deep, too threatening.

He gunned the engine, taking the curves and slopes of

the highway with breathtaking speed. And all the while he was wishing the wind blowing past him could blow away every dark, daunting thought swirling through his mind. Thoughts that were making him question every truth he'd ever held sacred.

CHAPTER EIGHTEEN

W yatt slowed to make the turn into town, then thought better of it and continued on along the highway until the pavement ended. He followed a dirt track through scrub and gnarled trees until he came to an outcropping of rock that ended in a sheer drop-off overlooking a stretch of rangeland.

Dismounting, he left his Harley and walked to the very edge of the rocky promontory. He sat with his back to a boulder and listened to the sudden, shocking silence. Tipping back his head, he studied the path of a shooting star and found himself making a wish.

"Old habits," he muttered aloud when he realized what he'd done.

That had him grinning, remembering nights under the stars with his cousins. As boys, they had scrupulously shared every myth and legend they had ever heard. And believed, as only kids could believe. They'd believed that if they wished on a shooting star, it would be granted.

They'd believed with all their hearts that they would remain best friends forever. They'd believed that their grandfather had the strength of a superhero, and the laser vision, as well, and that he would find the treasure of his ancestors. They'd believed in keeping promises, in always telling the truth, in love that would last forever.

And yet, scant years later, many of those beliefs had been shattered, often by people they trusted.

Now that he had allowed his senses to become attuned to the night, Wyatt became aware of a symphony of sound. Instead of silence, he heard the buzzing and chirping of insects. A night bird cried, and in the distance, its mate answered. Somewhere on the range a coyote howled to the moon, and others picked up the song until their voices echoed across the hills.

He studied the stars, looking close enough to touch, and felt his heart swell with sudden understanding. Wasn't it the same with people? Sometimes it was necessary to listen, not just to the words they said, but to the words they left unspoken.

Sometimes he needed to just sit and be in the darkness until he allowed his mind to hear the little sounds that he'd originally missed.

As a boy, he'd blamed others for taking him away from all that he loved. But here he was, back where it all started. Not because of others, but because of the choices he'd made. He had spent endless years mourning the loss of his beloved ranch, without taking the steps necessary to return. But now he had returned, and because of that choice, his life was richer, fuller.

Despite all that had happened in his life, he still believed.

He and his cousins were rebuilding the friendship they'd thought lost forever. They had vowed to continue Coot's search for the lost treasure. And though the last week had been a trial by fire, he was slowly beginning to believe that it was still possible, with honesty and discipline and sweat, to cut through the layers of words to the core of truth and find love.

Love.

It wasn't enough to just feel love for someone. Real love, honest love, meant putting the well-being of the other ahead of self. Giving a partner the things that were needed, even if it cost him dearly.

But could he do that, and still remain true to himself?

He stretched out his long legs and tipped his head back, letting the healing power of the night wrap itself around his mind and heart.

Here in the moonlight, with a million stars twinkling above, he had some heavy-duty thinking to do.

Marilee dropped off her discarded clothing at the local charity and drove her truck past the Fortune Saloon. The smell of grilled onions wafting through her open window, usually so tempting, held no appeal this night. She didn't think she could bear another knowing look from Daffy and Vi, or an encounter with Delia Cowling or any of the other folks in town, so determined to make her business theirs.

She drove back to her apartment and climbed the stairs. She had forgotten to eat today, but it didn't matter. She had no appetite. In fact, she'd noticed that her jeans were getting too big for her. The thought gave her no pleasure. She wasn't interested in a misery diet. But there it was.

She let herself into her apartment and put the kettle on for tea before dropping onto one of the stools at the counter.

Why in the world did she have to be so abrasive with people who cared about her? Why couldn't she learn to overlook the things that irritated her and just move on? *Because*, a small voice in her mind whispered, *you're terrified of becoming your mother.* She'd constantly needed her husband's approval, in even the smallest things. But, Marilee wondered, had she, in her determination to avoid becoming her mother, begun to emulate her overbearing father?

No, she thought with a vehemence that surprised her. She could never let that sort of anger take over her life. But she had to admit that she'd been strident. Her unexpected outburst had caught Wyatt by surprise. And for that she was deeply sorry, and unable to think of any way to atone. If she apologized, he would think she hadn't meant what she'd said. But unless she apologized, they were at an impasse.

She was locked so deeply in her disturbing thoughts, it took several moments before the whistling of the teakettle broke through enough to jar her.

Just as she started toward it, there was a knock on her door.

Ignoring the kettle, she crossed the room and peered through the peephole on her door.

"Wyatt." She tore it open and stood there, drinking him in. Just the sight of him had her heart doing a happy dance in her chest.

"Don't throw me out." He lifted a hand. "I come in peace. With food."

When she didn't say a word he added, "Pizza. With all your favorite toppings. Sausage, mushrooms, green . . ."

"Well, then." To hide the unexpected tears that sprang to her eyes, she turned away quickly. "Since you went to so much trouble, you may as well come in."

"It was no trouble. I just rode a hundred miles on my Harley, fought my way through the smoke screen at the Fortune Saloon, had to fend off Daffy's attempts to have her way with me, and discovered that I'd left my wallet back at the ranch, which meant I had to sign away my life before Vi would turn over this pizza, wine, and dessert. But hey, no trouble at all. It's the sort of thing I do nearly every day."

He followed her to the kitchen, where he set down the pizza box and a brown bag.

He glanced over at the stove. "Are you going to lift that kettle, or did I interrupt you making a recording of you whistling along with it in harmony?"

Despite her tears, she found herself laughing hysterically at his silly banter.

Oh, how she'd missed it.

He set the kettle aside. The sudden silence was shocking.

Because she had her back to him, he fought the urge to touch her. Instead he studied the way her shoulders were shaking. Troubled, he realized he'd made her cry.

"Sorry." Deflated, his tone lowered. "I guess this was a bad idea."

"Wyatt."

He paused.

"It was a good idea. A very good idea."

She turned, and he saw the tears coursing down her cheeks.

"Oh, God. Marilee, I'm sorry. I didn't mean to make you . . ."

"I'm not crying." She brushed furiously at the tears. "I mean I was, but then you made me laugh and . . ."

"This is how you laugh?" He caught her by the shoulders and held her a little away. "Woman, I didn't realize just how weird you are. Wait a minute. Do you think being weird might be contagious? Maybe I ought to get out of here before I turn weird, too."

The more she laughed, the harder the tears fell.

Through a torrent of tears she wrapped her arms around his waist and held on, burying her face in his neck. "You can't leave. I won't let you."

He tipped up her face, wiping her tears with his thumbs. "You mean that? You really don't want me to go?"

"I don't. I really want you to stay, Wyatt."

"For dinner?"

"And more."

"Dessert?"

"And more."

His smile was quick and dangerous. "I'm beginning to like the 'and more.'"

She smiled through her tears. "Me, too."

"Maybe we could have the 'and more' as an appetizer, before the pizza."

Her laughter bubbled up and over, wrapping itself around his heart. "Oh, how I've missed your silly sense of humor."

"You have?"

"I have. I've missed everything about you."

"Everything?" He leaned close to nibble her ear, sending a series of delicious shivers along her spine.

"Everything."

Catching his hand, she led him to the bedroom. "I worked very hard today making up the bed with fresh linens. Want to be the first to mess it up?"

He looked from the bed to her and then back again. "Oh, yeah."

He drew her close and brushed her mouth with his. Just a soft, butterfly kiss, but she felt it all the way to her toes. "I mean I want to really, really mess it up."

"Me, t . . ."

And then there was no need for words.

"I missed you. Even though it was only for a week, I missed you." Marilee sat back against a mound of pillows, sipping wine.

"Not as much as I missed you." Wyatt nibbled a slice of pizza before offering some to her.

She took a bite and passed it back. "I cleaned the entire apartment while I missed you."

"I can top that. I mucked out an entire barn. Not one, in fact, but two. Horse manure, and then cow manure."

She ran a hand down his biceps. "That was a pretty good workout."

He smiled at her. "So was this. And I enjoyed this a whole lot more. You smell so much better than the cows and horses."

They both laughed as he reached for another slice.

"Try not to get crumbs on the clean sheets."

"Yes, ma'am." He reached for a napkin.

She closed a hand over his. "I'm sorry, Wyatt."

She didn't need to explain. They both knew what she was talking about.

"You had a right to vent. I was behaving like a mother hen."

"A very sweet mother hen with too many chicks."

"I promise to back off." He offered her another bite of pizza. "But I can't promise not to worry."

"Fair enough." She kept her hand on his. "It's natural to worry. But you have to trust, too."

"You know what I've decided?" He plumped up a pillow and stretched out beside her. "You're even more of a rebel than I am."

"You think so?"

"Yeah."

"Next you'll be loaning me your Harley."

"I could be persuaded." He linked his fingers with hers.

She stared at their joined hands and sighed. "This is nice."

"Yeah. I was just thinking the same thing." He leaned his head back and began chuckling.

"What's so funny?"

"I've been a bear for the past week. I'd have happily snapped off anybody's head who dared to cross me."

"I know what you mean. Fortunately, there was nobody around for me to snap at. I had to content myself with yelling at the talking heads on TV." She paused. "How're you feeling now?"

He looked over at her. "What a difference a week makes. The thunderstorm's gone. The cloudy skies. The nasty rain. I'm all sunshine and blue skies and sweet-smelling flowers, thanks to you."

"Me, too." She set her wine on the nightstand and leaned over to brush a kiss over his mouth. "I'm so glad you're here, Wyatt. This has been the longest week of my life."

His arms came around her, gathering her close. Against her lips he whispered, "Speaking of which, you make me weak."

"And you make me . . ."

His kiss cut off her words.

As they rolled together, one word played over and over in her mind.

Content.

Wyatt McCord made her feel content. And safe. And absolutely, completely, thoroughly loved.

The ringing of the phone shattered their sleep.

Marilee untangled herself from Wyatt's arms and legs and sat up, shoving hair from her eyes. As she picked up the receiver she glanced at the clock on her night table. Almost six o'clock. Not only had she and Wyatt put in a very enjoyable night, but they'd been able to sleep uninterrupted for hours. For once the two-in-the-morning rule hadn't applied.

"Emergency One. What's the problem?"

She listened, then said, "I'm on it. I can be there in ten minutes or less."

She stumbled out of bed and pulled on her clothes. When she turned, Wyatt had followed suit and was walking toward the door.

She went very still while memories of their separation filled her mind and sent her heart tumbling to her toes. "Where are you going?"

He picked up his keys. Met her eyes. Gave her one of those cocky, heart-stopping smiles. "I figure, by the time I get to the ranch, Dandy will have breakfast ready, and I can get a head start on my chores."

She exhaled slowly, feeling her heart rate return to normal.

She grabbed up the keys to the emergency vehicle.

In the garage Wyatt hauled her up against him and gave her a long, slow, delicious kiss that had her head spinning. "Stay safe."

Did he know what that did to her? A part of her wanted to take him by the hand and drag him back to her room, lock the door, and hold the world at bay. The other part of her, the sensible part, knew what she had to do.

She gave a long, slow sigh. "You, too."

As she drove out of the garage, Marilee watched the Harley in her rearview mirror. It gave her such comfort to see Wyatt there.

At the intersection, he lifted his hand in a salute as the motorcycle veered right, heading toward the long ribbon of highway that would lead to the Lost Nugget Ranch. Marilee waved before heading in the opposite direction, keeping an eye open for the stretch of unmarked dirt road that would take her to a ranch not far from town.

She wondered just how much it was costing Wyatt to set aside his fears for her safety and live up to his promise to give her some room and get on with his own life.

He would never know how grateful she was that he'd been able to work through his frustrations and accept her as she was. In just seven long, dismal days she'd had a glimpse into her life without him, and it hadn't been a pretty sight. But as lonely and bleak as the time had been, she hadn't been ready to sacrifice her independence just to get him back into her life.

How was it possible that, in the space of a few weeks, someone could tumble off the back of a crazed bull and so completely change her world? Before she had met Wyatt McCord she'd had an existence that was both challenging and fulfilling. She certainly hadn't needed a man to complete her. In fact, she'd considered most men a complication. Or at the very least, a pleasant diversion.

Now a single day without Wyatt seemed flat and colorless. He'd begun to mean more to her than she was comfortable admitting to.

"Damn you, McCord." She was laughing as she said it. "I don't know what kind of magic potion you slipped into that pizza, but it certainly has done the trick. I don't ever want to live another day without your magic potion. Or another night without you, rebel."

CHAPTER NINETEEN

T his gadget's going crazy." Zane paused, holding a metal detector over a mound of earth.

Wyatt backtracked and studied the gauge. "Okay. Looks like we get to dig in the dirt again, cuz."

He and Zane took turns digging up the rock and sand. They had long ago shed their shirts and had tied bandannas around their heads to mop the sweat. Despite the fierce summer heat, they were in high spirits. Chasing the gold seemed to have that effect on all of them.

Wyatt bent to retrieve something from the hole they'd dug.

"Looks like an old tobacco pouch."

"Anything in it?"

When he tried to open it, the fragile fabric began to shred. "Empty." He stowed it in a sack before he and Zane moved on.

The three cousins had begun taking turns as often as possible, walking a prescribed area in the foothills of Treasure Chest Mountain, which they carefully mapped, and using the latest high-tech detectors and global-positioning tracking systems.

Everything they uncovered, whether it turned out to be ore-laden rock or foil gum wrappers, was cataloged and stored for reference. They had already discovered half a dozen of Coot's handwritten notes and doodles buried in the sand, along with artifacts from the 1862 gold-rush days. Miner's picks, mismatched boots, and broken tools. Lanterns. Even bits of furniture. Though they seemed useless, Jesse, Wyatt, and Zane recognized them as bits and pieces of men's dreams. Men had left the comfort of home and family to search for the elusive gold. Many had died, alone and desperate. And some had even killed. Those facts made this land, as Coot had taught them, sacred ground. They felt that they had a solemn duty to treat each discovery with respect.

Wyatt and Zane hiked for another hour without locating a thing.

"Time to head back." Zane tipped up a bottle of water and drained it.

"Yeah. I'm ready for a long, cool shower."

Hearing the drone of an airplane, both men looked up.

As soon as Zane recognized it, he glanced over at Wyatt, who was staring transfixed at the sky.

He grinned. "I see Marilee's plane is repaired."

"Yeah." With a look of naked hunger, Wyatt continued to track it as it drew closer.

"I'm surprised you're not up there with her."

Wyatt's gaze never wavered. He stared transfixed. "Today's a test run. If she's happy with the way it handles, she'll be back in business tomorrow."

As the plane passed overhead it dropped low enough for them to see Marilee at the controls. She waved before dipping the wings, first one way, then the other.

Both Wyatt and Zane pulled off their wide-brimmed hats and waved them wildly.

They could see Marilee's bright smile as she waved once more before pulling up and away.

When the little plane was just a streak of yellow disappearing over the mountain peaks, Zane shouldered the metal detector and led the way back to their truck in the distance. "What happened, cuz? You lose your taste for flying?"

Wyatt caught up with him, carrying the picks and shovels. "Marilee wanted to go it alone."

"You're okay with that?"

Wyatt shrugged. "Flying's her business. That means she gets to call the shots." After they'd climbed yet another hill, he met Zane's frown with a grin. "Hey. It's not a problem. I'm okay with it."

"Even after that crash landing?"

Wyatt winced. "If I secretly worry about her, I'll just have to live with it and deal with it in my own way."

At least he was working on it, he told himself as they began loading their equipment into the back of the truck before heading toward the ranch. And maybe one day it would actually get easier.

The roar of Wyatt's motorcycle had heads turning as he arrived at the airport. Marilee and several representatives from the airplane manufacturer were huddled around her aircraft.

When he strolled over she gave him a smile and took

his hand while handling the introductions, before returning her attention to one of the men who'd been speaking.

"As I was saying, we haven't had a single complaint about trouble with our fuel line. Despite your claim, we didn't find anything out of place. Naturally, we'll want to know if you should spot a problem."

"Oh, you'll hear me hollering loud and clear," she said with a laugh. "But today I gave it every test I could think of, and it passed with flying colors."

The company's chief mechanic strolled over. "I've checked and double-checked everything. It all appears to be in perfect shape. Is there anything more you'd like us to look at?"

Marilee shook her head. "Can't think of a thing."

The mechanic handed her a checklist, which she carefully read and signed.

They shook hands all around before the representatives climbed into their own aircraft.

Marilee and Wyatt watched as the sleek plane taxied down the single runway and turned. The engines revved and it gained speed before lifting and becoming airborne.

As soon as the sound faded Wyatt turned to her. "You're looking pretty pleased with yourself. I take it you had a good flight."

She nodded. "Not a single hitch. It couldn't have gone any smoother."

"I'm glad. You looked really happy when you did the flyover."

"I was. Happy to be flying again, and happy to see you and Zane. Find anything interesting? Like a pot of gold?"

"Not today." He grinned. "Hungry?"

"Starving."

He caught her hand. "Let's see what Vi has on the grill tonight."

"You realize she's becoming our own personal chef." With a laugh Marilee climbed aboard the Harley and wrapped her arms around his waist.

"I thought that was my title."

"You're my naked chef. But that has to remain our secret."

Her laughter bubbled on the breeze.

She'd loved the fact that she could fly again. Being up above the clouds had restored her sense of freedom. But having Wyatt here, she thought, was the perfect ending to a perfect day.

"Marilee." Ledge Cowling stood blocking the entrance of the Fortune Saloon as he waited for several of his friends to make their way to the table Daffy was indicating. "I hear you took your plane up for a test run. How'd everything go?"

"Just fine, thanks." Marilee stepped aside, revealing Wyatt behind her.

"McCord." Ledge's smile thinned. "You and your cousins have tongues wagging here in town."

"I'd say that's nothing new." Wyatt held up two fingers to indicate to Daffy how many were in his party.

"You know how folks love to talk." Ledge planted himself directly in front of Wyatt. "I hear you had some pretty impressive equipment shipped out to the ranch."

"I guess Joe Morris does more than deliver." Wyatt glanced at the owner of the delivery service, seated at the bar and surrounded by half a dozen ranchers who were hanging on his every word. "Do folks here in town pay him to report on what we order, or does he just do it for free drinks?"

Ledge refused to be sidetracked. "They're saying you've been seen digging in the foothills of Treasure Chest."

"Is that so?" Wyatt merely smiled and neatly stepped around Ledge before taking Marilee's arm. "Daffy has a table for us. Way back in the corner, far from the maddening crowd."

As they walked away, they could hear the buzz of conversation.

". . . following in crazy old Coot's footsteps."

". . . ought to know better than to ignore the family curse."

". . . won't be surprised if I hear about them meeting the same fate as their ancestors. They're all loony."

By the time they were seated in a far corner booth, Marilee was fuming. "Did you hear all that garbage?"

"Yep." He was wearing a silly grin.

"Doesn't it bother you?"

"No. And you can't let it bother you, either."

"I'm furious. They have no right to discuss you and your cousins as though you're a pack of idiots. Can't they see that they're the ones who are idiots?"

Wyatt leaned over and kissed her.

She gaped at him. "What was that for?"

"For getting mad on my behalf. And may I add"—he took her hand in his—"you're absolutely adorable when you're mad. You should do this more often. Your cheeks are so flushed they're almost as red as your hair."

For just an instant she looked as though she might explode with temper. Then, just as quickly, her little frown turned into a laugh of pure delight.

She touched a hand to his cheek. "You really know how to play me, don't you?"

"Do I?"

She gave a little shake of her head. "You're good, McCord. Really good."

"Why, thank you. Though I don't have a clue what you're talking about."

"And pigs fly."

They were still laughing together when Daffy walked up to take their order and, as usual, set a couple of frosty longnecks in front of them before dropping down on the opposite side of the booth and slipping off her shoes with a weary sigh.

"You realize, Wyatt, that you and your cousins are the object of some very heated discussions."

Wyatt grinned. "We heard bits and pieces of some of those discussions."

"You ought to hear as much as I have."

"Care to share?" He smiled at Marilee, whose look had sharpened.

"There's lots of talk that all the McCords are fated to chase their dream into the grave."

Wyatt chuckled. "Does that make us different from everybody else? Do they figure they'll avoid the grave?"

"You know what they mean." Daffy glanced around before lowering her voice. "That McCord curse. All the McCord men died chasing after that fortune."

Wyatt arched a brow. "You sound as though you're

going over to the dark side, Daffy. Are you beginning to believe them?"

She stared pointedly at her feet and wiggled her toes before sliding them back into her shoes. "You know how it is. When you get that many people harping on the same subject, it starts to make sense."

"If gossip about the so-called McCord curse is starting to turn you into a believer, I'd say it's time to call their bluff." Wyatt's smile widened. "For now, let's just talk about food. I'm going to have whatever Vi has on the grill that smells so wonderful."

Marilee nodded. "Me, too."

"Would that be the prime rib, or the liver and onions?"

Marilee and Wyatt both said in the same breath, "Prime rib."

"That pretty much makes it unanimous. I haven't had one taker for Vi's liver and onions yet." Giving another exaggerated sigh, Daffy stood.

As she walked away, Wyatt and Marilee fell into each other's arms laughing.

As they moved apart and sipped their beer, Wyatt gave a slight shake of his head. "I can't believe that damned curse is making the rounds again."

"Do you really think anybody believes it?"

"You heard Daffy."

"Yeah. Repeat a lie often enough, people mistake it for truth."

"But not sensible people." He glanced around the saloon, pausing to study the townspeople and cowboys who clustered around the bar and several tables, faces close, voices a low drone. "I don't believe anybody actually believes what they're saying. It may stave off boredom, or spice up a weekly bingo game, but I'm betting that most people in Gold Fever know better than to pay any attention to such garbage."

Daffy walked up with a tray and set two plates in front of them. "Enjoy your prime rib. Especially since yours is the last of it. Vi says anybody who comes in now will have to settle for liver and onions."

"Thanks for the warning." Wyatt picked up a fork. "I guess I won't be asking for seconds."

He winked at Marilee, who choked back her laughter until Daffy had turned away.

They took their time enjoying their meals, sipping their beers, and greeting old friends.

At last Marilee pushed aside her plate. "Perfect. Now I wonder what Vi has for dessert."

"I don't know about Vi, but I was hoping we could enjoy our dessert back at your place."

"I don't think I have a thing in the cupboards."

He caught her hand and gave her one of his best smiles. "I'm betting we can come up with something sweet."

Her sudden knowing smile matched his. "I'm sure we can."

They strolled hand in hand from the saloon, completely oblivious of the whispered comments from the crowd.

Wyatt roared up to the ranch just as Cal Randall began loading Cora's Jeep with supplies.

"'Morning, Cal. Aunt Cora." Wyatt kissed his aunt's cheek. "Looks like you're heading out for another artistic marathon."

Cora nodded. "I have to take advantage of the sunlight while I can. Summer never lasts long enough here in Montana."

Cal stood shaking his head and looking absolutely miserable. "I just wish you had someone going along. I don't like you all alone out in that wilderness."

"Now, Cal. We've been down this road a hundred times or more." She patted his hand. "I have my cell phone, my rifle, and my trusty handgun."

"So did Coot." Cal finished loading the last of the supplies and closed the door. He gave her a long, steady look. "But it wasn't enough."

"I don't intend to do anything foolish. I won't be climbing the foothills or even scrambling over rocks. I'll just find a nice sheltered spot to set up camp and then get to work on my canvas."

Choosing to ignore Cal's protest, she settled herself in the driver's side and fastened her seat belt. Through the open window she blew Cal and Wyatt a kiss. "I'll check in every evening. And I'll be back as soon as I'm satisfied with my work."

"No more than a week, Cora, or I swear I'll send out the troops."

She merely smiled at the weathered ranch foreman and put the vehicle in gear.

Cal watched until she rounded a corner of the long driveway before, grumbling, he made his way to the barn.

Wyatt headed in the opposite direction, hoping Dandy had made scrambled eggs. He didn't need pancakes or French toast this morning. He'd had enough sweetness last night to tide him over for the day.

* * *

Wyatt was whistling as he worked alongside Jesse and Zane and a handful of wranglers in the north pasture, mending fences.

When his cell phone rang he saw Archie's number and answered it before the second ring.

"Yeah, Archie. What've you learned?"

The distinctive Cockney voice broke through the static. "I've found your missing airport mechanic, in, of all places, a little one-horse town in Wyoming."

Wyatt's smile faded. "You're sure it's him?"

"It's him."

"Did he say why he went missing?"

At his tone of voice Jesse and Zane glanced up sharply and moved closer.

"I don't have all the details yet. I'll tell you what little I know. When I confronted him, and let him know you'd sent me, he reluctantly admitted that he was Craig Matson. He said he didn't even take the time to go back to his place and collect his things. He just hightailed it out of town, using cash for fear that a credit card would leave a paper trail. He found a job bartending in a place so secluded, he figured he'd never be found."

"Why, Archie? What's this all about?"

"I'll tell you as soon as I know. For now, he says he stumbled into a conspiracy."

"A conspiracy?"

"That's the word he used. And he added that somebody big was calling the shots. When he realized what was happening, and that his initials on that sabotaged fuel line would lead them right to his doorstep, he had no choice but to run. He said to tell you he fears for his life and Marilee's."

"Marilee's?" Wyatt swore. "Get me all you can on this. I'm hanging up now. I need to let her know right away."

He disconnected before dialing Marilee's number. When she answered he could hear the drone of an engine in the background. His heart started hammering. "Where are you?"

"Heading back from Razorback."

"Razorback?"

"I got a surprise request from Ledge Cowling to handle some of his messenger service for the bank. Talk about timing. The pay is enough for me to cover all the debt on my latest repair work." Her tone was so cheerful, it tore at his heart. "I should be home in time for dinner. What's up?"

"Where are you right now?"

He could hear the smile in her voice. "Flying over the prettiest landscape ever created. I'm about halfway between Razorback and Gold Fever with nothing but wilderness below."

"Wilderness. Do you see anything flat enough to attempt a landing?"

She laughed. "Get it through your head, rebel, I only land in the wilderness with you along as my copilot. Can you imagine me down there alone?"

It was too painful to contemplate. He pondered the wisdom of telling her what he'd learned from Archie. What was the point, when she was in no position to do a thing about it? If he were to tell her, she would carry the burden of fear all the way back to the Gold Fever airport. The fear that was weighing him down at the moment would be enough for both of them.

He struggled to keep his voice calm and reasoned. "I'll

tell you all about it over dinner tonight. I'll be waiting at the airport when you land."

"Wonderful." She gave a long, deep sigh. "I can't think of anything I'd rather see when I land than you waiting for me."

He swore again, loudly, fiercely, as he tucked his cell phone into his pocket and beckoned his cousins to follow him to their ranch truck. They had to run to keep up with his hurried strides.

"Okay." Jesse caught up with him and grabbed his shoulder, spinning him around. "Let us in on this."

Tight-lipped, he handed the keys to Jesse. "I'll tell you on the way. You drive. I'm too tense."

Alarmed, they climbed inside. And as Jesse headed back to the ranch, Wyatt filled them in on all that Archie had told him.

The two cousins listened in silence before hitting him with a barrage of questions.

Zane's eyes narrowed. "So he's saying that Marilee's forced landing wasn't an accident, despite what the manufacturer's representatives found?"

"That's how I read it." Wyatt's tone was low, controlled, to hide the fear that bubbled just below the surface.

Jesse spoke the words that they were all thinking. "And right now Marilee is returning from the very airport where that first fuel-line incident occurred."

"I just hope it was also the last."

Zane shot him a look. "You don't think lightning could strike twice, do you?"

At that Jesse floored the accelerator, sending the truck bouncing over ruts and rocks as they drew near the ranch.

Minutes later, while Wyatt sped off toward town on his

Harley, Jesse phoned the sheriff's office with details of what they had learned so far.

When he rang off he looked as worried as Wyatt had been. "Deputy Atkins left no doubt that he thought I was crazy, talking about a damned conspiracy. But I made him promise to give Ernie the information as soon as he gets back to town. The sheriff's out investigating an accident at the Fitzgerald ranch." He shared a look with Zane. "You thinking what I'm thinking?"

"Yeah. Wyatt needs us. I say we head into town now."

The two dashed to one of the ranch trucks. But though they broke every speed limit, they couldn't catch up with Wyatt's motorcycle, burning rubber with every mile as he sped to the airport, hoping against hope that Marilee would defy the odds and arrive safely.

CHAPTER TWENTY

———◆◆◆———

Marilee pocketed her cell phone. Up ahead were the peaks of Treasure Chest Mountain, bathed in sunlight and sparkling like the spires of ancient cathedrals.

How she loved this land. Every hill and rock and gully. Though she loved it in every change of season, she loved it best in summer, the sunbaked sand glistening like gold far below, feathery clouds above.

She was deliriously happy to be flying once more. She'd missed it terribly. It wasn't something she could explain to others. Flying, to her, was an expression of freedom. Without her plane, she'd felt like a bird with its wings clipped. Now she'd been given back her wings, her freedom.

When the plane cleared the mountaintops she reached for a bottle of water. As she drank she studied the scene spread out below. The foothills, some of them already in shadows, were a mixture of pink and mauve and purple.

She spotted a glint of sunlight off glass and realized

it was a vehicle parked near an outcropping of rock. She lowered the altitude of the plane enough to make out the Jeep. Though she couldn't see Miss Cora, she smiled at the thought of the older woman standing in the shadow of the mountain, lost in her work.

Marilee could understand Miss Cora's passion for her art. Didn't she have a similar passion for flying?

Some distance ahead she saw the path carved into the soil, resembling the marks made by wagon wheels, which she and Wyatt had first spotted on that fateful flight.

The thought of that flight had her glancing at her fuel gauge with a smile, knowing she'd gone to great pains to oversee the refueling at Razorback before climbing into the cockpit.

She stared in absolute disbelief.

The fuel gauge registered empty.

For the space of a heartbeat she couldn't process the information. It simply wasn't possible. How could this be happening again?

"No!" The word was torn from her lips, though she wasn't even aware that she'd spoken it aloud.

At almost the same instant an alarm sounded, and then the flashing light on the instrument panel, announcing the dangerous lack of fuel.

There was no time to think. No time to permit fear to paralyze her. Acting on pure instinct, she took a firm grasp of the controls, determined to take charge of the landing as much as possible, considering the fact that the little plane was already speeding on a course toward disaster.

The last time she was forced to make such a landing, she'd been blessed with relatively smooth ground. This time, so near the foothills, there was nothing but rocks and hills and deeply carved gorges that would surely rip her little plane to shreds.

With all her senses heightened, and a litany of survival tips playing through her mind, she braced herself for whatever was to come.

"Hey, Randy." Wyatt leaned on the counter that served as the nerve center for the tiny Gold Fever airport.

The grizzled old former pilot was able to listen to chatter from any aircraft in the vicinity while mopping the floor or servicing the occasional planes that came and went.

In a month's time, they would rarely have more than two or three aircraft pay a call. The rest of the time was spent keeping up with the backlog of paperwork demanded by the county, state, and federal government agencies.

"How're you managing without Craig Matson?"

The old man shrugged. "Not the same without Craig. He was better at most of this stuff than me. And these damnable documents." He held up a fistful. "They drive a man half crazy."

The two were sharing a laugh when there was a blast of static from the speakers, and then a voice calling, "Gold Fever. You there, Gold Fever?"

Old Randy limped over to a chair and sat, adjusting several dials before saying, "Gold Fever here."

"This is the control tower at Razorback. I've lost contact with MON342. Have you been in contact?"

"No, sir. No contact here." Out of the corner of his eye the old man saw Wyatt come charging around the counter to stand directly behind him. "Where was she when you lost contact?"

The voice gave specific information before saying, "One minute I had MON342 on radar, the next it was gone. No visual, no voice exchange, nothing. Just disappeared. I thought I'd check with you to see if she may have contacted you on another frequency." There was a pause. "I'll continue trying to reach her. I'd advise you to do the same. She was last tracked flying over some pretty rough terrain."

Jesse and Zane raced into the room just in time to hear the last words he'd said.

One look at Wyatt's face told them all they needed to know.

Marilee was in mortal danger. Hundreds of miles from civilization, in some of the roughest Montana wilderness.

And they were helpless to do more than wait and hope and worry.

As for Wyatt, his mind filled instantly with shattering images of his beautiful beloved Marilee, bruised and battered, all alone and fighting for her life. The thought of her suffering, mentally, emotionally, physically, was almost more than he could bear. But the alternative, that her wounds could be fatal, was simply beyond comprehension. He wouldn't allow himself to go there in his mind.

She had to be alive. Had to. He would cling to that thought, and that alone, for he knew, with absolute certainty, that he couldn't continue to live if he lost her now.

While Wyatt paced, his cousins did what they could to offer a measure of comfort.

"Marilee would be the first to tell you that she's a tough, independent woman, Wyatt." Jesse laid a hand on Wyatt's shoulder. "She'll come through this. You'll see."

In the background they could hear Randy contacting every airport within range, asking if they'd seen anything on their radar, or heard a distress call from an unknown aircraft. Their negative responses, broadcast at earsplitting level over the speaker, added to the dramatic sense of urgency.

They all looked up when a shiny black car pulled up to the door and Ledge Cowling hurried inside.

Seeing Wyatt, he stopped mid-stride and blinked before recovering. "McCord. I thought . . ." He glanced toward the old pilot who sat at the controls. "When Randy said Marilee Trainor's plane was down, I just assumed you were with her."

When Wyatt said nothing he cleared his throat and continued. "I feel totally responsible for this."

"You?" Zane stepped close, his gaze narrowed on the banker. "Why?"

"I was the one who hired Lee for this job. I should have never allowed a girl to do something so dangerous."

"Too dangerous for a girl?" Wyatt's hands balled into fists at his sides, causing Ledge to take a step back. There was a dark, dangerous look in his eyes. Eyes glazed with both pain and fury. "Marilee Trainor is the most competent, capable *pilot*," he said, emphasizing the word, "that the people of this town have ever known. She's been flying for years. Why should today be any different?"

"You know what I mean. It's too soon since her accident. Like having to get back up on a horse after a nasty spill. After that crash landing, you can hardly blame her for losing her edge. Just the thought of what almost happened probably caused her to get careless." Ledge shook his head. "Pilot error or not, as I said, I blame myself."

"Pilot error . . ." Wyatt's hand was halfway to the banker's throat before he brought his temper under control.

Completely ignoring Ledge, Wyatt turned toward the old pilot. "Randy, is there a plane for hire?"

"Sorry. There's nothing here. The best I could do is issue a request for a plane from a nearby airport. I could probably get one here tomorrow."

"Tomorrow." Wyatt spun away, his simmering frustration reaching the boiling point.

"Come on, cuz." Jesse dropped an arm around Wyatt's shoulder and began herding him toward the door. "We'll load your Harley in the back of our truck and drive to the sheriff's office. We need to file a report with Ernie."

On the drive across town Wyatt stared morosely out the window, lost in thought. Images of Marilee, alone and hurt, played through his mind, tormenting him.

At the sheriff's office Deputy Harrison Atkins wrote out a report and asked them to wait while he contacted the state police.

Half an hour later he brought them word that the state police would begin an air search in the morning.

When Wyatt started to protest, Jesse stepped in front of him. "Thanks, Harrison. We appreciate that. You'll see that the sheriff is told about this?"

"You bet." The deputy watched Wyatt begin his pacing and said softly, "If I were you, I'd see that he got something for those nerves before he explodes."

"Yeah. Will do." Jesse once again steered Wyatt toward the door and herded him into the truck.

"Morning." It was the first word Wyatt had spoken

since he'd left the airport. "Harrison says the state police won't even begin to search for the plane until morning. What if she's bleeding? Unconscious? Worse?" He ran a hand through his hair. "I should have been with her."

"That's what Ledge thought." Jesse stared over Wyatt's bowed head and caught Zane's eye.

The two exchanged a meaningful look that said they were both on the same wavelength.

Ledge Cowling had looked not only startled, but annoyed, when he'd caught sight of Wyatt at the airport.

Was there more to this? And if so, how much more?

Neither of them dared to put their thoughts into words for fear of sending Wyatt over the edge. He was already near the breaking point. There was no sense adding to his distress until they could prove their theory.

"I think," Jesse began, choosing his words carefully, "you may need to contact your friend Archie again, and see if he can use his influence to get a pilot willing to begin an air search tonight."

His words had the desired effect, giving Wyatt something on which to focus all that smoldering energy. With a look of gratitude he dug his cell phone out of his pocket and dialed the familiar number.

While Wyatt filled his friend Archie in on the latest developments, Jesse's cell phone rang.

"Hey, Aunt Cora. How're you surviving in the wilderness?"

He listened, then said, "Wait. I want you to tell Wyatt all that you just told me."

He handed the phone to Wyatt, who had just finished talking to Archie.

Puzzled, Wyatt shot his cousin a look. "The last thing I need at a time like this is to make small talk with Aunt Cora."

"Trust me. Talk to her."

With a sigh of frustration Wyatt said, "Hey, Aunt Cora."

It was all he managed to say before the voice on the other end, high-pitched with excitement, brought a gasp of pleasure.

"Say that again, Aunt Cora." He held the phone away and pressed the speaker button so the others could hear every word.

"At first, I was so caught up in my work, I wasn't even aware of the sound of an airplane. But when it dipped low overhead, I looked up and realized that it was Marilee's little yellow plane. She must have spotted my campsite. I returned to my work until a few minutes later, when I heard the sound of a crash, and my poor heart nearly stopped. I jumped into my Jeep and drove toward the sound. I'm here now, and though Marilee has some injuries, and, I suspect, some broken bones, nothing appears to be life-threatening . . ."

"Can I talk to her?" Wyatt held his breath until he heard Marilee's voice.

"Wyatt." Her tone was so soft and weak, he could barely recognize it.

"Oh, baby. I'm so glad my aunt found you."

"She saved my life. I was certain I'd be burned alive, but with my injuries, I couldn't work myself free. Wyatt, she got me out of the plane minutes before it exploded."

The three cousins gave a collective gasp when they realized the seriousness of the crash.

"Wyatt . . ."

He could hear her struggling for breath and interrupted her. "Save your strength now, Marilee. We'll talk when you're stronger."

"No. I need you to know. It was just like before. I refueled in Razorback." She paused, fighting for every breath. "My instruments gave no indication, and then all of a sudden everything went crazy and I was diving straight for the ground." She was silent for so long he thought she had passed the phone back to his aunt, but then her voice came back, each word an effort. "I . . . don't believe . . . was an accident."

"Neither do I. But for now I just want you to . . ."

Cora's voice came on the line. "That's enough, dear. I need to tend to Marilee's wounds. I'm afraid she's too shaken, and in too much pain, to speak coherently anymore. I'm going to get her as comfortable as I can tonight, and let her rest before we head home at first light. I wish I didn't have to make her wait until tomorrow for expert medical assistance, but I'm just not comfortable driving her alone in this darkness."

"I understand, Aunt Cora. Do what you have to."

For long minutes after he rang off Wyatt held the phone in both hands, his head bent low, eyes closed, as though unwilling to let go of the only connection he had with Marilee.

Finally he looked at his cousins and shook his head in wonder. "She's alive."

"That's the best news of all. For now, cuz, her safety is all that matters." Zane clapped a hand on his shoulder. "I guess you ought to file a report with the sheriff's office."

"Yeah."

He retrieved his cell from his pocket, but before he could make the call, it signaled an incoming call.

Seeing Archie's number, he snapped it open. "Archie, sorry, I forgot you were on the phone. I just got the best news of all. Marilee's alive."

"That's fantastic. Now you'll want to have the law take a close look at one of the owners of the airports at Gold Fever and Razorback."

"One of the owners? You mean Ledge Cowling?"

At Wyatt's question, the voice on the other end paused. "I see we're on the same page."

"I knew it." Wyatt's voice lowered with feeling. "All along he seemed to have more than a passing interest in our business. He had a stash of Coot's papers hidden in his sister's basement storage. And from what you uncovered earlier, he's probably been harboring an old grudge against the family because of Coot. Would you care to add to the list?"

Archie chose his words carefully. "Craig Matson has said he would only return to Gold Fever if he were promised protection. He fears reprisals if he makes public what he knows."

"You tell him the McCord family will guarantee his safety."

"Not good enough, Wyatt." Archie's voice was tinged with humor. "You may be strong and fearless, but you're not the law. Craig wants to hear it from the sheriff himself."

"He'll get it."

"There's more." Archie paused before adding, "I bought Tim Moody, the regular maintenance worker at the Razorback airport, a couple of beers and learned something interesting. On the day of your first forced landing, he'd been unexpectedly given the day off by one of the owners."

"Ledge?"

"That's right. Again today, with no notice, he was told to take a paid vacation day. Again, by the owner, Ledge Cowling."

"You're sure of this?"

"I don't see any reason why Tim would lie. But I intend to have him sign a document to that effect."

"Thanks, Archie. For everything. You'll stay on this?"

"Oh, be assured, I'm on it. Your family leads a . . . most interesting life." His deep rumble of laughter could be heard as he disconnected.

After hanging up, Wyatt turned to Jesse. "I don't know if you heard all that, but Archie confirmed our suspicion that Ledge had a hand in this." His voice was tinged with bitterness. "This time Ledge Cowling's gone too far. He very nearly succeeded in killing Marilee. I say we turn around and ask Ernie Wycliff to issue a warrant for Ledge's arrest."

Jesse shot a glance at Zane, seated on the other side of Wyatt.

Zane nodded. "I agree. But not just because of what he did to Marilee."

At Wyatt's arched brow he added, "You were probably too worried about Marilee to notice, but Ledge seemed genuinely surprised to see you at the airport. Jesse and I think he expected you to be on that plane with Marilee. Now that he knows you're still around, you never know what he might do to try to finish the job."

"Oh, I wish he'd try." Wyatt's hands balled into fists. "What I wouldn't give to face off against that bastard in a down and dirty fight."

"While it might be satisfying," Jesse said with a chuckle, "I think the best thing we can do is report our suspicions to the sheriff and let him do his job."

He hit the brakes and turned the truck around on the darkened highway, heading back toward town.

CHAPTER TWENTY-ONE

As the three cousins strode into the sheriff's office, Harrison Atkins and Ledge Cowling were bent close in earnest conversation.

Their heads came up sharply, and Deputy Atkins shifted his attention to his visitors.

"I was just helping Ledge file a report with the Federal Aviation Administration. I figured you boys would be home by now. What brings you back to town?"

"Police business." Wyatt glanced around. "Where's the sheriff?"

"Still out on the Fitzgerald ranch. Old Fitz got thrown from his horse, and it's looking bad. Doc Wheeler and Elly Carson are with him until the medevac team arrives. It could take all night. What can I do for you?"

Wyatt glanced at his cousins for confirmation before saying, "As a matter of fact, we were hoping to have the sheriff question Ledge about his involvement in Marilee's accident. It seems the regular maintenance worker at the

Razorback airport said Ledge gave him an unexpected day off."

"Why, you lying . . ." Ledge leaped to his feet, nearly knocking over his chair.

The deputy put a hand on his arm. "Calm down now, Ledge." He turned to Wyatt. "Are you suggesting that it's a crime to give an employee a day off?"

"I'm saying it's strange that on the same day Marilee paid to have her plane refueled, the regular employee was absent, and a stranger was working in his place. The same stranger, I might add, who replaced that employee just weeks ago, on the same day Marilee was forced to land in the wilderness because of a leak in the fuel line. What are the odds that a regular employee was replaced twice, and twice a certain plane was forced to make an unplanned landing?"

Ledge, his face a mottled shade of red, stood glowering at the McCord cousins, who looked equally furious and ready to do battle.

The deputy looked from one to the other.

"We can't afford to have a fistfight right here in the sheriff's office, boys. Now," Harrison Atkins said reasonably, "I think the safest thing to do is ask you, Ledge, for the sake of fairness, to go quietly home while these boys file a report."

Wyatt stepped closer. "If you're smart, you'll keep him here."

"Is that so?" The deputy smirked. "Why is that?"

Wyatt watched Ledge's eyes as he replied, "Because Craig Matson is willing to testify that the fuel line on Marilee's plane isn't the one he'd checked the previous day."

"Craig Matson? You've found him?" When Wyatt

nodded, Harrison Atkins turned to Ledge. "Maybe, until all this can be straightened out one way or the other, you ought to just step into a cell."

"What?" Ledge's face grew several shades darker. "Just like that? With no proof? Are you planning on taking their word over mine?"

Deputy Atkins looked distinctly uncomfortable. "I don't like this any more than you do, Ledge. How will it look when the good folks of Gold Fever hear that their bank president spent a night in jail?" He opened a desk drawer and removed a set of keys. "That's why, as soon as you're locked up, I'll grant you one phone call to your lawyer. With any luck you ought to be home and in your own bed within a couple of hours. And with the cooperation of Wyatt here, we can get all this straightened out."

Wyatt raised a fist to Ledge's face. "It'll be straightened out, all right . . ."

His angry tirade was interrupted when the deputy stood and took hold of Ledge's arm.

Keeping a hold on him, Harrison walked Ledge to the back of the room and unlocked a door leading to the cells. All the while, Ledge swore a blue streak and gave every indication of putting up a fight.

As they stepped through the open doorway, the deputy unlocked one of the two cells in the jail section and waited until Ledge stepped inside before slamming it shut.

He glanced toward the McCord cousins, who were watching and listening. "There's fresh bed linens, and plenty of soap and water while you wait, Ledge. I'll bring that phone in just a minute, as soon as I have Wyatt sign some papers."

From a desk drawer he produced a legal document

and handed it to Wyatt with orders to read, sign, and date it. "This says you're swearing out a warrant for the arrest of Ledge Cowling, with proof to be forthcoming of a commission of a crime. You'd better be certain of your facts, son, or Ledge could sue you for defamation of character."

Wyatt barely read a word before scratching his name and the date and shoving the document across the desk.

Deputy Atkins set the document aside. "I'll sign a request for that state police plane first thing in the morning."

Wyatt blinked. In the excitement, he'd forgotten the most important fact. "Sorry. There's no need now."

"No need?" The deputy's jaw dropped.

"Marilee crashed not far from where our aunt was camped out at Treasure Chest Mountain."

"Miss Cora was on the mountain?" Harrison lifted a brow.

Wyatt nodded. "The foothills. She managed to pull Marilee from her burning plane, and though she's injured, it isn't life-threatening. She plans on bringing her home at first light."

"Well . . ." Harrison shook his head in disbelief. "You're one lucky man, McCord."

"Yeah." Wyatt started toward the door. Over his shoulder he called, "Tell Ernie Wycliff I'll want to talk to him first thing tomorrow."

"You bet."

As they walked to the door Charity Atkins, the deputy's daughter, was just stepping from her car to handle the night shift.

Seeing her, Harrison called, "No need to come in, Charity. You can head on home."

"You don't need me? Who'll tend the phone?"

Her father put his hands on her shoulders and turned her toward her car. "I have someone in the holding cell, and since I have to be here anyway, no sense in you giving up a night's sleep, too. I'll see you tomorrow."

"I won't argue with a night off. Thanks, Dad." She gave him a quick peck on the cheek and hurried back to her car, waving to the McCord men as she passed them.

When Wyatt, Jesse, and Zane climbed into the ranch truck they could see the deputy still standing in the doorway, watching as they started toward home.

Wyatt pulled his cell from his pocket and dialed his aunt's phone. When he heard her voice he asked the question that was uppermost in his mind: "How's Marilee?"

"Dozing on and off. But she's in pain, dear. And the medical supplies she always carries in her plane were destroyed in the explosion."

Holding a hand over the phone he asked Jesse, "Mind dropping me at Marilee's place?"

"Not at all. You planning on staying the night?"

He shook his head. "I'm going to pick up the emergency vehicle."

Seeing where this was leading, Jesse gunned the engine. "We can be there in five minutes."

Wyatt spoke into the phone. "Aunt Cora, Doc Wheeler is on an emergency run, but I'm going to bring the ambulance to your campsite."

"Tell her we'll all be there," Zane added.

Wyatt glanced over at him, and then at Jesse. Both cousins were nodding.

"All three of us are coming, Aunt Cora. Once we're on the road, you can give us directions."

Relief sounded in Cora's voice. "I'm so glad you're coming, dear. I'll feel a lot better when you get here. I'm feeling just a bit overwhelmed at the moment."

"Hang tough, Aunt Cora. We're on our way."

He disconnected, then dialed Cal Randall. Hearing the ranch foreman's voice, he explained what had happened before adding, "I know how you worry about Aunt Cora. I thought you might want to ride along."

"Thanks, Wyatt. I appreciate that. I'll do you one better. While you boys are fetching that emergency ambulance, I'll take a couple of the wranglers and head on out to Treasure Chest right now."

"I know Aunt Cora will be glad for the company."

"She's not the only one. I should have been there with her."

Wyatt tucked his cell phone into his pocket and fell silent, his mind in turmoil over so many conflicting thoughts.

Craig Matson had spoken of a conspiracy. Someone big. It had to be Ledge, and the substitute mechanic he'd hired to sabotage Marilee's plane.

His cousins believed that he had been the actual target, and that Ledge had looked surprised and unhappy to see him at the airport.

Would a man like Ledge, successful and respected in the community, risk everything for an old family feud? Or did this go deeper? Was it all about Coot's fortune? Or were the two reasons so deeply intertwined, Ledge had simply gone over the edge of reason?

Wyatt's hands fisted at his sides. Ledge may have planned this incident, but that didn't make Wyatt feel less guilty. It was he who had brought danger to Marilee's doorstep.

The McCord curse. Though he knew it was nothing more than a stupid legend, and had no basis in fact, there was no denying that the search for the gold had brought real danger to Marilee.

My fault. My fault.

The words played through his mind.

The thought that he had put the woman he loved in harm's way was like a dagger through his heart.

Wyatt got behind the wheel of the ambulance. "You two catch some sleep. I'll drive. I'm too wired to even close my eyes."

"Not me." Zane pulled out his ever-present video camera and began filming his cousins, narrating the events that had them driving into the wilderness in the middle of the night.

Jesse gave a shake of his head. "Hearing all that, cuz, I'm beginning to think that if you actually get your documentary released one day, nobody will ever believe one family could have so many wild adventures."

Checking the vehicle's Global Positioning System, he turned to Wyatt. "I'm afraid I'll miss some of the excitement if I sleep. I'll be your backup."

As they raced across miles of rangeland, Jesse kept in almost constant contact with their aunt. When at last they'd left civilization far behind, they were grateful for both the GPS and Cora's directions. The ambulance swerved over dirt roads and rocky trails as they made their way unerringly toward her campsite, despite the cover of darkness.

"Oh, my dears, what a lovely sight I see." Cora's voice grew warm with pleasure.

Wyatt held the phone away from his ear and pressed the speaker phone so the other two could hear.

"Cal has just arrived, and I'm so glad to see him."

They could hear Cal's growl, a mixture of relief and recrimination, and could only guess that he was gathering their aunt into his arms for a fierce hug.

A little breathlessly, Cora said, "Cal brought several of the wranglers, along with our dear Amy, and they're already busy gathering up my supplies for the trip back to the ranch."

"That's great, Aunt Cora." In an aside to Jesse, Wyatt said, "Your wife went along with Cal and the crew."

Jesse nodded. "I heard. I'm glad she's there."

To his aunt Wyatt added, "They made good time. How's Marilee?"

"Marilee is . . ."

Suddenly Cora was heard giving a shrill cry, followed by the sound of masculine shouting and then shots ringing out.

"Aunt Cora . . . Aunt Cora!"

Wyatt's shouts went unanswered.

He felt his heart nearly stop as he floored the accelerator. Though it took them only minutes more to arrive at the campsite, it felt like hours. Wyatt's pulse rate was speeding out of control.

"Aunt Cora." He lurched from the vehicle, followed by Jesse and Zane.

For a minute they were surrounded by complete chaos.

Cora and Amy were kneeling beside Marilee, who was lying in a bedroll near a fire. One of the wranglers took aim with his rifle as the three cousins approached, until they stepped into the circle of firelight and identified themselves to him.

"What's this about?" Wyatt's voice was strangled with fear and fury.

Just then Cal Randall came running up, looking like a wild man. "He got away."

"Who? What's going on here?" Wyatt demanded.

Cal swore. "We spotted somebody sneaking into this campsite, and when he saw us and realized Cora wasn't alone he took off in a beat-up old truck. I fired off a couple of shots and managed to hit the rear of his truck, but missed hitting his tire."

"You think it was just a drifter?"

Cal swore again. "Could be. Or it could be something more sinister. I'm just glad we were here. I hate to think what might have happened to Cora and Marilee if they'd been alone."

While Jesse and Amy embraced, and Zane hugged their aunt, Wyatt hurried over to kneel beside the bedroll. With as much gentleness as he could manage he touched a hand to Marilee's fevered brow. "Hey, baby. How're you doing?"

At the sound of his voice her lashes fluttered and she looked up at him with a trembling smile. "Oh, Wyatt, I'm so glad to see you."

He closed a hand over hers. "Not nearly as glad as I am to see you."

For long minutes he gathered her close and held her in his arms, breathing her in while he waited for his heart to settle.

There'd been a time, back at the airport, that he'd feared he might never again get this chance to hold her. All the images of her, shattered and broken, remained in his mind, making this moment so much sweeter.

At last he brushed a kiss over her mouth. "Think you're up to the ride home?"

"Now that you're here, I'm ready for anything."

"That's my girl." He kept her hands firmly in his as the others quickly began dismantling Cora's campsite and loading her art supplies into the back of her Jeep. When that was done Cal and the wranglers took her keys and started the engine, prepared to form a caravan.

When all was in readiness, Wyatt lifted Marilee in her bedroll and carried her to the back of the ambulance, securing her on a gurney. Cora and Amy took seats beside her to tend her on the drive, keeping cloths pressed to her most serious cuts to stem the flow of blood.

Wyatt took the wheel, with Jesse and Zane up front beside him, and, with a phone call to alert Dr. Wheeler, they began the long trek back across miles of rocky wilderness to civilization.

CHAPTER TWENTY-TWO

In the sudden silence Marilee opened her eyes. Throughout the painful jostling on the long ride back, she'd managed to escape several times into mindless sleep. "Are we home?"

In the background could be heard the slam of truck doors and the low drone of men's voices.

"Yeah, baby. We're at the clinic." Wyatt tucked the ring of keys in his shirt pocket before walking around to the rear of the ambulance and lifting her in his arms.

She attempted a feeble protest. "The gurney has wheels."

His voice, muttered against her temple, vibrated through her. "I'd rather have you here in my arms."

She buried her face in his neck. "I'm glad. I feel a lot better with your arms around me."

"Me, too."

With Jesse holding open the doors and Amy rushing ahead to alert the staff, Wyatt carried Marilee into the clinic and looked around at the gleaming, silent room.

One of the cleaning crew poked a head around an open doorway.

"Where's Doc?" Wyatt demanded. "I phoned him and said we were on our way."

"He said to tell you he was sorry to leave, but he had an emergency."

"This is an emergency." Wyatt's tone was sharper than he intended. "How about Elly Carson?"

"She's assisting Doc." The young woman paused, holding a mop and bucket. "Doc said if you got here before him, you should put the patient in one of the examining rooms, and he'd be here as soon as possible."

Wyatt nodded toward an open door. "Are you finished cleaning in there?"

At the young woman's nod he started toward it, with Jesse going ahead to switch on the lights. The rest of the family remained in the waiting area.

While Wyatt deposited Marilee on an examining table, Amy located a supply of blankets and tucked one around the patient.

Wyatt saw the way Marilee winced, and took a blow to his heart. He couldn't bear to see her suffering. "I know you're in pain, baby."

"Some. I've been a medic long enough to know that these cuts need stitches to heal. My left arm may be broken, or badly fractured. Too much pain to know what else is wrong. But I don't mind now that I'm safe. Oh, Wyatt." She wrapped her good right arm around his neck and held on, loving the feel of his calm, steady heartbeat. "I was so scared. This was even worse than before. I wasn't sure I'd ever see you again."

Her words sent another burst of pain stabbing through his heart.

"Shh." He softly kissed her lips. "No more talking. I want you to rest until I get Doc and Elly here to tend you." He turned to Amy. "Will you stay with her while I call the doc and see what's holding him up?"

Amy took up a position beside the examining table.

Before Wyatt reached the door Marilee's eyes were closed, her breathing soft and easy as she slipped into blessed sleep.

"Thanks, Zane." Wyatt accepted a coffee from the vending machine as he dialed the doctor's cell phone.

His frustration grew when he was forced to leave a message. "I should have followed my first instinct and gone directly to the ranch."

"The clinic is the best place for Marilee to be," his aunt reminded him.

"It's cold and sterile and empty." He dialed the emergency number once again and let out a breath when he heard the familiar voice of Dr. Frank Wheeler.

"Hey, Doc. Wyatt McCord. Where the hell are you?"

"Wyatt." The doctor's voice was barely above a whisper. "Sorry to keep you waiting. Are you at the clinic?"

"Yeah. Marilee's in a lot of pain. Deep cuts, lots of blood, and she thinks her left arm may be broken. Except for trying to keep her warm, I haven't even taken the time to look her over carefully. The windshield shattered on impact, so there could be glass fragments embedded in some of the cuts. I just know we need you here now."

"Tell you what. I'll send Elly on ahead. She can make Lee comfortable until I get there. As for me, it'll be awhile yet, Wyatt. I'll have to sign some documents and finish up here before I can head to the clinic."

"Finish up what? Where are you?"

"I'm over at the jail."

"What are you doing there?"

"I'm here in my capacity as coroner."

"Coroner?" Wyatt couldn't seem to take it all in as his family suddenly looked up with interest. "Why does Ernie need a coroner?"

Doc's words had everyone gathering around Wyatt, wearing matching looks of shock and disbelief.

"Ledge Cowling was found dead in his cell. It appears that he hanged himself."

Wyatt and the others greeted Elly Carson in the waiting room and peppered her with questions as soon as she stepped inside the door. As she explained, they stared at her in openmouthed surprise.

"Deputy Atkins said he fell asleep shortly after allowing Ledge to make a call to his lawyer. When the lawyer arrived at the jail, he woke the deputy and the two of them walked to Ledge's cell, where they found him hanging by a rope made of bedsheets. They both worked on him, but it was too late. They couldn't revive him. By the time we arrived back in town with the sheriff, there was nothing to do but determine the approximate time of death and sign the official documents."

With that too-brief explanation she hurried into the examination room to see to Marilee's needs.

Cora sat with her hands to her hot cheeks, trying to take it all in. "I just can't imagine Ledge taking his own life. Not for any reason." The exhaustion of the past hours was evident in her eyes, red-rimmed from lack of sleep. "Poor Delia. Except for a distant cousin, Ledge was all the family she had. She must be devastated."

Cal dropped an arm around the old woman's shoulders. "Leave it to you to think about Ledge's sister at a time like this."

"Will you call her for me, please, Cal?"

He nodded and stepped out of the room.

Jesse passed around more cups of coffee from the vending machine. "Looks like Ledge took all his secrets to the grave."

"What secrets?" Cora looked up.

"It was Ledge who arranged to have Lee's plane tampered with. An employee of his at Razorback admitted that he'd been given the day off on both occasions, so that someone Ledge trusted could do the actual refueling." Jesse glanced at Wyatt, who had turned to stare morosely out the window.

He and Zane exchanged a look before Zane walked over to touch a hand to Wyatt's shoulder. "There's something more. What's eating you, cuz?"

Wyatt gave a shake of his head. "I don't know. It all just seems . . ." He shrugged. "I know I'm not making any sense. But I wanted answers. I wanted to know the why and how of it all." He shrugged again. "There are just too many unanswered questions."

Jesse dropped an arm around his wife. "I'd take unanswered questions anytime over facing two crazed gunmen who thought they knew everything."

"Sorry. I know you two had to go through hell and back with Rafe Spindler and Vernon McVicker." Wyatt thought about the danger his cousin and wife had faced at the hands of their grandfather's jealous lawyer and a ranch employee, who had plotted to kill them over the lost fortune.

Cal returned and spoke quietly to Cora, who looked stricken.

Seeing the way his great-aunt was clinging fiercely to Cal's hand, Wyatt asked, "You all right, Aunt Cora?"

She shook her head. "Cal tried phoning Delia and got her voice mail. He even tried her neighbor, Frances, who said Delia was too depressed to talk to anybody. I'm worried about her." She lifted pleading eyes to Wyatt. "I haven't spoken to Delia in years, and I don't want to add to her pain now. But you've had some contact with her recently, and she may be more receptive to you. Promise me that you'll see Delia when you have some time. She needs to know that any old issues between our families have been wiped away. Will you tell her, Wyatt?"

He set aside his coffee and crossed to her. "I'll see to it, Aunt Cora. I promise." He wrapped his arms around her and held her close, feeling her deep sigh of relief before she reached for Cal's hand.

Wyatt turned and headed toward the examining room. "Send Doc in as soon as he gets here."

He would mull everything later. For now, he just desperately needed to be with Marilee.

"You're one lucky lady, Lee." Dr. Wheeler watched as Elly Carson administered a sedative into an IV line in their patient's arm.

Marilee had been transferred to one of the rooms used for overnight patients. The family had been sent back to the ranch to rest and recover from their ordeal. Only

Wyatt remained with Marilee, unwilling to leave her for even a few minutes.

The doctor walked to her bedside. "Not too many pilots get to walk away from a crash like the one you described, with only a few cuts and no broken bones."

"Without Miss Cora, I wouldn't be here at all." Marilee could feel herself sinking into sleep. "There's nothing left of my plane but some ash and crumpled steel."

"Then Miss Cora's your angel."

"And your angel," Wyatt added, "is worried about Delia's state of mind now that she's lost her brother."

Doc nodded. "She took the news hard. When I can find time in my crazy schedule, I intend to call her and ask her to come in for a checkup." He glanced at Wyatt. "Isn't it just like your aunt to worry about everybody, even the town busybody?" He turned back to Marilee. "And thanks to Miss Cora, you're just fine. That fractured arm will heal cleanly. No fragments, nothing shattered. A good thing you won't need pins or surgery. There's no reason you shouldn't heal without complications. Still, for your peace of mind, I'd be happy to order a medevac to take you to the hospital in Helena."

"It's not going to happen." Marilee looked pleadingly at Wyatt to agree with her. "No planes just yet. I'd rather stay on solid ground."

"She needs some time. We all do." Wyatt stood on the other side of the bed and closed a hand over hers. "When can she be moved? I'd like to take Marilee back to the ranch for some pampering."

Dr. Wheeler looked at his patient, reading the pain and exhaustion in her eyes, before turning to Wyatt with a quick shake of the head. "I don't think she's up for that long ride just yet. Why don't you stay here at the clinic and keep an eye on her? There's a bed in the other room, if you want to sleep. Once Elly and I have a few hours of rest, we'll be back to take a look at our patient and I'll decide if she can be released."

Elly set a syringe on the bedside cart. "You'll be dealing with some big-time pain for a little while. There's a full dose of Dilaudid here. When the pain gets to be too much to handle, show Wyatt how to add it to your IV."

"I can do it. . . . Not sure Wyatt's got the stomach to handle big-time drugs." Marilee could feel her eyes closing.

As they started out of the examining room, Wyatt followed, still eager for answers.

"Did Ledge leave a note behind?"

Dr. Wheeler shook his head. "I wish he had. I hate loose ends. A note would have answered all our questions. But I suppose a proud man like Ledge would choose death over being forced to face the contempt of the townspeople when they learned what he'd done."

Wyatt walked with them as far as the door of the clinic. "Ledge didn't seem suicidal to me. In fact, I'd describe him as smug and arrogant and believing himself above the law. He seemed to think that Harrison had no business locking him up, and that his lawyer would have him out of jail in no time."

Doc shook his head. "There's just no way of predicting how people will react when caught in a trap of their own making." As he turned away he added, "My phone is always on. If I'm tied up, leave me a message and I'll get back to you. Call me with any questions."

Questions were all he had, Wyatt thought. As he made

his way back to Marilee's room, his mind was filled with too many troubling questions. He hoped a long, hot shower and some sleep would bring him a measure of relief.

Loose ends. Like Doc, he didn't like them. And there were just too many. Messy bits and pieces. And all of them dangling just out of reach.

Or maybe he was just too weary to fit them all together now.

The clinic was deathly silent.

Wyatt chose to ignore the inviting bed in the room next to Marilee's, stretching out instead in the visitor's chair he'd pulled alongside her bed. He couldn't bear to leave her side for even a few hours. He had a terrible need to assure himself that she was really alive and safe and here with him.

He wasn't certain he would ever be able to completely dispel the fear and horror he'd experienced when he'd heard about the crash. Those images would stay with him for a very long time.

But there was something else keeping him too wired to think about sleep.

For the life of him, he couldn't figure out this vague uneasiness that had settled over him like a fog. He should be relieved that the threat posed by Ledge was now resolved. Knowing Archie, he would continue to pursue all the angles until the witnesses had signed documents attesting to what they knew and when they knew it. Then, hopefully, they could put this thing to rest.

Still, something didn't fit, and he couldn't put his finger on it.

He struggled to settle down and rest, but his mind refused to cooperate.

When the door opened he looked over, expecting to see Doc or Elly. Seeing Deputy Atkins walking toward him, he struggled to his feet.

"What're you doing here, Harrison?"

"Just hoping to clear up a few things." The lawman saw Marilee stir.

He shifted his attention back to Wyatt. "Sit down, son. This won't take long."

Wyatt sank back into the chair while the deputy remained standing at the foot of the bed. "You said that Craig Matson was willing to testify against Ledge. But you didn't bother to say where Craig is."

"I don't see that it's important."

"I'll decide what is and isn't important." The deputy's eyes grew flinty. "He's considered a witness to an alleged crime. I need to know where to find him."

Wyatt glanced at Marilee, who had come fully awake and was struggling to sit. He was at her side at once, lifting her to a sitting position and fluffing extra pillows behind her back to support her.

She gave him a grateful smile before reaching for his hand.

Wyatt looked over at the deputy. "I'm afraid I can't answer your question."

"Can't? Or won't?"

Something in Harrison's tone had Wyatt straightening. He released Marilee's hand and stood a little taller. "I'll give that information to Sheriff Wycliff when I go in to see him and make out my report."

"You'll give it to me now."

Wyatt felt a chill, and then a sudden rush of adrenaline. Bits and pieces were beginning to fall into place, though, as yet, they didn't make any more sense than Ledge's suicide. "Just as we arrived at Aunt Cora's campsite, she had a surprise intruder. Cal and some of the wranglers were already there and managed to fire off a couple of shots, but they couldn't stop him." He watched Harrison's eyes narrow. "At the time, we thought it might have been a random attack. But my aunt was in the middle of wilderness. That suggests to me that she had been deliberately targeted for the attack."

The deputy calmly, deliberately pulled his handgun from its holster.

Wyatt watched the movement, feeling a quick jitter of nerves. "Something didn't quite fit in that attack, and now I know why. Beyond our family, nobody knew the exact location of Aunt Cora's camp in the wilderness, or the fact that Marilee had survived the crash, except you and Ledge. And Ledge was in no position to contact anybody without your knowledge."

Harrison's tone was grim. "I knew that sooner or later you'd figure that out. That's why I'm here. You and your lady love will have to be eliminated, of course. You know too much. But first you're going to tell me where I can find Craig Matson."

Wyatt shook his head. "You don't really think I'd tell you."

"I know you will." Harrison Atkins walked to the side of the bed, keeping it between himself and Wyatt.

He aimed the pistol at Marilee's head. "You'll tell me what I want to know, or this pretty little lady will pay the price."

Wyatt's tone hardened. "Keep her out of this."

"She's in it, and has been since the two of you became . . . close. And now that you've made it clear to everyone in town how much she means to you, I doubt you'll be willing to sacrifice her life for Craig Matson's."

"Why are you doing this?" Wyatt gauged the distance across the bed, wondering how he could possibly reach the gun before it would discharge. If he was killed in the attempt, it wouldn't matter. His life didn't matter. But Marilee . . .

Could he leap far enough, fast enough, to save her life? He knew only that he had to try.

"I figure, with the two of you out of the picture, the rest of your family will be too distracted, or too devastated, to continue searching for the treasure."

"All of this just for some gold that could remain lost forever?"

"Why does that surprise you?" The deputy sneered. "I suppose, growing up in a fine, fancy ranch house built like a palace, the hunt for a lost fortune is merely an amusing way for you to spend your summer vacation." His tone lowered. Hardened. "For some of us, it's a chance to change our lives forever."

"You'd actually kill for it?"

"I'd kill for a whole lot less." He brought the gun close enough to Marilee's temple to make her flinch. "Now you'll tell me where Craig Matson is, or I'll blow her head off and you'll get to watch."

Hearing the note of finality in the deputy's voice, and seeing the gun so close to Marilee, caused the rebel inside Wyatt to snap.

Without a thought for his own safety he lunged across the bed, arms outstretched toward the man's throat. "You won't get away with this."

Harrison Atkins whirled and fired. An explosion of sound bounced off the walls and ceiling as the two men came together and fell to the floor in a wild tangle of arms and legs.

CHAPTER TWENTY-THREE

M arilee heard her own voice, high-pitched in horror, as she watched a thin line of blood slowly stain the front of Wyatt's shirt.

The two men were pummeling each other over and over. Desperation had them fighting with all the force and fury of mad dogs, teeth bared, guttural sounds coming from their throats as they battered and punched and bloodied one another.

For a moment Marilee thrilled to the fact that Wyatt had the upper hand as he landed a fist in the deputy's face that had Atkins falling backward, sending blood gushing from a nasty cut above his eye.

But when she saw Wyatt's face turn ashen, she knew that the bullet had taken its toll.

She looked at the night table, hoping for something, anything that she could toss at the deputy as a distraction. It was bare except for the syringe. But as she reached for it, it slipped from her fingers and was buried in the folds of the bed linens.

Before Wyatt could attempt another blow, Harrison's hand closed around the pistol. He scrambled to his feet, keeping the gun pointed directly at Wyatt's chest.

Through clenched teeth he hissed, "Now, McCord, you'll tell me what I want to know."

Wyatt was forced to struggle for every breath, fighting a heaviness in his chest that made his breathing labored. "Never. I gave my word."

"Is your word more important than the woman's life?"

Wyatt lifted a hand as if to protect her.

When he refused to speak, Harrison gave a hiss of impatience. "Your precious word just sealed your lover's fate."

As the deputy stepped to the bed and placed the gun against Marilee's temple, she struggled against the drug that left her feeling so weak she could barely lift her head from the pillow.

The drug.

She latched onto that thought. The same Dilaudid that had deadened her pain could render this monster helpless if administered in one sudden dose. But only if she could find the strength within herself to catch him by surprise and do what was necessary.

Her fingers fumbled under the covers for the syringe she'd managed to snag from the night table. In her half-conscious state she'd dropped it in the bedding, and now she could feel her last chance slipping away.

Her fingers were still slightly numb from the sedative. She flexed them beneath the blanket until she was certain she could make them work.

So close. So close, but she could feel herself losing the last bit of strength.

She breathed deeply, filling her lungs for the task ahead.

"Say good-bye to your lover, McCord."

In the tangled sheet Marilee's hand closed around the cold syringe and she prayed that she could hold on to it without giving away her intentions.

"I . . . know where Craig is." The words, barely above a whisper, had the deputy going very still.

His eyes narrowed as he leaned close to catch every word. "Tell me."

Marilee waited, gathering her courage, forcing herself to meet his narrowed gaze without flinching. If he had even a trace of suspicion, she would lose her only chance.

"He's . . ." She deliberately kept her whisper so soft, Harrison was forced to lean even closer.

Again she waited, though her heart was now pounding. Adrenaline began pumping through her veins, a certain sign that she would have but one chance to make this work. Once the adrenaline rush was over, she would be rendered as helpless as a newborn.

"Wyatt told me he was . . ."

When the deputy was so close she could feel his breath on her cheek, she freed her hand from the cover of the blankets and jammed the needle against his arm with all the strength she could muster.

For a moment her heart stopped when she felt the slight resistance as needle met tough skin.

Had her hand been stronger, her aim truer, she thought, she might have succeeded.

But just as fear of failure began to surface, she felt the syringe bite deep, penetrating his flesh.

"What the hell . . . ?" Caught by surprise, he jerked back. The gun discharged, firing wildly into the ceiling.

For a moment Atkins merely stared at the syringe that protruded from his flesh. Then, as he tore it loose and tossed it aside, he tried to take aim. His arm, already numb, refused to obey. While he watched in disbelief his legs began to tremble, no longer able to support his weight. The string of oaths he was trying to mutter became unintelligible babble as he dropped weakly to the floor.

The gun clattered from his grasp and Wyatt scrambled to retrieve it. While he dialed for help he kept a wary watch on the deputy who lay as quiet as death on the hard wooden floor. Then he dropped to one knee beside the bed and gathered Marilee close.

"You were amazing," he whispered against her temple.

"You didn't give me any choice. I thought he'd killed you." She looked at his stained shirt. "You're bleeding."

"I am?" Wyatt looked down at himself in surprise. In the excitement, he hadn't even been aware that he'd been shot. Now, as he saw the blood, he gradually became aware of a heaviness radiating from his chest area.

He pulled the ring of ambulance keys from his breast pocket, and a bullet pinged on the floor.

He and Marilee stared at it with solemn looks as they realized the enormity of what had just happened.

"Saved by a key." Wyatt sank down on the edge of the bed and caught Marilee's hands in his. With a shake of his head he muttered, "I guess Harrison's aim was

better than I realized. Thank heaven for you. The key
to my heart."

As he pressed his lips to hers, Marilee felt again the
quick jitter of adrenaline. Wyatt's kiss? She wondered. Or
the knowledge that she'd succeeded in saving his life?

Both, she decided.

Then, as the last vestiges of energy drained away
and the drug once more took over her reflexes, she lay
back, eyes closed, breathing slow and labored, as chaos
ensued.

The once-quiet clinic was suddenly alive with humanity.

A caravan of trucks from the Lost Nugget Ranch
chose that time to pull up to the clinic, bearing food from
Dandy and clean clothes from Wyatt's closet. Jesse and
Amy were the first to come running into the room, followed by Zane.

"I thought I heard gunshots . . ." Jesse skidded to a halt,
with Zane on his heels.

Zane peered at the figure on the floor. "Is that Harrison
Atkins?"

"Yeah."

Before Wyatt could say more, Cora and Cal hurried
inside and stepped gingerly around the unconscious man.

"What . . . ?" Cal stared around in disbelief at the signs
of a deadly struggle. Bloodstains smeared the walls and
floor, as well as the front of Wyatt's shirt.

They all looked up as Sheriff Wycliff stormed into the
room. "I was afraid I wouldn't get here in time." He pointed
to his deputy. "What did you hit him with, Wyatt?"

"Not me. Marilee. I think he'll be out for a couple
of hours."

"Lee?" Ernie Wycliff looked skeptical. "Doc said you had some pretty painful injuries. How could someone so badly injured manage to subdue my two-hundred-pound deputy?"

Marilee pointed to the syringe lying on the floor beside Harrison Atkins. "Just doing what I know best."

The sheriff gave her a look of admiration. "However you managed it, you did just fine."

"Thanks." She was grateful for Wyatt's hand on hers. She was feeling oddly out of focus and knew it was the drug. For someone so accustomed to being in charge, this was an uncomfortable feeling.

She roused herself enough to say, "Wyatt came close to being killed. Even though the bullet didn't penetrate, Doc needs to take a look at him."

"Hey, baby, didn't you know that Superman never gets hurt?"

While the others joined in a chorus of nervous laughter, the sheriff pushed a speed-dial button on his phone and spoke tersely. "No rest for the weary, Doc. You're needed back at the clinic." He paused. "No. It's not Lee this time. It's Wyatt McCord. He's been shot, but like Superman, he claims the bullet bounced off his chest."

They heard the note of excitement in the voice on the other end, followed by a sudden disconnect.

"How did you happen to be here, Ernie? I tried phoning you and got no answer."

At Wyatt's question the sheriff bent and cuffed his unconscious deputy before getting to his feet. "I was busy taking a call from a man named Archie"—he stared pointedly at Wyatt—"a bit of a shady character, who claimed to be a friend of yours."

"He is. And has been for years. What did Archie say?"

"He wanted me to know that the substitute employee who'd been hired by Ledge Cowling disappeared before he could be deposed. Archie figured Ledge had warned the man off. But since Ledge was in a cell, and only made one call to his lawyer, it meant that someone else had warned the man to take a hike. The phone company confirmed that Harrison had made a number of calls last night, which would disprove his claim of having fallen asleep right after you left. Harrison was, in fact, very busy, phoning not only the substitute mechanic at Razorback to warn him to get lost, but also an ex-convict who owed him a favor. The state police picked up the ex-con an hour ago. His vehicle bore several bullet holes. I'm sure when they get time to compare them to the ones from Cal's rifle used to ward off that late-night robbery attempt at Miss Cora's campsite, they'll prove to be a perfect match."

"So it wasn't a random thief?" Cora sank down into the chair vacated by Wyatt. "What was this all about, Sheriff?"

"I've asked the state police investigators to handle this. I'm sure in time we'll be able to piece it all together."

Wyatt glanced around at the family. "Harrison admitted that he did it for the lost fortune. He thought by getting rid of us"—he glanced at Marilee and tightened his grasp on her hand—"the rest of the family would be too devastated to continue the search."

"Oh, dear heaven. First there was the danger to Jesse and Amy. And now the two of you." Cora lifted a trembling hand to her lips. "I know this wasn't what Coot wanted for any of you when he enticed you to stay and continue his search."

Jesse hurried over to kneel in front of her. "Don't dwell on it, Aunt Cora. We're not responsible for every crazy person who wants to steal the gold."

"But don't you see? Everyone believes there's a curse connected to the gold. Maybe the true curse is that history will keep repeating itself." She touched a hand to her great-nephew's cheek. "This all began when a madman coveted what our ancestor had found. Grizzly Markham slit Jasper McCord's throat in the night and stole the sack of nuggets. And now there are others willing to do violence, and all for the lure of a fortune that may never be found."

"I know." He took her hands in his and kissed her cheek gently. "But history doesn't have to repeat itself. We're forewarned now. We'll know better than to let down our guard again."

Dr. Wheeler came bustling into the room. When he saw the crowd he paused. Then, seeing the weariness etched on the faces of Wyatt and Marilee, he took charge.

"Sorry. You folks will have to wait in the outer room. Now I have two patients to look after."

Amy and Jesse led Cora away while the sheriff and Cal hauled the unconscious deputy from the room.

Zane stood back, filming everything, until Doc ordered him out, too.

The doctor paused beside Wyatt. "You strong enough to stand?"

"Yeah. The bullet hit a ring of keys in my pocket, and I guess one of the keys cut me. It's nothing. Except that I feel like there's an elephant sitting on my chest."

"From the force of that bullet hitting you at a hundred miles an hour. Come with me." With his hand under

Wyatt's arm, the doctor led him from the room and helped him onto an examination table.

A short time later Wyatt returned to Marilee's room, trailed by Elly Carson in her crisp white uniform.

The doctor looked up from Marilee's bedside.

"It seems all we do is disturb your sleep." Wyatt's discomfort had lessened considerably after Elly had administered a shot to numb the pain.

Dr. Wheeler chuckled. "No problem. I'll catch up on sleep later."

"Are you done with us, Doc?"

"You can go." Dr. Wheeler nodded. "I just hope you know how lucky you are, Wyatt."

"Yeah. I know." Wyatt paused. "How about Marilee? Can she leave with me?"

The doctor gave her a cool, assessing look. "Are you feeling up to leaving?"

"Oh, yes." Marilee felt her spirits lift as she turned to Elly Carson. "Can you help me dress?"

"All I have is a spare set of scrubs."

"They'll do nicely."

Doc herded Wyatt through the doorway and into the waiting room, where the entire family had gathered.

Wyatt turned to Jesse. "If you want to head back to the ranch, Marilee and I will join you there later."

"You don't have to stay for observation or anything?"

Wyatt shook his head.

As the others began filing out the door, his great-aunt paused and returned to his side.

"Cal and I tried to see Delia, but she didn't answer our knock. I'm worried about her, Wyatt. She has to be feeling so alone in her grief. I know you have so much to do already, but in the next day or so, if you could just pay a call. Would you mind . . . ?"

Seeing Marilee standing in the doorway, Wyatt cut off his aunt with a quick kiss to the cheek. "I'll stop by. And I won't leave until she agrees to talk to me."

"Thank you, dear." With that assurance, Cora took her leave.

Wyatt hurried over to wrap an arm around Marilee's shoulders, and the two made their way to the ambulance.

When Marilee was comfortably seated in the passenger side, Wyatt turned the key in the ignition. "I thought I'd take you back to your apartment first, so you can change into your own clothes."

Marilee leaned her head back and smiled. "Oh, it feels so good to be out of the clinic. I don't mind bringing other people there, but it's not my favorite place to stay."

"I know what you mean." Across town he guided the emergency vehicle into her garage, then carried her up the stairs to her apartment.

"Wyatt, I'm perfectly capable of walking."

"Relax and enjoy the ride." He brushed his mouth over hers before setting her down in the middle of her bed. With great care he slid the top over her head. "Tell me what clothes you want and I'll find them."

She gave a firm shake of her head. "You're going to the other room. When I'm dressed, I'll let you know."

"You've decided to get overly modest on me now?"

She laughed. "I've decided to take back my power. Now get out."

He shot her a wicked grin before strolling from the room.

*   *   *

Wyatt paced the length of Marilee's apartment and back, mulling all that had happened. The plane crash. The late-night gunman in his aunt's camp. The endless ride to the wilderness and back with Marilee wounded and in pain. And now they'd been given a second chance. He wasn't about to blow it this time.

Marilee walked from her bedroom wearing a gauzy mint-green sundress and strappy sandals, her hair long and loose spilling down her shoulders.

At the sight of her Wyatt sucked in a breath. "Now that's a big improvement over faded scrubs. Have I told you how beautiful you are?"

"Not lately."

"Sorry. I've been a little preoccupied. You're so beautiful you take my breath away."

"Thank you." She gave an exaggerated flutter of her lashes.

She was still laughing as Wyatt dropped to one knee in front of her.

Her smile faded. "What are you doing?"

"Isn't this what a guy is supposed to do when asking—"

She clapped a hand over his mouth to halt his words. Sudden, unexpected tears filled her eyes and she brushed at them. She could feel herself hyperventilating. "Wyatt, don't do this to me."

"Don't do this to you?" He looked puzzled, and then, as he came slowly to his feet, it dawned. "You're afraid."

"I am not. I'm just feeling . . . too emotional." She scrubbed at the tears that had trickled down her cheeks. "Maybe it's the accident. Everything's happening so fast. There hasn't been time to let it all sink in, I guess. Oh, don't you see? I've worked so hard to be free. To be independent. I vowed I would never let someone have power over me."

"Power? Is that what you think this is about? Marilee . . ."

"No. Of course not. You're the kindest, most amazing man I've ever known. But I've . . ." She was blubbering, but she couldn't seem to stop herself. "I've spent years fighting to live on my own terms. And now, right now, I don't want to think beyond today. I'm not ready to face the future and make a lifetime commitment. Not today. Not now. Don't you see?"

"I guess I have no choice but to hear what you're saying. I shouldn't have sprung this on you." His tone went flat. "You've been through way too much. You need time. Maybe I'll head back to the ranch and give you some space."

Marilee knew that once again she'd hurt him deeply. If she let him go, how could she ever make things right between them? But she was simply too overwhelmed at this moment to think of how she could ever make amends.

As she watched him walk through the door and pull it closed behind him, she experienced a moment of absolute panic, aware that this time she'd stepped way over the line. How many times could a proud man like Wyatt McCord accept rejection before he simply walked away forever?

Why did she always have to hurt the ones she loved? Was it pride, or was it, as he'd said, fear?

Whatever the cause of her obstinate nature, she was about to pay a terrible price.

She absorbed an almost crippling pain around her heart.

This time, she knew, as she heard the sound of his Harley roaring away, she'd gone too far.

And she was too exhausted, too overcome with emotion, to do a thing about it.

CHAPTER TWENTY-FOUR

———◆———

Jesse and Zane strolled into the barn, where Wyatt was mucking out a stall. The back of his work shirt was stained with sweat, his boots caked with mud and dung, attesting to the hours he'd been working.

Jesse leaned on the rail to watch. "Did Doc say you could do this so soon after that gunshot?"

"I wasn't hit by the bullet." Wyatt kept his back to his cousins.

"I know." Jesse exchanged a look with Zane. "But Doc said you should take it easy for a few days."

When there was no response he tried again. "We noticed that you skipped dinner last night, and Dandy said you didn't bother with breakfast this morning before heading out here. You planning on driving into town later to check on Lee?"

"I'm sure she's just fine." Wyatt barely paused in his work.

"Amy talked to her a little while ago and got a bit worried."

That had Wyatt's movements going still, though he didn't turn around.

"Amy said Lee was awfully quiet. Just said she was mending, and would probably see Doc later today."

"Good." Wyatt forked dung into the wagon with more force than necessary.

"Word from town is that Delia took Ledge's body to Helena for burial. Her neighbor said she was hoping to avoid a public display."

"I don't blame her." Wyatt continued shoveling. "Small towns just can't resist enjoying gossip. The uglier the better."

"Well." Jesse and Zane exchanged another look before Jesse said, "We thought we'd head on over to the saloon tonight. Want to join us?"

"No thanks."

"If you change your mind, just let me know." Jesse dug his hands into his pockets and sauntered out of the barn, with Zane trailing behind.

When they were gone Wyatt stood for long, silent moments staring into space. He'd played so many scenes over and over in his mind. The helplessness he'd experienced when Harrison held a gun to Marilee's head. The desperation that had him leaping into the path of a bullet rather than risk losing her. The pride and awe at her courage in overcoming the effects of the drugs in order to end the gunman's madness. And the wave of pure relief when he'd finally been allowed to take her home.

Marilee had made it perfectly clear how she felt about losing her independence. And still he'd foolishly forced the issue. He'd allowed his own selfish needs to drive her away. Again.

Maybe they weren't meant to be together. Maybe they had very different goals. But being with her made him happy. Being apart was killing him. And he had no one to blame but himself and his foolish heart. He had convinced himself that, having come so close to death, she would fall into his arms and beg him to keep her safe for the rest of her life.

When would he learn that the woman who owned his heart wasn't like other women? She didn't need a hero, or a warrior. She needed her freedom, her independence. And she saw him as a threat to both.

He swore and bent to his task.

Cora stepped into the barn and peered around until her eyes adjusted to the gloom. After the sunlight of her studio, this place was like a cave.

When she spotted her nephew at one of the benches, oiling a leather harness, she walked over and took a seat beside him.

"Jesse said you've been spending your time out here."

He glanced over. "Making up for all those years when I couldn't be here."

"Yes. It must have been hard, leaving your only home." She placed a hand on his, stilling his movements. "I've heard that you and Marilee have had a spat."

When he said nothing she went on. "I don't believe in giving advice. Each of us must come to terms with life in our own way. And I know you're wise enough to figure things out. But I would think, Gold Fever being so small, that sooner or later the two of you will have to meet. I hope, when you do, that you can at least be friendly."

He looked over, and she was startled by the sadness in his eyes. She'd expected anger. Or perhaps cool disdain. But this was almost more than she could bear.

"I don't think I'd know how to be just her friend. But I won't embarrass you, Aunt Cora. I can be civil."

Getting quickly to her feet she cradled his face in her hands and bent to press a kiss to his cheek. "I'm sorry, Wyatt. I wish I knew how to make things better." She stepped back and took a deep breath. "I spoke with Frances Tucker. She said Delia is home now and refuses to see anyone. I know she'd never agree to see me, but I was hoping that, since she's had contact with you, she might allow you a brief visit. That is, if you're willing."

Wyatt gave a slight nod of his head. "I'll try, Aunt Cora. But I doubt that she'll want to see any of the McCord family."

"All you can do is try, dear. Sometimes in life, that's all any of us can do."

When she walked away, Wyatt set aside the harness, the cleaner, and the rag and got heavily to his feet. The last thing he wanted to do was go to town. But there was no way he could ever refuse his great-aunt.

All you can do is try, dear.

Wasn't that what he was doing each morning? Getting out of bed, just to try to get through another day?

Wyatt parked the ranch truck in front of the neat white house and walked determinedly up the steps.

When the door opened, Delia took one look at him and turned pale before she started to close the door.

"Wait." Wyatt's hand shot out to keep her from shutting the door in his face.

Delia's eyes filled. "I know why you're here. I can't tell you how sorry I am about . . . everything."

"I'm here," Wyatt said softly, "because I know my neighbor is hurting from the loss of her only brother, and my family and I want to know how we can help."

Delia's eyes went wide with stunned surprise. Then, remembering her manners, she moved stiffly aside. "Please. Come in."

He stepped inside and stood awkwardly in the little front parlor. Both Wyatt and Delia seemed at a loss for words.

Wyatt decided to take charge. "I don't know about you, but I could use some tea."

The old woman was too shocked to react.

With his hand beneath her elbow, Wyatt steered her toward the kitchen.

While Wyatt held a chair, Delia sat numbly. He put the kettle on the stove and, after a brief search of her cupboards, located some dainty cups.

Though Delia remained frozen at the table, a lifetime of good manners had her rising to the occasion. "There are some cookies in that cupboard."

Wyatt filled a plate and set it on the table while Delia sat stiffly.

When the kettle boiled, he made tea and filled two cups.

Delia stared, transfixed, at the tabletop, unable to meet his eyes.

Wyatt leaned toward her and took her hand in his. It was cold as ice.

"I'm sorry about Ledge."

"How can you be sorry?" She took a breath and forced herself to say the things she was thinking. "The sheriff told me he found pages from your ancestor's diary in Ledge's things. And dozens of Coot's maps and drawings, even though he'd told me he had all those old papers shredded." Her lower lip trembled. "I swear to you I didn't know."

"Of course you didn't."

Her head came up. She looked at him. Really looked. And saw the compassion in his eyes. "You believe me?"

He nodded.

Before he could say more there was a knock on the door.

When Delia started to get up he held out a hand. "Would you like me to get that?"

"Yes, please. And send whoever it is away."

He left the kitchen and walked to the front parlor. When he opened the door and saw Marilee standing there, he felt as if he'd just taken a blow to the midsection. All the air left his lungs, and for a moment he couldn't find his voice.

She looked equally stunned. "Sorry." She put a hand on the opened door to steady herself. "I saw the ranch truck and thought it was Amy." She was babbling, she knew, but she was so startled to see Wyatt standing here, she couldn't seem to stop. "She phoned me to ask if I'd look in on Delia. It seems your aunt is very worried about her."

"Yeah. That's why I'm here." He stepped stiffly aside. "She's in the kitchen."

As Marilee made her way through the parlor, Wyatt followed behind, feeling an empty ache at the sway of her hips, the drift of fiery hair around her shoulders. He could hardly bear to look at her. And yet he couldn't look away. He felt like a drowning man reaching out for a safety net, only to have it snatched away each time he got close.

"Marilee." Delia looked up. "I suppose you're here with Wyatt."

"I'm here alone." The word hung in the air as Marilee and Wyatt stared at each other with naked hunger.

Seeing it, Delia said softly, "I'd know a good deal about being alone. I've decided to sell my place here and move to Shelbyville to be closer to my cousin. She's my last living relative."

"But you won't know anybody there. Won't you miss your friends and neighbors?"

"I will." Her voice grew sad. "But I doubt they'll miss me." She quickly changed the subject. "We're having tea. Will you join us?"

At Marilee's nod, Wyatt reached for another cup and saucer and proceeded to pour tea before setting in on the table.

"I was just telling Wyatt how sorry I am. I wasn't aware of the fact that Ledge had many of Coot's old papers hidden among his things." Delia folded her arms over her chest, as though the mere mention of such things left her chilled. "Bless him, Wyatt says he believes me."

Marilee rubbed a hand over the older woman's arm. "I believe you, too, Delia."

"That's more than kind of you. Of both of you. Thank you. It gives me comfort to know this."

When Marilee took the seat beside hers, Delia surprised her by touching a finger to her cheek. "Are those tears?"

"I'm just"—Marilee struggled to stem the flow—"feeling emotional."

"Of course you are. So much has happened. It's the way of things, I suppose. Life deals us blows, and some of us remain standing, while others fall." Delia fell silent for a moment before giving out a long, deep sigh and turning to Wyatt. "I thought I was so strong because I remained standing in the face of life's pain. Now, I realize that standing isn't enough." She took a deep breath before saying, "I once hurt your grandfather. Hurt him deeply."

"I know."

At Wyatt's response she shook her head. "But you don't know the whole story. No one knows." She paused, going back in her mind. "I loved Coot McCord. Loved that man with all my heart. But my family felt he was beneath them. At that time his ranch was little more than a hardscrabble patch of forest and prairie. Everyone in town knew how he used to go off for weeks at a time, all alone in the wilderness, searching for his ancestor's lost treasure. My parents warned me that I'd live to regret a life of loneliness married to such a crazy man." She shook her head. "I wouldn't listen. We used to meet on horseback at our secret place, in the foothills of Treasure Chest. And when Coot asked me to marry him, I agreed. We made plans to run away and marry without my family's knowledge. I was so wildly in love, and so happy. But I made the mistake of sharing my good news with Ledge." She withdrew her hands and folded them in her lap. "Ledge agreed with our parents that I was nothing more than a foolish girl."

She paused a moment. "On one of Coot's forays into the wilderness he got caught in a nasty blizzard, miles from home, and spent a couple of weeks on a ranch the other side of Treasure Chest Mountain. Ledge learned that the rancher, Ben Moffitt, had a pretty daughter, and, knowing I had a jealous streak a mile wide, he made sure that I heard about her, too. Coot tried to convince me that he'd merely taken shelter from the storm, but I wouldn't believe him. We had a terrible argument. When Ledge learned of it he inserted himself into our business, making thing even worse. Ledge called Coot a liar and a fool if he thought he could ever win my family's trust. That pushed Coot over the limit of his patience. Blows were exchanged, and when it was over, Ledge had a broken nose and enough bruises that he needed weeks to mend. He threatened to have Coot arrested for assault."

"And I . . . I told Coot that I never wanted to see him again. Of course I didn't mean it. I just spoke out of fear and anger. If I'd taken the time to cool down, I would have let Coot know that I didn't mean any of the things I'd screamed at him. But he gave me no chance to set things right. Coot was so hurt and so furious that he took off on his horse for parts unknown. He was gone for months. I kept thinking that he'd come back and we'd make up. Instead, when he finally returned, he was accompanied by his brand-new wife, pretty little Annie Moffitt."

Tears filled Marilee's eyes. "I'm sorry, Delia. Is this why you never married?"

"How could I, when I still loved . . ." Delia paused, too overcome to speak.

After several long moments of silence she found her voice. "The first time I saw Coot in town with his Annie, I thought my heart would break and I would surely die right there on the spot. But in time I learned that people don't die of a broken heart. They just die a little at a time. I learned that living was even harder than dying. Every time

I saw Coot and Annie, another piece of my heart broke, until, in time, I felt as though I had no heart at all. But I held my head high, and I pretended not to care about anyone or anything."

Her voice trembled. "When Annie died, I actually entertained the thought that maybe Coot would pay a call, but he never did. Why should he? By then I was a dried-up old spinster with a mean, spiteful tongue. The laughing-stock of the town. When Coot died, I thought maybe the pain would end, but it hasn't." She turned toward Wyatt and swallowed. "That day you and Marilee came to visit, I looked at you and saw your grandfather. The same hand-some face. The same charming smile. The same laughing blue eyes. You were so kind to me. So sweet and funny. And for the first time in fifty years I felt a little bit of my heart start to beat again." Hot tears spilled down her cheeks. "And then Ledge tried to kill even that tiny piece with his spiteful behavior."

Unable to bear the old woman's sorrow, Marilee pushed away from the table and wrapped her arms around her. "Don't dwell on it now, Delia. Don't let the bitterness eat at your soul again. It's time to let go and start to live again, before it's too late."

Delia bowed her head and sobbed. "Don't you see? It is too late. I've spent a lifetime without the only man I ever loved, because of my foolish pride. And all I have left are the bitter memories of an old maid."

At her words of anguish Marilee glanced over her head and met Wyatt's gaze.

She had to struggle to swallow the lump in her throat. "Thank you for sharing your story, Delia. I needed to be reminded how rare and fragile love can be. Sometimes, by holding on too tightly to old . . . complications, we fail to see how simple the path before us can be."

Delia glanced from Marilee to Wyatt, who were staring at each other with matching looks, as though they'd both been struck by a bolt from heaven.

Wyatt pulled himself together first and leaned over to kiss Delia's cheek. "Thank you."

She touched a hand to the spot. "For what?"

"As Marilee said, for sharing your story." He shoved away from the table. "I'll leave the two of you to visit."

In a hurry to escape he let himself out of the house and walked to the truck. Before he could climb inside Marilee raced down the steps.

Breathless, she came to a sudden halt in front of him.

At the dark look in his eyes she swallowed. "Please don't go, Wyatt. I've been such a fool."

"You aren't the only one." He studied her with a look that had her heart stuttering. A look so intense, she couldn't look away. "I've been beating myself up for days, because I wanted things to go my way or no way."

"There's no need. You're not the only one." Her voice was soft, throaty. "You've always respected my need to be independent. But I guess I fought the battle so long, I forgot how to stop fighting even after I'd won the war."

"You can fight me all you want. You know Superman is indestructible." Again that long, speculative look. "I know I caught you off guard with that proposal. It won't happen again. Even when I understood your fear of commitment, I had to push to have things my way. And even though I still want more, I'm willing to settle for what you're willing to give, as long as we can be together."

She gave a deep sigh. "You mean it?"

"I do."

"Oh, Wyatt. I was so afraid I'd driven you away forever."

He continued studying her. "Does this mean you're suffering another change of heart?"

"My heart doesn't need to change. In my heart, I've always known how very special you are. It's my head that can't seem to catch up." She gave a shake of her head, as though to clear it. "I'm so glad you understand me. I've spent so many years fighting to be my own person, it seems I can't bear to give up the battle."

A slow smile spread across his face, changing it from darkness to light. "Marilee, if it's a sparring partner you want, I'm happy to sign on. And if, in time, you ever decide you want more, I'm your man."

He framed her face with his hands and lowered his head, kissing her long and slow and deep until they were both sighing with pleasure.

Her tears started again, but this time they were tears of joy.

Wyatt brushed them away with his thumbs and traced the tracks with his lips. Marilee sighed at the tenderness. It was one of the things she most loved about this man.

Loved.

Why did she find it so hard to say what she was feeling? Because, her heart whispered, love meant commitment and promises and forever after, and that was more than she was willing to consider. At least for now.

After a moment he caught her hand.

"Where are we going?"

"Your place. It's closer than the ranch, and we've wasted too much time already."

"I can't leave the ambulance . . ."

"All right." He turned away from the ranch truck and led her toward her vehicle. "See how easy I am?"

At her little laugh he added, "I'm desperate for some time alone with you."

Alone.

She thought about that word. She'd been alone for so long. What he was offering had her heart working overtime. He was willing to compromise in order to be with her.

She was laughing through her tears as she turned the key in the ignition. The key that had saved his life.

"Wyatt McCord, I can't think of anything I'd rather be than alone with you."

CHAPTER TWENTY-FIVE

Marilee glanced at her bedside clock. "When I left, I told Delia that I'd be right back."

Beside her, Wyatt chuckled. "Two hours went by like two minutes."

"It may feel that way to us. But poor Delia must be wondering what in the world we were thinking, rushing away like that. Come on." She caught Wyatt's hand and together they made their way down the stairs.

They were across town within minutes.

When they walked up the steps to Delia's house, the older woman greeted them with a rare smile. "If I didn't know better, I'd say the two of you managed to find something good to share on this strange day."

"We have." Marilee touched a hand to Wyatt's. "And after hearing your story, I have to agree with you, Delia. Wyatt is just like his grandfather."

The old woman led them inside. "That he is, dear."

Wyatt leaned down to kiss Delia's cheek. "I guess

now it's your turn to make some choices. You spoke about leaving Gold Fever and going to live with your cousin. Maybe you should consider another choice. You can continue to live with regrets as before, or you can take what's left of your life and make it all you'd hoped it could be."

Delia was shaking her head. "With the town knowing about Ledge's crimes, I'll just be fodder for gossip."

"They won't blame you for the sins of your brother. This town is better than that."

The old woman gave a long, deep sigh. "I've wasted so many years, I wouldn't even know where to begin."

Marilee touched a hand to Delia's shoulder. "I'd know a thing or two about fighting old battles. Sometimes, they go on for so long, nobody can remember how they started, or just what they were fighting for. All that anger and resentment, and all that wasted energy, could be put to better use. You've made friends with your neighbor, Frances, haven't you?"

The old woman shrugged. "She refused to be put off when she first moved here and I tried to ignore her. After a while, she just wore me down. And frankly, I'm so glad to have a good friend like Frances."

"You see? There are lots more neighbors in Gold Fever who would like to be your friend, Delia. Sometimes you just have to reach out and let them know."

The older woman gave a shake of her head. "I've held everyone at arm's length for such a long time, I wouldn't even know how to begin."

Wyatt surprised her and himself by saying, "You can start by accepting our invitation to come out to the ranch with us for dinner."

"Oh, I couldn't. Your aunt Cora and I haven't spoken in . . ."

She stopped herself. Swiped at her eyes with the backs of her hands. And tried again. "Sorry. That was the old Delia talking." Her lips trembled as she struggled to smile. "The new Delia would . . ." She took a breath then tried again, a bit more forcefully. "The new Delia would love to go with you."

Marilee looked at Wyatt, his arm around this trembling old woman, and felt her heart fill to the brim.

His generosity was another thing she admired about him. There was so much goodness in him.

They made their way to the ambulance parked at the curb. With Delia seated between them, they started toward the Lost Nugget.

Wyatt spoke into his cell phone. "Dandy. Tell my aunt and cousins that we'll be home for dinner. We're bringing a guest. Delia Cowling."

He slipped the phone into his shirt pocket, and that had him thinking about the bullet that had nearly taken him away from all this. He had the ambulance, and a ring of keys to thank for this moment. And the kindness of the Fates.

"I think, to add to the festive occasion, we ought to turn on the lights and siren." He turned to Delia. "What do you say?"

"Oh, heavens no." She covered her mouth with her hand before giving it a second thought. "Sorry. That was the old Delia. The new Delia says yes. That would be so exciting."

Beside her, Marilee said sternly, "The old Marilee says you'll be breaking the law."

Wyatt winked. "This old rebel says he doesn't care. A celebration requires some noise."

The two exchanged a long look, then broke out into peals of laughter.

As they sped along the open highway, lights flashing, siren blasting, Delia found herself laughing along with them in absolute delight. Despite all the heartache, and all the turmoil, she was sharing a ride with Coot's grandson, heading out to Coot's ranch for the first time in over fifty years, and having the time of her life.

"Sheriff Wycliff." Cora greeted him warmly and led him into the great room, where the entire family, as well as Delia and Cal Randall, had gathered after supper. "If you had let us know that you were coming by, we'd have delayed dinner."

"Thanks, Miss Cora. I ate at the Fortune Saloon. The place was crawling with people, and all of them speculating about what happened."

He glanced at Delia, seated on the big sofa beside Cora. Would wonders never cease? How had the town gossip managed to end a lifetime feud with the McCord family?

That had him wondering just how much he could say without causing her pain.

He glanced at Wyatt and Marilee, close together in front of the fireplace. "Good to see you two looking as good as new."

Marilee laughed. "I wish someone would tell my body. Every time I try to do the least little thing, I ache all over."

"As Dr. Wheeler told you, dear, you just have to give it time." Cora was still reeling with delight at the sight of

Wyatt and Marilee together again. Apparently they had mended their latest tiff. They both looked relaxed and happy.

She indicated a tray on which rested steaming cups of coffee. "Will you have some, Sheriff?"

"Thank you. I will." He sipped, then explained why he was there.

"The state police have been conducting their investigation. As near as they can piece together, they've learned that Ledge . . ." He turned to Delia. "Begging your pardon, ma'am. Your brother was investing heavily with Harrison in some land ventures for future airports, and gave in to the temptation to use bank funds. In order to cover it up, Harrison coerced him into sharing what information he'd acquired regarding the lost fortune."

He sipped his coffee again, then settled onto a nearby chair. "Their plan was to scare away the family so they could be free to hunt without intruders finding out about them. Because trucks make too much noise, they'd been hauling heavy equipment using a team of horses to avoid being detected by any wranglers in the area. But they figured it was a good bet their tracks could be spotted from the air. Which is why you became a double threat to them, Lee. You fly often enough to notice anything out of the ordinary. And once you and Wyatt became more than friends, Harrison figured it was only a matter of time until you conveyed your thoughts to the McCord family."

Cora set down her cup. "Did Ledge agree to this?"

The sheriff shrugged. "Near as the state police can tell, Ledge was a very reluctant partner. He had, in fact, gone so far as to notify a bank examiner about the money, and was hoping to cut a deal. Harrison was actually plotting each step and calling the shots. It was Harrison who disabled the air bag in the ambulance. Now that I've seen the state police report, I realize that he changed that to hide his deed. And when Ledge learned that Harrison had once again sabotaged Marilee's plane with the hope of silencing forever both Lee and Wyatt, Ledge rushed out to the airport, only to find Wyatt alive. By then, we suspect, he feared for his own life and was too afraid to tell anyone."

The sheriff turned to Wyatt. "When your friend Archie gets signed testimony from Craig Matson and the young mechanic at Razorback, we'll know more. Right now we're going on the assumption that Harrison made most of these vile plans on his own, and he kept Ledge in the dark until it was too late for him to stop the momentum."

He turned to the others. "The state police have uncovered excavating equipment and precious metal detectors that were apparently delivered under cover of darkness and hauled out to Treasure Chest and hidden in several caves. Harrison figured he could work undetected as long as Lee's plane was grounded."

The sheriff set aside his empty cup. "It will be months before the state police wrap up their investigation." He shook his head. "I'm sorry about Ledge and Harrison, but I'm glad you two were spared. Sometimes, the Fates are cruel. And sometimes they give us a second chance."

That had Marilee and Wyatt turning toward each other. Though they spoke not a word, the look they shared spoke volumes.

"See you all later."

As the others were distracted bidding the sheriff good night, Wyatt caught Marilee's hand and led her from the room and up the stairs to his suite. Once inside he closed the door and watched as she looked around.

"So this is where you grew up."

"This is it." He continued to lean against the door, wanting to touch her, but knowing if he did, he wouldn't be able to stop. He still couldn't believe his good fortune.

"It's a lot bigger here than I'd imagined. Didn't it seem strange having so many generations under one roof?"

"That was my normal." He chuckled. "Didn't it seem strange having no family but your parents as you moved all over the world?"

She laughed. "Good point. It was my normal."

"Do you think there's any way your normal and mine could ever coexist?"

She looked over and felt her heart take a slow dip. "Are you thinking about proposing again?"

"That depends. Are you thinking of accepting?"

She couldn't quite meet his eye. "I'm not sure. Not that it matters. I don't think you're serious. After all, last time you proposed, you were on one knee. Isn't that traditional?"

"Last time, you weren't very receptive to my proposal. I've decided that you and I aren't meant to be traditional. I'm hoping you like this proposal better."

"And just what are you proposing?"

He walked to a cabinet and removed a tiny box. He opened it to reveal a simple platinum band.

"This was my mother's. I'm proposing that, if you accept this, it means we throw caution to the wind and just take the leap."

"Oh, Wyatt." She stared at the ring for long minutes. "What if we take the leap and fall?"

"People fall, Marilee. And when they do, they pick themselves up and try again." He gave a wry smile. "I'd be an expert on that."

Without warning, she held out her hand.

He shot her a questioning look before she wriggled her fingers and extended the third finger of her left hand. "Why are you looking at me like that?"

He hesitated. "Like what?"

"Like I've just dropped down from another planet."

"I'm just wondering who you are and what you've done with Marilee?"

"It's still me, Wyatt." She stretched out her finger. "Why don't you try it on?"

He did as she asked.

As the ring slid onto her finger she surprised herself and him by bursting into tears.

At once he opened his arms to comfort her. "Hey now, I didn't mean to make you cry."

She flung herself into his arms. And clung. And wept. And blubbered, "Here I am, sobbing like some weak, silly teen."

All the while he held her, Wyatt's heart plummeted. This had been a mistake. Another terrible misstep that she was already regretting.

Finally, she pushed a little away.

Before she could say a word he whispered, "Look, I know you don't want to be tied down. I would never do that to you. You don't have to wear my mother's ring, or make any promises that smother you. I'll understand. I know this is all new to you, and that you're feeling a little overwhelmed by so much family. I promise you, they'll back off and give you all the space you need. And best of all, if you give them a chance, they'll love you just the way I do, and accept that you need your freedom."

When she opened her mouth he went on a little too quickly, "Don't say a thing. I know marriage isn't for everyone. And I won't press you. But I don't want to settle for a few nightly visits and a lot of good-byes for the rest of our lives. I want it all, Marilee. When you're ready, I want love, marriage, forever after. As the sheriff said, we got another chance. I don't want to squander it. I want to spend the rest of my life with you. I'll do whatever it takes . . ."

She put a hand to his mouth. "Wyatt, you don't have to convince me. If I didn't know before, I certainly know now just how foolish I'd be to throw away what we have. I want what you want. Love, marriage, forever."

He stared at her in astonishment. "You're not just saying that because it's what I want?"

"It's what I want, too."

He stared deeply into her eyes. "Oh, Marilee, you've just made me the happiest man in the world."

"And I'm the luckiest girl."

"Not girl. Woman," he growled against her mouth. "A thoroughly independent woman. And all I'll ever want in this life."

He could wait no longer to kiss her. With a sigh he dragged her close and slowly, reverently nibbled her lips, tasting the salt of her tears.

But, he thought with a soaring heart, these, at last, were happy tears.

"Aunt Cora." Holding firmly to Marilee's hand, Wyatt watched as Dandy brought in a tray of champagne glasses, as he'd requested, and began passing them around to the family members gathered there.

Everyone looked up in silence.

"Marilee and I have an announcement." He turned to Marilee, and the two of them shared a smile so radiant, it seemed to light up the entire room. "She's agreed to make me the happiest man in the . . ."

Before he could say more his cousins were slapping him on the back, and Amy was hugging Marilee like a long-lost sister.

Then it was Cal's turn to shake Wyatt's hand, while Cora embraced the young woman.

Suddenly everyone was talking at once.

The love reflected in the eyes of these two was almost blinding as their family raised their glasses in a toast to their bright, happy future.

Delia Cowling studied them and turned to Cora. "It's funny. I had the strangest feeling, when these two came to visit me, that the tears I spotted on Lee's cheeks may have been caused by more than the events of the past few days."

Cora nodded. "We were all so worried about them. We were aware that they'd quarreled, of course, but they didn't seem able to resolve it. Then Amy and I decided to have them 'meet' at your place."

Delia's eyes sparkled. "And here I thought I'd had a hand in all this." She lowered her voice. "I told them that it had been my foolish pride that had cost me the love of your brother."

Cora closed a hand over Delia's and felt a warm glow as she sipped her champagne.

Oh, Coot. Will wonders never cease? Despite her heartache, Delia seems almost the lovely young girl who owned your heart all those years ago. As for Wyatt and Marilee, I can read the happiness in their eyes. You've not only brought our family together, but you're bringing so much joy to each of us. Thank you, darling Coot. I miss you. I will always miss you. But I see your hand in all of this and I feel you here, enjoying this moment right along with me.

EPILOGUE

———◆◆◆———

O_{h,} just look at what you've done to this place."
Amy and Cora stepped into Wyatt's suite of rooms
where Marilee was arranging the last of her personal
belongings.

Cora ran a hand over the baskets and masks adorning
a wall of shelves in the living room.

"I think they look good there, don't you?" Marilee
stood back for a better view.

"Lee, you have a real eye for decorating." Amy
nodded toward the rich silk framed in black hanging on
one wall.

"Thanks." Marilee gave a laugh. "I could fit my
entire apartment into one of these bedrooms. This place
is huge."

The three women shared a laugh.

"Speaking of your old apartment, is there a new
tenant?"

Marilee nodded. "A retired Army medic. He answered

the town's ad for an ambulance driver, and he was thrilled to get a place to live in the bargain."

"Will you miss the emergency runs?" Cora asked.

"I'm sure I will at first. But living way out here, it's impossible to keep the job. Of course, on the plus side, I won't miss those calls at two in the morning."

"And what of your plane?" Amy saw a quick flash of sorrow in Marilee's eyes before she blinked it away, and she wished she'd left the question unasked.

"The insurance wasn't enough to cover buying a new one. I think I'll just keep the money in the bank and forget about flying. It doesn't seem fair, since Wyatt's such a nervous flier." She turned toward the elegant, private kitchen. "Shall I make tea?"

"There's no time. We're going to leave you to shower and get ready. Reverend Carson will be here soon." Amy turned in the doorway. "After I'm dressed, I'll come by to see if you need any help."

"Thanks." Marilee waited until the door closed before circling the rooms for a final look. Satisfied, she made her way to the master bathroom and couldn't help pausing to take in all the grand expanse of marble and glass. Wyatt's parents had definitely had a taste for the best.

As she showered and dressed, she thought about the girl who had been all over the world, always yearning for roots, for a place to call home. This was so much more than she'd ever dreamed. Not the place, though it was grand. Much more important to her was the thought of belonging to this big, raucous family. With each day they were becoming more and more dear to her.

When her hair was dry she pinned it behind one ear with a jeweled comb, leaving the soft curls to fall over the other shoulder. Her ivory gown was a simple column of silk that fell to the ankles.

Simple. That was what she'd requested when she and Wyatt made their wedding plans. Because she had no family, she was eager to embrace his. But the thought of inviting the entire town was too much to contemplate. They had agreed on hosting a dinner at holiday time that would include all their friends. But for now, Marilee was content to keep the ceremony small and intimate, with just his family, as well as Cal Randall and Delia Cowling.

Marilee had thought she could manage her nerves, but as she worked the zipper of her gown, her fingers trembled.

Maybe, she thought, some people just weren't meant to give up independence for togetherness.

This wasn't about loving Wyatt. She did love him. With all her heart.

So why this sudden flutter in the pit of her stomach? She placed a hand over the spot and prayed she wouldn't be sick.

Would she ever be able to completely give up the battle she'd fought for so long?

The fireplace of the great room was banked with masses of white hydrangeas, Marilee's favorite flowers. In the late summer heat, there was no need of a fire.

Dandy was busy preparing a wedding supper for the entire family. Wyatt had requested prime rib, and Marilee's only request was for Dandy's special carrot cake with creamy frosting. He'd baked three tiers, and instead of the traditional bride and groom on top, he'd crafted the bridal couple on a motorcycle. He smiled as he added the finishing touches. There was nothing traditional about Wyatt and Marilee. They added the perfect spice to this family.

Jesse, wearing fresh denims and shirt, poked his head in the kitchen. "Have you seen Wyatt and Zane?"

"They said they'd meet you at your special spot."

"Thanks, Dandy."

Jesse hurried out the door and across a patch of lawn until he came to the fenced-in area dotted with several headstones.

"I thought maybe you'd forgotten." Wyatt, dressed in a dark suit and tie, looked up and grinned as he began filling glasses with Irish whiskey. "Hey, cuz, you got all duded up just for me?"

Jesse laughed. "You did say this was to be a casual affair."

"I did. But I'm thinking your wife will make you change before the preacher gets here."

"You bet. And after a tug-of-war, I'm sure I'll do exactly as she asks and put on a shirt and tie."

Zane had removed his jacket in the heat and draped it over the fence before lifting his camera and motioning for the two to move closer. "Let's record this for posterity."

"Set it on a tripod and get yourself in the picture." Jesse looked over. "Is that jacket cashmere?"

Zane grinned. "A holdover from my Hollywood days."

Jesse nudged Wyatt. "You can take the boy out of Hollywood, but you can't take Hollywood out of the boy."

"Hey, it got me plenty of women. Chicks dig cashmere."

That had the three laughing as the camera recorded them holding their glasses aloft.

They looked up as Cal arrived.

"Well." He handed around cigars and held a match to the tips before snagging a tumbler of whiskey. "Here we are again, gathered for yet another wedding celebration."

They emitted rings of smoke and waited for his toast.

"Wyatt, here's to you and your bride. You've found yourself a fine woman. May the two of you have a long and happy life together."

They drank.

"And here's to Coot." Cal's voice thickened, and he paused to clear his throat. "You three have stayed the course, and kept your promise to continue his search. I'd say you've done your grandfather proud."

"To Coot." In unison the three intoned the words before taking another drink.

"And to his sister, the finest woman in the world."

At Cal's words, the three shared knowing smiles before draining their glasses.

Did he have any idea how his voice gentled whenever he spoke Cora's name? Probably not. But the others had begun to take note of it, especially since Amy and Marilee had pointed it out.

"Now," Cal said, again clearing his throat, "you three had better get up to the house. The preacher's waiting."

As they walked away Cal remained, taking a drag on the cigar, emitting a wreath of smoke, and staring at the gravesite before turning away. With a thoughtful look he trailed slowly behind.

Reverend Carson stood before the fireplace, watching as Wyatt and Marilee walked past the line of family to stand before him.

Reading from the paper he'd been given, he looked at those assembled. "Wyatt and Marilee have prepared their own vows, and ask only that we give witness." He turned to the bride. "Lee, would you like to be first?"

She faced Wyatt and wondered at the way her poor heart was hammering. But when he gave her one of those heart-stopping smiles, all the butterflies disappeared. In their place was a feeling of calm.

"Wyatt, I've spent a lifetime fighting for my independence. For my place in the universe. I didn't want to fall in love. It wasn't part of my plan. But there you were, making me laugh, making me question everything I'd worked so hard to achieve, and making me love you when I wasn't ready. I guess that's what I needed to learn. Love isn't convenient. It doesn't happen when we want it, but when we need it. And I realize now that I need you in my life. Even when I don't necessarily want you there." She took his hands. Her tone lowered to an intimate purr. "So be patient with me. It may take me a while to learn how to be part of a team. But I'm a fast learner. And I have one thing in my favor. I love you more than anyone in this world."

Delia let out a loud sigh, causing the others to smile.

Wyatt kept hold of Marilee's hands as he said solemnly, "Marilee, I've been all over the world. I told myself I was searching for adventure. What I was really looking for was my life. I had to come back to Montana to find myself, my roots, my home. Best of all, I found you. You're not just my love, you're the other half of my heart. I love you. And I give you this pledge: Even if I smother you with love, I will honor you and your need for independence every day of my life."

While Delia openly wept, and Cora squeezed Cal's hand so hard he cringed, Reverend Carson spoke the words pronouncing them husband and wife.

After a long, lingering kiss, Wyatt accepted the handshakes and backslaps of his cousins, while Marilee was hugged and kissed by the women.

A short time later they were enjoying Dandy's excellent dinner while being relentlessly teased by Jesse and Zane, who kept the entire company laughing.

"Here's the cake you requested." Dandy rolled a serving cart into the room, and they gathered around to exclaim over his clever artistry.

"I think the groom looks like me." Wyatt placed his hand over Marilee's, and together they cut the first slice.

Soon they were enjoying the wonderful dessert while toasting the happy couple with champagne.

"I have something I'd like to say." Marilee got to her feet, staring around the table. "As an only child, I often felt so alone. No brothers or sisters, no aunts or uncles or cousins. And now, I have a sister." She walked to Amy and the two embraced. "And brothers." She hugged Jesse and Zane, and the two kissed her on each cheek, making the others smile. "I've even acquired an aunt." She paused to kiss Cora's cheek. "And good friends I know I can count on." She kissed

Cal, and then Delia. "And all of this because of you, Wyatt."

The two kissed, bringing a round of cheers from the others.

Jesse stood and lifted his glass of champagne. "I'd like to say something to my cousin and his bride . . ." He paused at the roar of a plane's engine flying directly overhead.

Marilee shot a questioning glance at Wyatt.

In reply, he gave her a mysterious smile and caught her hand. "It's about time your wedding gift made an appearance."

With the others following, he led her outside and to a waiting convoy of trucks.

"Wyatt, what on earth . . . ?"

He put a finger to her lips to silence her questions. "All in good time."

Their party drove across a meadow and paused at a newly constructed hangar and a private airstrip. Sitting on the tarmac was a bright yellow plane, the pilot standing beside it.

Seeing it, Marilee felt her eyes begin to fill while the others gathered around.

So many tears, she thought. She'd shed more in the past few days than she'd shed in a lifetime.

Wyatt kept his tone casual. "We all agreed that it was time for the Lost Nugget to step into the twenty-first century. And that meant a private airstrip and plane, to keep us up to date on our vast holdings. Who better to handle this than you, Mrs. McCord?"

"Wyatt, I know how you feel about flying. Besides, I told you I was through with it forever."

"Yes, you did. But I know your heart said otherwise. Marilee, I want you to share my life, not my fears. You love flying. It gives you a sense of freedom. I don't ever want to take that away from you."

"Oh, Wyatt." With a sob she wrapped her arms around his neck and buried her face in his throat, too overcome to find her voice.

"There's no sense fighting it any longer. You're stuck with me for a lifetime. Now . . ." He turned to the others with a grin. "If you don't mind, I think it's time my wife took me for a spin in her new plane."

"When will you be back?" Cora asked.

"An hour or two. Or until Marilee gets tired of her newfound freedom."

She looked up at him. "Are you sure you want to do this? It's your wedding day, too."

"I've never been so sure of anything in my life." Wyatt drew Marilee close. "If you ever start to worry that you're losing your independence, just kiss me and you'll see how much power you wield."

She drew back to stare at him.

At her arched brow he grinned. "If I'm Superman, then baby, you're my kryptonite. I promise you, one kiss from you and I'm so weak, you'd have to scoop me up with a spoon. So be very careful with such awesome power."

They climbed into the plane and, with their family watching and cheering, rolled down the new runway and lifted into the air, waving to those on the ground.

She turned to him. "You all right?"

"I'm fine. In fact, I'm better than fine."

This, Wyatt thought as his heart did a flip and began to settle, was exactly where he wanted to be. As the ground dropped away, and the blue sky swallowed them up, he felt a rare sense of peace. He would continue the search for the elusive treasure. It was his promise to his grandfather.

But if he never found the McCord gold, at least he'd already found, in this woman's love, the rarest treasure of all.

The last thing in the world Zane McCord wants is to be tied down to just one woman . . . until Riley Mason changes everything.

Please turn this page
for a preview of

Montana Glory,

the stunning conclusion to
R.C. Ryan's trilogy.

Available in November 2010.

CHAPTER ONE

———◆———

Hoo, boy." Jesse McCord grinned when he caught sight of his cousin Zane walking into the big kitchen of the Lost Nugget ranch house. "Two weeks up in the hills, and you look more like a grizzly than a human."

Zane ran a hand over his rough beard. "The cattle don't care what we look like, as long as we deliver food in the snow."

Though spring had arrived in Montana, the mountains were still hip-deep in drifts. A storm had dropped nearly a foot of snow the previous weekend.

Cal Randall, foreman of the Lost Nugget, turned from the stove where he was filling a mug with coffee. "These late snowfalls play hell with the calving."

"Yeah. But the flip side is"—Zane pulled a tiny video camera from his shirt pocket—"I got some fabulous shots of the hills buried in fresh snow. They'll make a great background for the introduction I'm planning for my documentary. I can see the camera panning a vast, snow-covered wilderness, while a voice intones, 'When Coot McCord died, the town of Gold Fever called him crazy for having spent a lifetime searching for the lost treasure of his ancestors. How could anyone in his right mind believe one man could find a sack of gold nuggets in such a primitive setting? But Coot's grandsons pledged on his grave to carry on his search. This, then, is the record of one family's dream, and the successful conclusion of a treasure hunt that began in 1862, at Grasshopper Creek, in the Montana wilderness.' "

"Sounds great, cuz." Wyatt punched his arm. "Especially that part about the successful conclusion. The sooner the better."

"Yeah. Hey, it's slow going, but we're all committed."

Zane paused for a moment and gave Cal a long look. "Is that a clean shirt in the middle of the day?"

Cal nodded. "Thought I'd clean up for the interview."

"Interview?" Zane glanced around. "What've I missed?"

Cal took a sip of coffee before saying, "With Coot gone, I'm being buried in paperwork. I complained to our accounting firm in Helena, and they agreed to send me their new hotshot bookkeeper to clean up the mess."

"A hotshot bookkeeper is coming all this way?"

"Schooled in the East." Cal took a sip of coffee. "Guy named Riley Mason."

"A city boy?" The cousins shared a grin. "How long do you think he'll last out here?"

Cal shrugged. "Depends on what he finds. I'm hoping no more than a couple of weeks, to get everything into a computer database so the Helena firm can handle all those mysterious government forms that need to be filled out in triplicate."

"Where will he stay?"

Cal pointed his mug toward the doorway. "He can have his pick of empty rooms. There's that small suite next to the office that would probably work best."

Marilee gave a throaty chuckle. "Maybe you can keep him chained to his desk, Cal. Then he can clear up the paperwork in half the time."

"Believe me, I'd be happy to, as long as I wouldn't ever have to deal with legal documents again. I don't know how Coot could stand doing all the paperwork involved in running this place."

"Good luck with the interview. I'm more interested in supper." Zane turned away, rubbing a hand over his bristly beard. "Excuse me while I head upstairs for the longest shower and shave in history."

He ambled out of the kitchen and was heading through the great room on his way to the stairs when he heard a knock on the front door.

Since nobody but a stranger would ever use the front entrance, Zane was grinning good-naturedly as he grasped the knob and threw open the door to admit the accountant.

"Hello."

Zane knew he was staring, but it took him a moment to switch gears. He'd expected a dark suit, and he wasn't disappointed. And a firm handshake, which he returned woodenly. But the nerdy accountant in his mind was replaced by a gorgeous female, dark hair slicked back into a knot at the back of her head, trim figure encased in a knee-skimming dark skirt and figure-hugging jacket. And what a figure.

Then there was the voice. Soft and breathy, with just a hint of nerves.

"I'm Riley Mason. Are you Cal Randall?"

"No. Cal's in his office." Zane decided to give her one of his most charming smiles. "My name's Zane. I'll show you the way."

She had taken a step back, studying him warily, and he realized, too late, that he probably smelled like a barnyard and looked like a trail bum.

He held the door wider, and she was forced to accept his invitation to step inside. She did so hesitantly.

"Maybe I'll just wait here and you can tell him I've arrived for my interview."

He gave a shrug of his shoulders. "Sure thing."

With one last look he sauntered away, leaving her standing in the foyer.

Riley didn't relax until the cowboy disappeared along a hallway. She'd known, of course, that the Lost Nugget was a working ranch. But she'd assumed that she would be isolated from the wranglers, since she'd been told they lived in bunk-houses scattered across thousands of acres of rangeland.

Not that she felt herself above working cowboys. She'd been working since she was fifteen and proud of it. But if the men on the ranch looked anything like that one, she preferred to give them a wide berth. There had been a fierce, dangerous look to him. Like a throwback to the cowboys of the Old West who could calmly shoot a gun-slinger, toss back a glass of whiskey, and ride out of town without a backward glance.

Silly, she knew. She'd always been cursed with a wild imagination. But being on a ranch in Montana was about as far from her comfort zone as possible.

"You're not in Kansas anymore, little girl," she muttered.

She watched the approach of a handsome, white-haired man. Now this was how she'd envisioned Cal Randall, foreman of the Lost Nugget. Tall, rangy, weathered, and extremely courtly as he extended his hand.

"Riley Mason? Cal Randall."

"So nice to meet you, Mr. Randall."

"That was my father. Call me Cal." He put a hand beneath her elbow. "Let's go to my office and chat."

They passed through an enormous room with a four-sided fireplace surrounded by comfortable furniture. The floor-to-ceiling windows offered an incredible view of the towering spires of Treasure Chest Mountain in the distance. Riley caught her breath at the sheer beauty of it.

Before she could take it all in, Cal led her along a hallway and paused to open a set of double doors. Inside was a purely masculine retreat, complete with walls of shelves holding an assortment of leather-bound books and yet another fireplace.

Cal settled himself into a leather chair behind an oversize desk littered with paperwork. He indicated a chair across from him, and Riley perched on the edge of the seat.

Seeing her nerves, he strove to put her at ease. "Tell me about yourself, Riley."

"I'm twenty-four. Fresh out of college." She flushed. "I took some time off to work, so that set me back a bit. I've worked since I was fifteen. Mostly as a clerk in a local store, and at a coffeehouse on campus. I'm trained in accounting. But I have to be honest with you." She stared openly at the mountain of paperwork. "I just don't know how much help I can be until I have a chance to look over some of this. It looks . . . intimidating."

"I know what you mean." Cal tapped a pen against the desktop. "It intimidates the hell out of me."

That had the desired effect, causing her to relax a bit as she matched his grin.

"I'm current with state and federal guidelines on fees and assessments, and even though I've just arrived, I know I can get up to speed on local issues, as well."

She dug an envelope out of her pocket and set it on the desk. "Our firm suggested independent assessments of my work. These are the e-mail addresses of my immediate superiors at our Philadelphia firm, as well as my college professors who are familiar with me. They agreed to answer any questions you might have about my abilities. They were in contact with the firm before I was hired."

She took in a breath. "I've been apprised of your business, and I'm prepared to handle daily sheets and payroll, as well. I think I could get all the necessary paperwork ready for our CPA firm in Helena. And though I can't promise miracles, I'm pretty sure I could get most of this"—she indicated the desk—"cleaned up and in some sort of order. But, as I said, neither of us will really know what I'm capable of until I take a look at the work you need done."

"Fair enough. To make your job a bit easier, I'm prepared to offer you a room here."

She seemed surprised. "The firm didn't say anything about living on the ranch."

"Is that a problem?"

She hesitated. "Before driving out here, I arranged for a room in Gold Fever, with a lady named Delia Cowling, who was recommended by a banker in Helena."

Cal smiled. "I know Delia. Her brother was owner of the Gold Fever bank before his untimely death." He thought a minute. "As you know, it's an hour's drive from town. Living here could save you time, as well as gas and wear and tear on your car."

The way she was chewing on her lower lip told Cal that something was bothering her. "Of course, the decision is up to you, Riley."

She took a deep breath. "I didn't come to town alone. I have a four-year-old daughter."

"Oh." It was Cal's turn to be surprised. "Is your husband okay with the hours you'll be away?"

Her head came up. "My husband?"

"I figure he'll be stuck with some of the child care if you sign on for this."

Riley realized she'd been sitting on the edge of her seat. She sat back in the chair and met Cal's questioning look directly. Her chin came up defensively. "I didn't mean to mislead you. I don't have a husband. I've never been married. There's just Summer and me."

"I see." He saw more. Much more. Though the job interview may have unnerved her, questions about her private life were infinitely more painful. This was obviously not the first time she'd been asked about her unmarried status. Though she was direct and honest, she didn't volunteer any more than necessary.

"You haven't said if you'd be willing to live here on the ranch."

"I'd . . . be more than willing, as long as you under-stand that I'd be bringing along my daughter."

Cal stared at the envelope she'd dropped on his desk. "I don't need to check any further references, Riley. Our firm in Helena had nothing but good things to say about your work. That's good enough for me. So, if you're agreeable, I'd like you to get started as quickly as possible."

His abrupt end to the interview caught her by surprise. She'd expected Cal Randall to be like so many others who judged her without even knowing her.

And he had, she realized. But he was judging her by her work ethic, and not by her personal life.

Cal got to his feet and leaned across the desk to extend his hand. "If you'd like to wait in the great room, I'll phone the firm in Helena and affirm your employment."

She was reeling from the speed with which he'd come to a decision.

She stood and offered her hand. "Thanks for giving me this opportunity, Cal." She turned toward the door.

"Can you find your way?" he called to her retreating back.

"Yes. I'm fine with it." Riley closed the door and back-tracked until, pausing in the massive great room, she sank into an overstuffed chair, feeling a wave of giddy relief.

Needing to calm her nerves, she closed her eyes and took long, deep breaths until her heartbeat returned to normal.

Zane was whistling as he descended the stairs and headed toward the kitchen. He'd noted the door to Cal's office closed, and he wondered about the foreman's reac-tion to the new *guy*, Riley. That had Zane grinning. It was a natural mistake, and they'd all been guilty. Who'd have believed the new hire would be female? And so darned pretty.

In the great room he came to an abrupt halt. The object of his thoughts was seated in a chair, hands folded in her lap, eyes closed.

He took that moment to study her more closely, enjoying the way a lock of dark hair had fallen from that prim knot to curl against her cheek. Such a pretty, dimpled cheek. Everything about her was pretty. And soft. From the lips, pursed as though in prayer, to the gentle curve of her eyebrows.

Just then her eyes opened and she caught sight of him staring.

"Hi again."

At the sound of his voice her eyes widened in recognition. "You're . . . the one I met at the front door."

"Zane."

"Zane." She almost laughed aloud at the change in him. Gone was the dark beard, the filthy clothes. Now he was freshly showered and shaved, with little drops of water still glistening in his hair. Dark hair, she noted, that just brushed the collar of his plaid shirt. Long legs were encased in faded denims. On his feet were scuffed boots.

He was darkly handsome, with piercing blue eyes in a tanned face that wasn't so much handsome as commanding. With that killer smile aimed at her, it was impossible to look away.

"When do you get to tackle Cal's office mess?"

"Whenever he wants me to start."

"I'd say the sooner the better. Cal doesn't have much patience with paperwork."

"That's what he told me." She laughed. "Fortunately, it's what I do best."

Just then Cal stepped into the room. "You two getting acquainted?"

"Yeah. When does Riley start?"

Cal turned to her. "You'll need tomorrow to move your things out here and get settled in. Then you can start the following morning. How does that sound?"

"Perfect." She offered her hand. "I'd better get back to town now."

Cal accepted her handshake. "Just a thought. Maybe you'd like some help getting your stuff out here."

"Oh, I don't think—"

Zane interrupted. "I'm free in the morning. I could take one of the ranch trucks into town and lend a hand."

"Perfect." Cal gave Riley a smile. "How does eight o'clock sound?"

"Yes. All right." She turned to Zane. "Thanks for the offer. I'm staying at Delia Cowling's place. Do you know it?"

"Sure thing." Zane's smile grew. "I'll see you at eight."

When she and Cal walked to the front door, Zane stood admiring her backside.

Minutes later, when Cal closed the door and joined him, he was grinning like a conspirator.

"Very slick," Cal muttered as they made their way to the kitchen.

"Thanks. I was thinking the same thing. Thanks for giving me that perfect opening."

"A word of warning." Cal paused at the kitchen door. "She's going to be an employee now, Zane. You make the wrong moves, she could sue you for harassment."

"Me?" Zane threw back his head and roared before dropping an arm around the foreman's shoulders. "When have you ever known me to make a move on an unwilling female?"

"Willing or unwilling, Riley Mason is off-limits."

"Thanks for that fatherly advice. I'll keep it in mind."

Zane was still chuckling as he joined the others for dinner.

Amy Parrish was the only woman Jesse McCord ever loved. Now she's back in town—but an unseen enemy is fast closing in . . .

Please turn this page
for a preview of

Montana Legacy,

the first book in the trilogy,
and discover how it all began.

Available now.

In the kitchen Jesse loosened his tie and poured himself a tumbler of Irish whiskey. Like his grandfather, he wasn't much of a drinker. But every New Year, and at the annual roundup barbecue, Coot would pour a round of whiskeys for himself and the crew, and offer a toast to the future.

"Life's all about the road ahead. What's past is past. Here's to what's around the bend, boys."

Jesse could hear his grandfather's voice as clearly as if he'd been standing right there. There had been a boyish curiosity about the old man that was so endearing. He'd truly believed he would live to find his ancestor's fortune. The anticipation, the thrill of it, had influenced his entire life. And it was contagious. Jesse had been caught up in it as well. It's what had kept him here, chasing Coot's rainbow, instead of going off in search of his own.

Not that he had any regrets. He couldn't imagine himself anywhere but here.

He crossed the mudroom and stepped out onto the back porch, hoping to get as far away from the crowd as possible.

Just as he lifted the drink to his lips, a voice stopped him.

"I thought I might find you out here."

He didn't have to see her to recognize that voice. Hadn't it whispered to him in dreams a hundred times or more?

His tone hardened as he studied Amy Parrish standing at the bottom of the steps. "What's the matter, Amy? Make a wrong turn? Lunch is being served in the front yard."

"I noticed." She waited until he walked closer. "I just wanted to tell you why I came back."

"To gloat, no doubt."

"Don't, Jess." She pressed her lips together, then gave a sigh of defeat. "I'm sorry about your grandfather. I know you loved him."

"Yeah." Her eyes were even greener than he remembered. With little gold flecks in them that you could see only in the sunlight. It hurt to look at them. At her. Almost as much as it hurt to think about Coot. "So, why did you come back?"

"To offer some support to my dad while he had some medical tests done."

His head came up sharply. "He's sick?"

She nodded. "The doctor in Billings sent him to a specialist at the university. The test results should be back in a couple of days, and then I'll be going back to my job, teaching in Helena."

"I'm sorry about your dad. I hope the test results come back okay." He paused, staring at the glass in his hands because he didn't want to be caught staring at her. "So, I guess you just came here to say good-bye before you leave. Again."

"I just . . ." She shrugged and stared down at her hands, fighting nerves. "I just wanted to offer my condolences."

"Thanks. I appreciate it."

The breeze caught a strand of pale hair, softly laying it across her cheek. Without thinking he reached up and gently brushed it away from her face.

The heat that sizzled through his veins was like an electrical charge, causing him to jerk back. But not before he caught the look of surprise in her eyes. Surprise and something more. If he didn't know better, he'd swear he saw a quick flash of heat. But that was probably just his pride tricking him into believing in something that wasn't there, and hadn't been for years.

He lowered his hand and clenched it into a fist at his side.

She took a sideways step, as though to avoid being touched again. "I'd better get back to my dad."

"Yeah. Thanks again for coming."

She walked away quickly, without looking back.

That was how she'd left in the first place, he thought. Without a backward glance.

Now he could allow himself to study her. Hair the color of wheat, billowing on the breeze. That lean, willowy body; those long legs; the soft flare of her hips.

Just watching her, he felt all the old memories rushing over him, filling his mind, battering his soul. Memories he'd kept locked up for years in a small, secret corner of his mind. The way her hair smelled in the rain. The way her eyes sparkled whenever she smiled. The sound of her laughter, low in her throat. The way she felt in his arms when they kissed. When they made love . . .

He'd be damned if he'd put himself through that hell again.

He lifted the tumbler to his lips and drained it in one long swallow, feeling the heat snake through his veins.

"What's past is past," he muttered thickly. "Here's to what's around the bend."

THE DISH

Where authors give you the inside scoop!

♥ ♥ ♥ ♥ ♥ ♥ ♥ ♥ ♥ ♥ ♥ ♥ ♥ ♥ ♥

From the desk of Paula Quinn

Dear Reader,

While doing research for LAIRD OF THE MIST, I fell in love with Clan MacGregor. Their staunch resolve to overcome trials and countless tribulations during a three-hundred-year proscription earned them a very special place in my heart. So when I was given the chance to write a brand-new series featuring Callum and Kate MacGregor's grown children, I was ecstatic.

The first of my new four-book series, RAVISHED BY A HIGHLANDER (available now), stars Robert MacGregor, whom you met briefly in A HIGHLANDER NEVER SURRENDERS. He was a babe then, and things haven't changed. He's still a babe, but in an entirely different way!

My favorite type of hero is a rogue who can sweep a lady off her feet with a slant of his lips. Or a cool, unsmiling brute with a soft spot no one sees but his woman. Rob was neither of those men when I began writing his story. He was more. I didn't think I could love a character I created as much as I loved his father, but I was wrong, and I'm not ashamed to say it.

Rob isn't careless with women's hearts. His smile isn't reckless but a bit awkward. It's about the only thing he *hasn't* practiced every day of his life. Born to fill his father's boots as chief and protector of his clan, Rob takes life and the duties that come with his birthright seriously. He's uncompromising in his loyalty to his kin and unrelenting in his beliefs. He's a warrior who is confident in the skill of his arm, but not rash in drawing his sword. However, once it's out, someone's head is going to roll. Yes, he's tall and handsome, with dark curls and eyes the color of sunset against a summer-blue loch, but his beauty can best be seen in his devotion to those he loves.

He is . . . exactly what a lady needs in her life if an entire Dutch fleet is on her tail.

I'll tell you a little about Davina Montgomery, the lass who not only softens Rob's staunch heart, but comes to claim it in her delicate fingers. But I won't tell you too much, because I don't want to reveal the secret that has taken everyone she's ever loved away from her. She came to me filled with sorrow, chained by duty, and in need of things so very basic, yet always beyond her reach: safety, and the love of someone who would never betray her or abandon her to danger.

I saw Rob through Davina's eyes the moment he plucked her from the flames of her burning abbey. A hero: capable, courageous, and hot as hell.

We both knew Rob was perfect for her, and for the first time, I saw hope in Davina's eyes—and her beauty can best be seen when she looks at him.

Travel back to the Scottish Highlands with Rob and Davina and discover what happens when duty and desire collide. And I love to hear from readers, so please visit me at www.paulaquinn.com.

Enjoy!

Paula Quinn

♥ ♥ ♥ ♥ ♥ ♥ ♥ ♥ ♥ ♥ ♥ ♥ ♥ ♥ ♥

From the desk of R. C. Ryan

Dear Reader,

Are you as intrigued by family dynamics as I am? I know that, having written a number of family sagas, I've been forced to confront a lot of family drama. But fiction mirrors real life. And in the real world, there's nothing more complicated or more dramatic than our individual relationships with the different members of our families.

We read a lot about mother-daughter and father-son relationships, not to mention sibling rivalry. Psychologists tell us life paths are often determined by birth order. And yet there are always exceptions to the rule—the child of poverty who builds a financial empire. The man with a learning disability who lifts himself to the ranks of genius. The girl who loses a leg and goes on to run marathons.

And so, while I'm fascinated with family dynamics, and our so-called place in the universe, I'm even more intrigued by those who refuse to fit into any mold. Instead, by the sheer force of their determination, they rise above society's rules to become something rare and wonderful. Whether they climb Mount Everest or never leave the neighborhood where they were born, they live each day to the fullest. And whether they change the world or just change one life, they defy the experts and prove wrong those who believe a life's course is predetermined.

In MONTANA DESTINY, the second book in my Fool's Gold series, Wyatt McCord returns to the Lost Nugget Ranch after years of living life on the edge, only to lose his heart to the fiercely independent Marilee Trainor, a loner who has broken a few rules of her own. These two, who searched the world over for a place to belong, will laugh, love, and fight often, while being forced to dig deep within themselves to survive.

I hope you enjoy watching Wyatt and Marilee take charge of their lives and forge their own destinies.

R. C. Ryan

www.ryanlangan.com

♥ ♥ ♥ ♥ ♥ ♥ ♥ ♥ ♥ ♥ ♥ ♥ ♥ ♥ ♥ ♥

From the desk of Robin Wells

Dear Reader,

"So, Robin—what's your latest book about?"

I get that question a lot, and I always find it difficult to answer. I usually start off by describing the plot in varying degrees of detail. Here's the short version:

STILL THE ONE is the story of Katie Charmaine, a hairdresser in Chartreuse, Louisiana—the same colorful small town where my previous book, BETWEEN THE SHEETS, took place. Katie lost her husband in Iraq, and she thinks she'll never love again. But when her first love, Zack Ferguson, returns, she feels the same irresistible attraction that stole her heart at seventeen. To Katie's shock, he's accompanied by the teenage daughter Katie gave up for adoption at birth. The daughter, Gracie, has a major attitude, a smart mouth—and is now pregnant herself.

The medium-length version adds: Gracie's adoptive parents were killed in a car accident, and when she discovers her birth parents' identities, she locates Zack first. She wants him to declare her an emancipated minor and give her a nice wad of cash. Instead, Zack takes Gracie to Chartreuse, where he and Katie share custody until Gracie turns eighteen."

The long version gives still more detail: Zack and Katie experience the ups and downs of parenting a difficult teenager, while rediscovering the love that initially drew them together. Can they forgive each other for their past mistakes? Can Zack overcome his commitment-phobic ways? Can Katie get beyond her feelings of disloyalty to her late husband and her fear of opening her heart again? Can Gracie let go of her anger and open her heart to Katie?

The long version still doesn't fully cover everything that happens, but then, a book is much more than a plot. So I also answer the "what's your book about?" question by citing the following themes present in STILL THE ONE:

Romance. There's nothing like the heady feeling of falling in love, and nothing worse than believing you're falling alone.

Family. This book is about some of the ways that families shape us, for better and for worse.

Grief. Love doesn't die, even though people do. How do we get past the feeling that loving someone else is disloyal to the deceased? How do we ever find the courage to care that deeply again, knowing how much it hurts to lose someone you love?

Mistakes. Teenagers aren't known for making wise choices, but adults don't always make the best decisions, either. Regardless of age, we all can get lost in the moment, make incorrect assumptions, repeat a destructive pattern, or neglect to say something that needs to be said.

Blessings. Sometimes mistakes that have haunted us for years can turn out to be life's biggest blessings.

Forgiveness. How do we let go of hurts—especially big, bad ones? Once we've been hurt by someone, can we ever fully trust that person again?

And last but not least, **Love.** If I had to give a single answer to what my book is about, this would be it. I believe that love has the power to heal and redeem and transform anyone and any situation, no matter how hopeless it may seem, and that's the major underlying theme of this novel—and all my novels, come to think of it. I hope you'll drop by my website, www.robinwells.com, to see a short video about the book, read an excerpt from my next novel, and/or let me know your thoughts. I love to hear from readers, and I can be reached at my website or at P.O. Box 303, Mandeville, LA 70470.

Here's hoping your life will be filled with love, laughter, and lots of good books!

Robin Wells

Want to know more about romances at Grand Central Publishing and Forever? Get the scoop online!

GRAND CENTRAL PUBLISHING'S ROMANCE HOME PAGE

Visit us at www.hachettebookgroup.com/romance for all the latest news, reviews, and chapter excerpts!

NEW AND UPCOMING TITLES

Each month we feature our new titles and reader favorites.

CONTESTS AND GIVEAWAYS

We give away galleys, autographed copies, and all kinds of fun stuff.

AUTHOR INFO

You'll find bios, articles, and links to personal Web sites for all your favorite authors—and so much more!

THE BUZZ

Sign up for our monthly romance newsletter, and be the first to read all about it!